I0835044

BARE

BARE

ELISABETH CALDWELL

CITY OWL
PRESS

BARE
A *Spice up the Night* novel

CITY OWL PRESS
www.cityowlpress.com

Cover Design by MiblArt. All stock photos licensed appropriately.

Edited by Tabatha Barber.

For information on subsidiary rights, please contact the publisher at info@cityowlpress.com.

Print Edition ISBN: 978-1-64898-567-6

Digital Edition ISBN: 978-1-64898-566-9

To my favorite cardiologist.
My heart beats only for you.

Author's Note

This work contains: 1) explicit sex and explicit language, 2) descriptions of murder, violence, cancer, and hair loss/baldness, and 3) references to limb loss and sexual assault.

Chapter One

She. Would. Not. Scratch.

The air conditioning was pumping, but hot sweat dampened Rosemary Cashman's armpits, making them sticky. Her fingers cramped from gripping the arms of the conference room chair. She angled her head to the side, hoping her wig would reposition enough to alleviate the all-consuming itch, but it didn't work.

She. Would. Not. Scratch.

Not here. Not in front of her boss and their client.

She just needed this interminable meeting to end.

"Rosemary, are you all right? You look pale."

Armando Pannetone's voice was gentle with the soft lilt of an Italian accent. In the six months she'd worked at Pannetone & Associates, she'd never heard Armando raise his voice. He didn't need to. People respected him and listened when he spoke.

A pang of guilt made her shift in her seat.

From her first day of work, Armando treated her like family. He'd hired her despite her limited experience and had patiently trained her. In a matter of weeks, they'd settled into the type of easy rhythm that usually took years to develop. He wasn't just her boss. He was her mentor. And here she was, thinking about bolting in the middle of a meeting so she could scratch her head. She squeezed the armrests even tighter, trying to ignore the itch that was so intense it bordered on pain.

"Rosemary?" Armando repeated, his thick gray eyebrows drawing together.

Armando's scrunched brows portrayed his emotions as clearly as a neon sign at midnight. He was worried.

She nodded, hoping the small head movement might generate some relief. "I'm fine. It's just a headache. I forgot to take my allergy pill this morning."

That wasn't really a lie. The itch was so irritating that her head *was* aching, and she *had* forgotten her Claritin.

"Why don't you go get an espresso? Espresso is the best remedy for a headache."

Even with her scalp on fire, her lips curved up at the corners. To Armando, espresso was a miracle drug. Last week, she'd overheard him prescribing espresso to Lily as she cried at the front desk over an argument she'd had with her older, married boyfriend. Rosemary would have told Lily she was better off without the boyfriend, but Armando had assured the receptionist that meeting the man for espresso would solve all their problems.

Right now, she'd be grateful if someone would pour an espresso over her head. It would give her an excuse to move her wig and get some relief.

"An espresso sounds amazing." She fought to keep her tone calm and professional. "Are you sure you don't need me any longer?"

Armando swiveled his chair to face their client, Salvatore Moresco. "I invited you because Sal's been asking to meet you, but I think we've covered all the high points. If anything else comes up, I'll fill you in later when we touch base on the Girard warehouse payment schedule and financials. Sal, we can handle the rest without Rosemary, correct?"

Sal's eyes hardened into shiny marbles. "I thought the Girard payment schedule would be done today. Those payments need to go out."

Companies generally did their own payables processing, but Armando arranged the payment of every invoice for each of the Moresco family businesses. It was an odd arrangement, but if Sal wanted to pay the firm's high-dollar hourly rates for busy work, who was Rosemary to question it? She just wanted to get out of the meeting so she could deal with the infernal itch.

Armando met Sal's irritation with patience. "I understand, but you specifically asked that Rosemary start working on your matters. I need to train her and oversee her work. That means things are going to take a bit longer. I know you're traveling for the next several days. Everything will be done when you return. If anyone is eager for payment, I'm sure you can make a call, and they'll be happy to wait."

Sal's cool, dark gaze fixed on her. He appeared tall, even while sitting with his long legs stretched out and crossed at the ankles. Even though Rosemary didn't consider herself short, she'd had to look up to meet Sal's eyes when they'd been introduced earlier that morning. He'd been standing then, and his strict posture and neatly buttoned jacket had partially concealed his paunch. His middle-aged girth was more noticeable now that he was sitting and his suit coat was unbuttoned. His thick black hair was sprinkled with gray, and his skin shared the same olive tone as Armando's. His appearance was that of a sleek, Italian grandfather, but there was something in his posture that suggested he owned the room...and everybody in it.

Silence ate the passing moments. Sal continued to stare. He'd been perfectly professional during their meeting, but now, under the weight of his black-coffee-colored gaze, she felt like a butterfly pinned to a board. Still, she wasn't going to look away. When she was young, she'd been a natural at the quiet game, but her sister, Sage, had won nearly every staring contest. It had taken years of her sister's encouragement for Rosemary to learn to meet any gaze fiercely. She used that skill now to resist the urge to avert her eyes. She wasn't going to wither under a little scrutiny.

Even if it felt like Sal's gaze was focused on her hair.

Armando rose and leaned across the table, becoming a human

barrier that interrupted Sal's line of sight. He pushed a Redweld full of paper across the table toward her. "Would you kindly give this to Lily on your way back to your office?"

She scrambled out of her chair and lifted the file, grateful for the errand, even if it meant she'd have to interact with Lily. Lily had treated her with disdain from day one, and Rosemary didn't know why.

"Yes. Of course." She forced herself to look back at Sal while she picked up her purse from the table. "It's been a pleasure meeting you, Mr. Moresco."

"The pleasure's all mine," he responded. "I hope you feel better soon."

Rosemary pushed the heavy glass conference room door open, took a few quick steps down the hall, and ducked into the ladies' room. The spicy aroma of the cinnamon-apple air freshener filled her nose. She bent over, peeking under the stalls.

No legs. She was alone.

She set her purse and the file on the dark green marble counter. *Verde uba tuba.* It was the same marble her mother had picked for the kitchen in Davis's house, and she'd never forgotten the name. She used to think of that house as her home. Now, she couldn't think of it as anything other than the place Davis had once kicked Sage and her out of.

The thought slipped from her mind, shoved out by the raging impulse to scratch. Her head was a sea of prickly, itchy heat. Her fingers closed around the cool zipper of the flower-patterned, Vera Bradley bag Sage had given her last Christmas. She yanked it open and snatched an extra-long, thin, wooden toothpick from her stash. She slipped the toothpick under the edge of her wig and rubbed it vigorously against her scalp.

Sweet, sweet, sweet relief.

She continued to scratch for several seconds, relishing the sensation. Once the offending itches were alleviated, she slid the toothpick along the length of the wig, hitting any areas that were even slightly uncomfortable. It was best to scratch as much as she could now, or she'd be back in the bathroom in half an hour doing the same thing.

It wasn't the wig's fault. It was high quality and well-made. Sage and her fiancé, Ryker, had insisted on buying her the best, but even the best wigs were no match for her sweaty, itchy, finicky scalp. The wig consultant had given her every tip in the book. She'd tried wearing different types of wigs and wig liners, spraying her head with witch hazel, applying anti-itch powder, and even rubbing zinc on her head at night. Nothing worked. She still experienced a maddening, all-consuming need to scratch, usually at the most inopportune times.

The wig consultant had suggested the itching could be psychosomatic. Sage told the woman to go to hell and told Rosemary to put the goddamn things in the trash, but Rosemary couldn't bring herself to do it. There was no way she was going out without a wig. The few times she'd left the house in a scarf had been bad enough.

People knew she was bald under the scarf, and bald meant cancer. Bald meant she was knocking at death's door. Bald meant people looking at her and seeing a walking, soon-to-be corpse. They didn't see a person. They saw death.

And no one wants to be reminded of their own mortality.

Even when she wore the wig, some people regarded her with a mix of pity and curiosity. The ones who knew she'd been sick. The ones who knew the treatment that had saved her life had taken every bit of hair from her body. The ones who knew the long, nearly platinum locks, so very much like her precancer hair, were fake. The wig was a costume designed to make her appear "normal," but she didn't feel normal. She felt like an alien trying to pass as human...and failing.

She'd been so naïve. So goddamn naïve to think she could share the truth of her hair loss with a few friends—or people she'd thought were friends. She'd caught them inspecting her hair with furtive glances, looking for chinks in her golden armor, almost angry that her hair seemed natural. That she didn't look sick anymore. That she was no longer someone to pity.

She hadn't wanted to think it. Hadn't wanted to believe that someone would prefer her to be ill so they could play the role of benevolent helpmate. So they could have someone to gossip about in hushed, concerned tones. It went against the core of Rosemary's "think positive" approach to life, but she couldn't and wouldn't deny what she saw.

Her mother had taught her to always look for the best but to never hide from the truth. So, she kept her rose-colored glasses in her pocket, accepted, and forgave. If someone needed another person's suffering to make them feel good about themselves, they deserved her sympathy.

But not her friendship.

She was just grateful she'd never been foolish enough to let anyone actually see her bare head. Not even her sister had seen it. Only the wig-fitter. She'd left the days of being an object of pity firmly behind her. She had a new life now. There was no way she'd ever be laid bare like that again.

She did one more sweep of her scalp with the toothpick, then wrapped it in a paper towel and tossed it in the trash. There were only two other women in the office: Lily, the receptionist/file clerk, and Marge, who wore the triple hat of bookkeeper, billing coordinator, and office manager. She didn't want them wondering why there were fruit-in-your-drink style toothpicks in the ladies' room wastebasket every day.

She studied herself in the mirror. Straight nose, wide mouth, big blue eyes, and long blonde hair that no one would ever suspect wasn't her own. If she braided it in pig tails, she'd look like the girl on the chocolate milk container her mother would sometimes buy her for a treat. If she had on overalls, with her strong shoulders and full hips, she'd fit right in on a dairy farm. Instead, her vintage, flared, navy skirt and white jacket made her look like an office admin from the 1950's.

She brushed her hand down the wig's silky-soft, donated, human hair. It might feel scratchy and annoying against her scalp, but she cherished it. Her hair was never going to grow back. Second, third, and fourth opinions had confirmed it. The medicine that had saved her life had left her permanently bald. The wig allowed her to be normal.

Quiet, low-profile, under-the-radar normal. That's all she wanted. That's why she couldn't say "screw you" to the world and get rid of the goddamn wig.

Sage would do it. In a heartbeat. Nothing held Sage back. Ever. And Sage was so ridiculously beautiful, being bald would probably only accentuate her exquisite features. But Rosemary wasn't bold and model-level gorgeous like her sister. She was plain, easygoing. She didn't ruffle feathers and didn't make a fuss—and she liked it that way. Which meant she needed to get out of the bathroom and back to her desk before Armando got worried and sent Lily or Marge to check on her. That cringeworthy thought made her grab the file folder and her purse and head for the exit.

Hopefully, she'd make it to lunchtime without needing another scratch break.

The click of her navy heels echoed then muted as she journeyed to Lily's large walnut-hued desk in the small but elegant reception area. Nick Guerrero, the only other "associate" in Pannetone & Associates, had informed her that the travertine tile in the lobby had been imported from Tivoli and the hand-woven Turkish rug under the couch and chairs were Pannetone family heirlooms.

The room had the old-world elegance her stepfather had always strived for in his home but never quite achieved. Every time she passed through, she slowed to admire the Impressionist-style watercolors that adorned the walls, the intricate cut glass light fixtures, and the delicate hand-painted porcelain vases full of fresh-cut flowers that sat on large half-pillars on either side of the lobby. The overall effect was simply stunning.

Not that Lily ever seemed to notice. Right now, she had her nose buried in her cell phone, oblivious to the beauty of her surroundings. Maybe if the woman took a minute to appreciate what was around her, she'd be less grumpy.

Negativity breeds negativity. Her mom's voice shimmered in her mind, and Rosemary felt a wash of shame. Lily had worked at the firm for several years and spent every day in the reception area, while she had just hit the six-month mark and spent most of her time diligently working in her office. Of course, the beautiful room would have become commonplace for Lily. Rosemary just couldn't imagine not taking time each day to appreciate the graceful charm of the space. Life was too short. You had to take all the pleasure you could in every small moment, since you never knew when those moments would run out.

Three bouts of bone cancer had taught her that.

She set the folder atop the raised portion of Lily's desk and pasted a friendly smile on her face. "Good morning, Lily! Armando asked me to give you this."

Lily didn't look up.

"Would you also pull the files with the invoices for the Girard warehouse when you get a chance?" she asked.

Lily lifted her head and huffed. "Why do you need the invoices? Marge enters all the important information from the invoices into the system, and I do a double check. You shouldn't need the paper copies for anything."

"I understand that, but there are a few things I can't quite figure out, and I think seeing the paper might help. Even with two big computer screens, sometimes it's easier to shuffle through paper."

"And last week, you asked to see the invoices for the Penrose project, which you aren't even working on. The whole reason we input the invoice information into the system is so the accountants don't waste valuable client time wading through paper. Mr. Pannetone says customers don't want to pay hundreds of dollars an hour for accountants to do administrative work."

She kept her forced smile in place. Lily managed the file room, but she'd flat out refused to give Rosemary the Penrose files, saying she had to get Armando's permission first. Rosemary had ignored her and gone to the file room and looked at what she needed without telling Lily what she was doing. Still, she tried to soothe Lily now with an explanation.

"Penrose and Girard are both warehouse projects. I wanted to look at the Penrose invoices because those financials are complete. I thought looking at them would help me get a flavor of what type of expenses are normally involved in a warehouse project. I hoped it would help me do a better job on the Girard warehouse financials, which I *am* working on. I tried to access the Penrose invoices on the computer but couldn't open any of those files, so I figured the paper files would be the next best thing."

"You need to ask Dante about your computer," Lily snapped. "He's the one who controls access to the electronic files."

Her face might crack if she kept smiling, but if she got what she wanted, it would be worth it.

"I'm not asking about the electronic files. I know that's not your area. I'm asking you to pull the files with the invoices for the Girard warehouse for me. This is my first Moresco project, so I want to make sure everything is perfect." She risked having her cheeks break and expanded her smile. "I'll look at them during my lunch hour, and I won't bill the client for the time, so Armando won't have any reason to complain."

"I'm not sure. I'm not supposed to be giving anybody any Moresco files without Mr. Pannetone's express approval. Plus, I don't have time to be running around for you." Lily pointed one long hot pink fingernail toward a tall stack of paper on her desk. "I need to scan all these."

"Mr. Pannetone assigned the Girard warehouse work to me, so I'm sure he won't mind me reviewing the files if I don't bill the client for my time. I know you're busy, so I can just grab them myself. I need to go down to the file room anyway to talk to Dante about my access issues."

Lily glared at her, the expression making her look older than her thirty-three years. Lily was pretty, petite, and curvy with gorgeous long blue-black curls, but her nearly constant sour expression diminished her natural beauty. She wanted to tell Lily that life was too short for so much anger, but she knew Lily wouldn't appreciate the advice.

"I'm the only one who's supposed to touch the files," Lily said.

Rosemary leaned over and plucked an empty, dark blue file folder from Lily's desk. "I'll take this with me. I'll pull one file out at a time and use this to mark the spot. Nothing will get out of place. I promise."

Lily's grimace softened a bit. "Fine. Just be careful."

Rosemary swung by her office to grab her computer before heading down the internal fire exit stairs. She'd rather take the chilly concrete stairs than the elevator any day. The office occupied the second floor and basement of a building that dated back to the 1800s. The elevator's mechanics had been updated, but the size of the shaft was never enlarged, and the wood molding covering the walls made it feel even more cramped. The first time she'd ridden in that elevator, it had taken fifteen minutes of meditation and deep breathing to stop sweating.

Now, she always took the stairs.

Once she reached the bottom of the stairwell, she entered the access code and pushed the cool, thick metal bar to open the heavy door that led into the file room. The aroma of paper, warm electricity, and dust filled her nostrils. To her left, old-fashioned metal shelves stood floor to ceiling in perfect rows. She walked down the narrow aisle between the files and the wall, her low heels making oddly satisfying clicks on the gleaming linoleum.

Dante's thick dark curls appeared at the top of his cubicle, followed by his dancing eyes, friendly smile, and broad shoulders. He stepped around the partition, met her halfway down the hall, and bowed. "Welcome to my kingdom, fair lady. How may I be of service?"

Dante's formal greeting was a stark contrast to his low-riding joggers, sweatshirt, and vintage Jordans. They'd had a cake for his twenty-third birthday last month, but he still looked and dressed like a teenager.

She pointed to his sweatshirt where six different geometrically shaped dice were lined up over the words *Choose Your Weapon*. "Is that a band?"

Dante laughed. "You never played *Dungeons and Dragons*, did you?"

She'd played lots of games. Lots and lots of games. There'd been too many months when she'd been too sick, too weak, or too immunocompromised to leave the house, and there were only so many movies a person could watch. So, she, her mom, Sage, and Justin played tons of board games, but never *Dungeons and Dragons*. If they had, maybe their fantasy lives would have turned out better than their real ones.

She nudged that depressing thought out of her head. Fate was fate, and choices were choices. Being bitter or sad wouldn't change the past and would only sour the present. Even though her mom was gone and Justin was in prison, she wouldn't let those facts poison the joyful memories of playing board games with them.

"I'm a big fan of *Forbidden Island* and *Dominion,*" she answered, "but I've never played *Dungeons and Dragons*. I'll have to put it on my list."

Dante rolled his eyes. "You can't just start playing. You need to find a group first."

"A group?"

"You're hopeless," he said as he gestured toward her computer. "Are you having trouble with your laptop?"

He'd already started bouncing on his toes and peeking back toward his work area. He was a tech whiz who could spend hours staring at code or building a computer from scratch, but his patience for conversation was limited to about three minutes, and she'd hit the threshold.

"I came down to look at a few things in the Girard warehouse files, but I'm also having a computer issue. Lots of the Moresco files are grayed out on my laptop. I can see the file names, but they're in a lighter script, and when I click on them, nothing happens. The only Moresco files that aren't grayed out are the ones for the Girard warehouse. Do I need a different password or something?"

Dante quirked a bushy dark eyebrow. "I'm surprised Pannetone has you working on a project for Sal. He normally does all that work himself."

Pride swelled in Rosemary's chest. Nick, the other associate accountant, had been at the firm much longer, but Armando had trusted her with the assignment.

"It's my first Moresco project, so I want my work to be flawless. Mr. Moresco is here now for a meeting. You're related, right?"

She'd heard through the grapevine that Dante was Sal's nephew, which would explain his position at the firm. Even with Armando's archaic views on Cloud computing, a firm of three accountants, a receptionist, and a bookkeeper couldn't possibly generate enough IT work to keep Dante busy full-time. Of course, her stepfather had helped her get this job, so who was she to judge a bit of nepotism?

"Sal's my uncle," Dante confirmed, "but you know you're not supposed to talk about him being here. Armando told you that, right?"

Her cheeks and neck warmed. Armando had told her Sal was fastidiously private and that she was forbidden to discuss him or any of his projects, but she hadn't thought that applied to Dante.

"Right. Sorry. I guess I wasn't thinking."

Dante laid a hand on her wrist. "When it comes to my uncle, you can't afford to not think."

Unease chilled her spine. She swallowed and took a step back.

Dante released her arm and chuckled. "I didn't mean that to sound so ominous. My grandpa is whack when it comes to privacy."

"Your grandpa?"

"Yeah. He's the reason I have this job. Sal doesn't like me, but he doesn't have the balls to cross him. Grandpa's old school. No cell phone. No email. And when he does call, he's always using someone else's phone. He always thinks Big Brother's watching. That's why you can't get into any of the Moresco files."

Dante's conversations frequently jumped topics, but she could usually follow his twists and turns. This time, she was baffled.

"I can't get into your uncle's files because your grandpa doesn't like to talk on the phone?"

Dante snorted. "Kind of. Grandpa hates technology. He only let Armando start keeping electronic records a few years ago. That's why I'm here."

He pointed toward the table of servers next to his cubicle. "Everyone else might be on the Cloud, but the Moresco files are all on those servers, and the email system is locked down so the files can't be emailed out. I've got the files set up so that Armando and I are the only ones with full access. That's why all the Moresco files are grayed out on your computer except for the Girard warehouse. I gave you temporary access to those, and I'll revoke it when the work is done."

Her watch vibrated on her wrist. She was late for a call.

"Yikes. I have to go." She headed back down the hall, calling out over her shoulder, "Seems a little heavy-handed for a real estate and construction business, don't you think?"

Dante's odd response still echoed in her mind hours later.

"With my family, you can never be too careful."

Chapter Two

Aleksei Thompson's phone started ringing as soon as he passed a crooked Balsam fir that served as his mental marker for when cell service cut off on the trail—or in this instance, restarted.

Shit.

He should turn around and walk back up the mountain. He wasn't ready to talk to anyone yet. Wasn't ready to lose the clear mind and sense of peace he always found while hiking. Alone in the woods, out of cell phone range, it was easy to let the real world slip away. But reality was like smoke. It always found cracks to seep through.

He slipped his hand into his pocket, found the volume button, and held it down, effectively turning the ring into a vibration. He pressed forward, ignoring the buzz in his pocket and the temptation to flee back up the mountain. He was good at ignoring.

During the past couple of years, he'd become an expert at avoidance, a master of compartmentalizing. He lived. He worked. He occasionally visited his mother and called his sister. He pasted a smile on his face every time anyone asked how he was doing.

He lied through his teeth and said things were fine.

And when he couldn't take it one minute longer, when his too-keen mind and guilty heart wouldn't allow him to forget that Phillipe was dead, he hiked. He hiked to find respite from the constant sorrow simmering in his soul. He hiked to forget.

He focused on forgetting now, concentrating on the whisper of the breeze on his face, the mulchy, mossy aroma of spring, and the sporadic glints of sunlight on the glossy green leaves. His spine eased as his legs covered ground in long rhythmic strides. The trees thinned, and the path widened as he neared the trailhead. He lowered the zipper on his weatherproof jacket. It was getting warmer as the chill of early morning waned and the elevation decreased.

Birds chirped. A chipmunk skittered across his path. His hiking boots were quiet on the muddy trail. It had rained almost every day last week, and the nights were still too cold for the ground to dry quickly. A squirrel paused halfway up a loblolly pine, studying him.

Too much wildlife.

Which meant Jaka was too far behind.

Aleksei paused, whistled, and waited. He closed his eyes, focusing on the sounds of the forest. The birds quieted, and the low scuffle of small animals fleeing filled his ears. He opened his eyes, and flashes of black, brown, and white appeared through the trees, followed by the pound and squish of paws on wet ground.

Jaka bounded down the path and came to a full stop next to him. Aleksei dropped to one knee, the ground damp and cold on his leg. His pants, unlike his jacket, weren't water-resistant, but they were almost to the truck. It didn't matter if he got a little wet. He buried his fingers in the dog's long thick fur. Jaka's dark, intelligent eyes seemed to assess him before she nudged her forehead into his face. He let his cheek rest there, feeling the tickle of whiskers and warm breath, regaining the inner calm the ringing phone had ripped away.

"Sometimes, I don't know what I'd do without you."

Jaka barked softly.

It was crazy, but sometimes he thought Jaka actually understood him. Maybe not his words, but it was as if the Australian shepherd sensed what he needed. Comfort. Distraction. Play. A good long hike.

His mother kept telling him that a dog wasn't a substitute for a human, but, on this one thing, his usually correct mother was dead wrong.

Jaka was better than a human. She was reliable and predictable. With her, there were no surprises. People, on the other hand, were an entirely different story. No matter how well you knew somebody, they could still do something completely unpredictable.

Like end up with a .40-caliber bullet in the back of their head.

The image dug into his mind like a falcon's talons. Phillipe, face down on the blood-soaked sidewalk. Flesh and bone torn open by the force of the shot. Pink-gray brain matter speckling his hair. Then the medical examiner flipping him over. The money in his mouth. The missing hands.

He gulped in air as the protein bar he'd had for breakfast threatened to come up.

Fuuuuuuuck.

No matter what he did, he couldn't escape that scene.

Alcohol. The FBI psychologist. Time.

They hadn't helped. Hiking and Jaka were the only things that made him forget. But they were temporary reprieves. The overwhelming sense of gut-wrenching loss always clawed its way back in. Aleksei shifted so his forehead was pressed to Jaka's, and he let out a long slow breath, trying to clear his mind. Once that image invaded his mind, it was so goddamn hard to wipe it away.

Without warning, Jaka jumped. Muddy paws pressed into his shoulders, pushing him off balance. He flailed his arms outward but gripped only air as he flopped backward onto the trail with Jaka's paws on his chest and her rough, wet tongue on his cheek. He tried to push himself up, but the ground was too slick to get much purchase. His heavy hiking pack had turned him into a flipped turtle.

A smile pulled on his lips. If his sister were here, she'd be laughing her ass off. She'd love seeing him floundering and unbalanced. She was always teasing him about being a military science project, saying he was too fit to be a normal human. After seeing *Captain America: The First Avenger*, she started calling him Cap, and Phillipe had picked right up on it, ribbing him mercilessly. Phillipe even bought him a Captain America backpack for Christmas one year. The backpack was hidden under a blanket on a shelf in Aleksei's closet. He couldn't bear to look at it.

The memories were sharper than his favorite knife.

Jaka resumed her enthusiastic tongue bath, pulling Aleksei back to the present. He gently pushed the dog down and shifted his weight to the side so he could stand.

"All right. All right. I get it. You don't like it when I'm sad. But you didn't need to knock me over. I'm a muddy mess. I'm going to have to change out of these clothes before we get into the truck, and the bathrooms don't open until ten. I'll be lucky if I don't get arrested for indecent exposure for changing in the parking lot."

Jaka's response was to bark and trot ahead down the trail. He shook his head and followed.

The world really would be so much better if people were like dogs.

He'd taken only a few steps when the phone started vibrating again. Whoever was calling was persistent. His mouth turned dry. He should answer. What if something had happened to his mom? Or his sister? He pulled the phone out of his pocket, glanced at the screen, and spit whatever moisture was left in his mouth to the ground.

Kemper.

Gary—ass-kissing, by-the-book, relentless as a dog with a bone—Kemper.

If he didn't answer the phone, Kemper would just keep calling. And if he turned the goddamn thing off, Kemper would probably have some white-collared, buttoned-up lackey standing at his front door by the time he got home. When that man wanted something, he was tenacious. Rumor was he'd spent nineteen straight days on a stakeout pissing into a Gatorade bottle and leaving the car only when he had to take a shit.

Too bad Kemper was too much of a company man to have used that same fire to speak up when the FBI pushed Phillipe's murder under the rug. Instead, Kemper had chosen to follow orders and look the other way. When the shit hit the fan, Kemper had saved himself.

Asshole.

Aleksei had tried investigating himself, but that had gone over like bringing a preacher to a bachelor party. The bigwigs had gotten pissed, and Kemper said they'd threatened to fire Aleksei for insubordination if he didn't back off. He hadn't cared about the job, so he kept on digging. Then, one morning, he came to work and found a picture of Phillipe's dead body on his desk, with a confidential internal affairs memo theorizing that Phillipe was taking bribes. There'd also been a printed copy of a *Wall Street Journal* article about his mom's recently announced decision to run for Virginia Attorney General. Someone had struck out the headline and written "Son of Rising Star Judge Involved in Bribery Scandal."

The implication was clear. It didn't matter that Aleksei was squeaky clean and the evidence against Phillipe was flimsy. He was Phillipe's partner and best friend. If someone leaked that Phillipe was an FBI agent and claimed Aleksei was involved with whatever Phillipe was into, the facts would be irrelevant. The media wouldn't be looking for proof. They wanted only a sensational story. If he didn't back off, someone was going to feed lies to the media, and his mom's political career would be over before it even started.

He couldn't do that to her. Not when she'd worked so hard and come so far. Her story was an impossible one. She was a Romani-Serbian immigrant who'd been the victim of human trafficking. She had nothing when his dad got her out. She worked to pay her own way through college and law school, her gender and accent making every step three times harder than it should have been. She'd dedicated her life to fighting oppression, to protecting those with no one to fight for them.

She wouldn't have cared if he'd continued to stir the pot. She would tell him to run every lead into the ground and damn the consequences. She would tell him to find out what happened to Phillipe no matter how long it took or who he angered. She had his back. Always. He shivered, thinking of the lecture he'd get if she ever found out he'd backed down because he hadn't wanted to put her career in jeopardy.

His mother was like a riptide. It was impossible to swim against her.

But she didn't know that he'd had to choose between her and Phillipe, between dashing the dreams of the living and clearing the name of the dead. There had been no choice. There was no point in ruining his mom's political aspirations. With the FBI throwing up every possible roadblock, the chances of bringing Phillipe's killer to justice were shit anyway. So, he lived with the fact that he'd failed his best friend.

And it was fucking brutal.

His phone went still for a few seconds and then started vibrating again.

He'd thought Kemper was done trying to talk him into taking the job in Chicago. His leaving the FBI and shifting to a consultant-trainer at Quantico had been a win-win. He'd needed some separation. He couldn't stomach being an active FBI agent after the bureau had betrayed Phillipe, and the bureau was glad he was out of Philly. They didn't want him drawing attention to the death of a dirty agent, and it was hard as hell to stir up trouble when you were in another state.

So why the hell was Kemper calling now?

He hit the green circle to accept the call. "I'm hiking, so this better be good."

"You'd be less grumpy if you'd transferred to Chicago instead of schooling newbies." Kemper's deep, gravelly voice boomed through the phone.

"We've walked this road. You know I'm not coming back, and I know you don't really care. If you did, you'd be on the streets doing everything in your power to put the asshole who murdered my best friend in a cage."

Kemper sighed. "You're right. We have walked this road, and you know this was out of my hands the second the ME pulled twenty grand in cash out of Phillipe's pocket. You guys were undercover for months, and we had nothing to show for it but an agent on the take. No matter what I said, they were going to shut us down."

Kemper was right. There was only so much Kemper could do. He was fifty-two years old with a wife, two kids in college, and one in private high school. The guy couldn't afford to risk his job, but that did nothing to cool the ever-present lava of anger that simmered in Aleksei's chest day after day. Without the rigid control he'd learned in the military, some of that anger might have spilled out.

"If you aren't calling to tear open old wounds, what are you calling about?"

The question was met with the hissing swoosh he recognized as Kemper taking a drag on one of his beloved Marlboro Lights. Kemper had smoked like a chimney but quit cold turkey after his brother died from lung cancer. If he was smoking again, something was up.

"I don't want to get your hopes up, but I think I might have found something."

His chest tightened. Kemper knew there was only one thing that could get his hopes up. Only one lead that could possibly matter to him. Only one wrong he'd give almost anything to right.

Kemper had a line on Phillipe's killer.

Aleksei forced himself to take a few seconds before responding. An excited mind prevented concentration. An excited mind meant mistakes. He'd spent nearly two years trying to convince himself to accept the fact that he might never have the opportunity to avenge his best friend's death. Now, he realized that wasn't what he'd been doing at all. He'd just been waiting. Waiting for an opportunity. Waiting for something to break. Waiting for a call like this.

"What did you find?"

"It's probably nothing," Kemper answered.

"You wouldn't be calling if you thought it was nothing."

Another sharp hiss filled the line while Kemper took another drag. "Even though we shut the operation down, I still had a couple informants on the payroll. We shared 'em with DEA, and they were under their budget, so they never got cut off. I'd forgotten about them until I got a call from one of them the other day. He must've still had my number."

"Does he know who killed Phillipe?"

Kemper grunted. "You really think it's going to be that easy?"

Of course not. Nothing truly worth having ever came easy. His parents had made sure he'd learned that.

"What did the informant say?"

"He said Salvatore Moresco had him follow an accountant. A woman. Rosemary Cashman. Moresco wants tabs on her. The CI said Moresco got pissed when he asked why. He also said that she's related to a guy who spent a few months in jail for fraud. Davis Anderson. The CI thinks Anderson might have ties to Moresco."

Salvatore Moresco. Just hearing the name made his muscles tense.

He quickened his pace. His mind always worked better when he was moving. *Rosemary Cashman. Davis Anderson.* He didn't recognize either name. "Could the woman be Moresco's girlfriend? Maybe Moresco wanted to make sure she wasn't getting down and dirty with someone else?"

"I asked. The CI said no. Said he'd been following her for a few weeks, and she's just an average woman with an average life. He actually sounded worried about her."

Aleksei pulled Jaka's leash from his jacket pocket, snapped it on her collar and then sped up to a light jog. His backpack bounced against his shoulder blades and lower back as his feet and Jaka's paws thudded on the muddy trail. The increased blood flow and rhythmic pounding were like jumper cables for his brain. He could almost hear the gears clicking and whirring as he processed what Kemper had shared. A guy wasn't going to follow someone day in and day out for free. Manpower had a price, and Moresco thought this woman was worth paying it.

"Embezzlement?" he asked.

Kemper snorted. "I thought the same thing. The CI doesn't think so. Says the girl lives a simple life in a simple apartment, so there's no sign of extra cash. Plus, I did a quick Google search, and it looks like her sister's fiancé is as rich as Midas. But I guess you never know."

The whirring gears intersected.

"You think Moresco's worried she knows something. Something he doesn't want told."

Another long hiss filled the line.

"I think she's an accountant and they got Capone on tax evasion. Plus, the CI says she works for Pannetone & Associates. I remember Phillipe mentioning something about that firm right before—"

Right before he was murdered, and we all shut our eyes and walked away.

But arguing with Kemper wouldn't bring Phillipe back. "You think this accountant might be the key to bringing Moresco down?"

"Phillipe was killed outside a Moresco property, so I think Moresco knows what happened to him. Not a goddamn thing happens in that organization without his approval. It's worth checking out. If the accountant's got something on Moresco..."

"We use it to get justice for Phillipe," Aleksei finished Kemper's sentence for him.

"You have to keep this on the down-low," Kemper warned. "I'm walking a fine line telling you any of this since you're a consultant now and not an active agent. Plus, you know the bureau doesn't like our dirty laundry made public. If the big shots find out we're at this again, both our asses are toast."

"Don't worry. Quantico just finished classes, which means I'm off for the next few weeks. No one will even know I'm in Philly."

If the accountant knew anything—anything at all—Aleksei was going to find it out.

Chapter Three

Rosemary had been looking at invoices so long that numbers danced behind her eyelids every time she closed her eyes. Something just wasn't adding up.

Figuratively.

Because, literally, everything was adding up. She'd checked every number on every paper invoice, compared those to the spreadsheet she'd found in the file, compared those to the numbers in the payables summary, and checked every number on every page of the financial statements. Then she'd redone the math by hand on her calculator.

It was nearly 2:00 p.m., and she'd let herself get sucked into double- and triple-checking the numbers on the Penrose warehouse, which had taken forever because Armando had refused her request to access the electronic files. He thought using the Penrose financials as a basis for her Girard work was a waste of time. But with the projects being so similar, that just didn't make sense. So, instead of listening to her boss, she'd snuck all the Penrose files into her office and had spent the morning reviewing them when she was supposed to be finishing the draft payment schedule and financials for the Girard warehouse.

She was going to get herself fired.

She kept telling herself to put the Penrose files away and work on the Girard project, but she had that same niggling sensation she used to get during math tests when some other, smarter part of her brain would tell her she'd made a mistake on one of the earlier problems. Sure enough, every time she had that feeling and rechecked her work, she found an error.

So why wasn't she finding the error now?

Maybe Remiza had fried that part of her brain at the same time it fried her hair follicles.

"And cured your cancer, you ungrateful wretch," she muttered.

She was lucky to have this job. Even though she was twenty-six years old when she'd started at Pannetone & Associates, she'd had very little work experience. With being sick so much, it had taken her longer to finish college, so she'd gotten a late start on her career. Then, she had to quit her first and only accounting job when Davis had lost his mind, and her orderly life had gone to hell in a handbasket.

But Davis had paid the price, at least in her mind. Sage said six months in jail and two years' probation didn't really count as paying a price, but Rosemary disagreed. Davis had apologized to both of them, expressed remorse, and tried to make amends by helping her get this amazing job. The job was perfect.

The office was only a twenty-minute walk from her apartment, which was just enough time to ease into the day and decompress on the way home. Armando was pleasant, charming, and eager to share his extensive knowledge, and the pay was fantastic. She was making twice what she earned at her prior job and working fewer hours. Armando prioritized family and encouraged everyone to leave the office by 5:30 or 6:00. At her old firm, she was lucky if she got home by 8:00. Sure, Lily was difficult, the espresso machine went on the fritz every other week, and Rosemary had gained five pounds from the fact that the office was above a gelato shop, but overall, the pros heavily outweighed the cons.

She pushed her wig into her sweaty head with her fingers and released a heavy sign.

If she wanted to keep her job, she needed to stop chasing windmills and finish the tasks assigned to her. If she didn't ignore her gut and get back on track, she'd never get the financials for the Girard warehouse to Armando by the deadline.

She lifted her bleary eyes from the papers she'd been studying and looked around her office. Redwelds covered the small table next to her desk and the floor around it. Armando had an invoice for every single item purchased for the Penrose warehouse—from steel girders and truckloads of cement down to the doorbell camera and the hand dryers in the bathroom. Plus, all the contractor service invoices.

It seemed odd to maintain every paper invoice, but meticulous recordkeeping shouldn't be making her instincts flare. *So why was it?* She considered for a moment then grabbed the calculator from her desk, shoving it into her top drawer.

She did *not* have time for this.

She needed to get the Penrose files—which she wasn't supposed to even have in the first place—back to the file room and get her ass in gear on the Girard project. It would probably take four or five trips to carry the veritable sea of files back downstairs. She could grab the cart from the copy room, but then she'd risk Lily seeing her and catching wind of the fact she'd taken the files out of the file room. A ranting, raging Lily was not something she was willing to deal with today. Plus, taking the files back on the cart would also mean riding in the claustrophobic elevator.

The elevator!

Rosemary's fingers flew to the spreadsheets covering her desk, flipping through pages. The payables list was organized by payee. *Not helpful.* She leapt up and grabbed the file with the complete financials, her eyes absorbing line after line of data. She likely wouldn't find what she was looking for. Construction financials didn't break down every single payment. Only an incredibly large expense would be called out separately. Although expensive by an everyday person's standards, an elevator wasn't a big enough expenditure to be a line-item entry.

She jumped back up and rifled through the files. Forty-seven minutes and two paper cuts later, she found what she was looking for. One lone invoice from LG Mechanicals for the purchase and installation of a 3500-pound max capacity in-ground hydraulic elevator. She pivoted and grabbed the two-foot-long, heavy-gauge cardboard tube labeled PLANS.

She pulled the chunky blue-and-white construction schematics from their casing, dropped to her knees, and rolled them out on the ground. She flipped past the initial survey and various exterior site plans that labeled setbacks, impervious surface, and drainage, until she found the sheets with the interior detail. The building was a standard, large, open-floor-plan warehouse with a bathroom and office space. There were large doors and ramps for loading, but she didn't see anything that resembled any type of electronic lift, let alone an actual elevator.

She stared down at the invoice she'd set next to the plans, her heart racing in her chest.

$574,355.

That was a lot of money for an invisible elevator.

She stood on shaky legs, pulled a handwipe from the stash in her desk drawer, and cleaned her hands. If she got any of that blue ink from the plans on her favorite white jacket, it would never come out. That stuff stained everything it touched.

Her scalp twitched. Nerves had made it even sweatier. She pressed her fingers into the itchy spot, moving the wig against her wig cap to scratch the itch. She did not have time for toothpicks and a bathroom trip right now.

The Girard warehouse invoices were all still in the file room. She was almost certain she'd seen an elevator invoice in there. *Had it been from the same company?* She couldn't remember. She plopped down in her office chair and pulled up the Girard payables list on her computer. At least she had access to the Girard electronic files and didn't have to rummage through paper like she'd just done for Penrose. She searched LG Mechanicals.

Nothing.

It would take her hours to go through all the Girard invoices. And for what? To find an invoice for an elevator? Maybe there *was* an elevator in the Girard warehouse. Maybe they'd added one to Penrose and hadn't added the updated plans to the files.

Right. Pannetone keeps every single piece of paper down to the invoice for the toilet paper dispenser, and he doesn't put updated plans in the file?

Her scalp twitched again. A strong itchy twitch.

She needed to stop. How many times had her mother and sister told her she was relentless? Relentless with those murder mystery games. Relentless with crosswords and sudoku. Relentless with the 3D brainteaser puzzles her mother always bought for her. This wasn't a game or a puzzle.

This was her job. And she had a deadline. She had to put the finishing touches on the Girard financials and get them to Armando this afternoon so he could review them. Especially since she was leaving a little early tomorrow to go to the theater with Sage.

She needed to focus on finishing the Girard work.

And she would. Right after she took a quick dash to the file room to take an even quicker look at the Girard plans to see if they showed an elevator. It would only take a few minutes, and she had to start returning the Penrose files anyway.

She pulled open the heavy fireproof door to the basement stairwell, the knob cool on her hand. She whipped around the landing, numbers dancing in her head. The Morescos had hundreds of businesses. From tiny enterprises like vending machines to multiphase high-rise construction projects. If someone had found a way to slip fake invoices into even a small portion of those businesses, it could mean millions of dollars. Maybe tens of millions. Maybe even more.

Whomp!

Flesh collided with flesh, and the three Penrose files she'd been carrying went flying. Paper scattered like glass on concrete.

Lily staggered backward.

Instinct sent Rosemary's arm flying out to steady her. "I'm so sorry. Are you okay?"

Brown pupils glittered from red, swollen eyes. Rivulets of eye makeup stained Lily's cheeks.

"I'm fine," Lily said, crouching to help clean up the mess. After picking up a few sheets, her eyes narrowed. "These are Penrose files. You aren't supposed to have these! Armando's going to be really angry when he finds out you took these from the file room."

Shit.

Rosemary's mouth went dry, and her armpits and scalp went clammy. Her mind raced, trying to find a way out of the disaster her obsessive nature had created. Coming up blank, she tried distraction. "Why are you crying?"

"I'm not crying," Lily snapped.

She laid a hand on Lily's slippery rayon sleeve. "Maybe I can help."

"It's boyfriend stuff. You wouldn't understand."

Of course Lily would think she wouldn't understand. Everyone in the office knew she was single. They just didn't know the complicated reason why.

"Try me. When something's wrong, it helps if you talk about it."

At least that was what her mother always said.

Lily flopped down on a step, leaning her back against the wall. "I feel like my boyfriend's using me. I see him less and less, but he wants more and more from me. I hate all the lies. He keeps telling me he's leaving his wife, but he's been stringing me along for five years. We got into a terrible fight about it, and now I regret it. I don't want to lose him."

If it had been five years and her boyfriend still hadn't left his wife, he wasn't going to, but Lily was going to have to come to that conclusion on her own. Giving unbidden, unwelcome advice Lily wasn't ready to hear wasn't going to help either of them.

"What about a fancy, romantic dinner at the Capital Grille? That should help smooth things over, right?"

Lily sniffed. "I can't afford that."

"I still have that $300 gift card Armando gave as the prize for winning the March Madness bracket. You could use that."

"And you'd just give that to me?" Lily asked suspiciously.

"Definitely. If you straighten up this mess"—she gestured toward the papers spilled across multiple stairs—"and get the other Penrose files out of my office and back to the file room without Armando knowing."

Lily's sad face brightened. "Done."

Rosemary willed her pounding heart to settle as she watched Lily gather the spilled papers and shove the disorganized mess into the folders.

Done. Just like she was done. Done risking her job. Done worrying about imaginary elevators. Done chasing rabbits down holes. She wasn't going to chance running into the Queen of Hearts. She liked her head just where it was.

* * *

Aleksei glanced at his smartwatch. It was close to six p.m. He'd started his walk about an hour ago, slowly meandering around Third Street. He stopped and studied the display windows of the art galleries he passed, browsed the paperbacks stacked on tables outside a used bookstore, and managed to grind another fifteen minutes of stakeout time buying and eating a gelato from Enzo's Gelateria. A couple of teenage boys had been more than happy to earn ten bucks holding Jaka's leash while he'd grabbed a cone.

Now, he was down to his last few licks. Time was running out. If he lingered much longer, it would look suspicious.

Last night, in a Walmart parking lot in Delaware, Kemper had given him a brief written report on Rosemary Cashman as well as a candid picture that he figured was taken by the snitch. In the photo, Rosemary was stepping out of a coffee shop, face lifted as if she was admiring the clouds or welcoming the day. She looked peaceful and content yet eager to see what was around the next corner.

There'd been a time when he, too, approached each day like a present to be unwrapped. Now, his days felt blank. Blank with piercing gashes of sadness, anger, and guilt.

Discipline made him bury the thought before it had time to settle in, and he shifted his gaze to study the exterior of the gelateria. The report stated that Pannetone & Associates was on the second floor above the shop, but from his on-the-ground recon, he realized that the businesses had separate entrances. The glass door to the gelateria was on the side of the building, about fifteen feet from the corner, and looked like a modern addition, while the modest, bronze, Pannetone & Associates sign was affixed to the brick at the corner, up five concrete steps next to a heavy oak door.

He watched two women walk out the door as he leaned against a cold metal light pole. One woman was in her early thirties, petite, dark-haired, and wearing heavy makeup. The other woman reminded him of his mom. Gray hair, strong bones, and a quick, efficient walk. Neither matched the blonde-haired, blue-eyed woman in the photo Kemper had given him.

He pushed away from the pole and tightened his grip on Jaka's leash. The sun was setting. He'd lingered as long as he could without seeming creepy. He bent down and grabbed a few napkins some careless patrons had let fall to the ground, crumpled them up along with the little sampler spoon he'd used to share his dessert with Jaka, and tossed the entire crinkly ball in an arc toward the trash can at the edge of the curb. It flowed neatly through the circle opening.

"Nice shot!"

The voice flowed over him like early summer wind—warm and cleansing. The speaker stood at the top of the concrete steps. She wore round-toed navy heels along with a navy skirt with thick, white stripes. She also donned a navy top with a white jacket and a tan open raincoat, the belt hanging loose at her sides. A flowered purse hung from her shoulder, and a new black briefcase that still had its shine crossed her body. Her platinum hair hung past her shoulders, and a bright, white-teethed smile stretched her lips.

This was Rosemary Cashman, but in the picture, she looked quiet and thoughtful. In person, vitality crackled around her.

"Thanks. I'm usually one for five. You caught me on a good day."

He strode toward her, intentionally keeping his pace loose and lazy. Working undercover, he'd acquired the ability to project whatever image he needed. Nervous, dangerous, intimidating, or, like now, relaxed, easy, and friendly. In this case, his demeanor wasn't entirely affected. The open warmth in Rosemary's smile was infectious. He wanted to approach her. Wanted to get to know her better.

"You look like you should start singing and dance down those stairs," he said as he reached the bottom of the concrete steps.

She laughed. "What do you mean?"

He waved his free hand up toward her. "Your skirt and jacket. The traditional raincoat. You look like you should be in one of those 1940s musicals. You'd open some colorful umbrella, start tap dancing down the stairs, and when you get right here"—he pointed down at the sidewalk—"you'd bump into Bing Crosby and launch into a duet."

She executed a little shuffle kick, spun, and then took each step down in a partial skip, her heels clicking on the concrete. When she reached the bottom, her cheeks were pink, and her eyes were as bright as a full moon.

"The dancing I can fake. The singing, not so much."

"Fake the dancing? That was impressive."

She shook her head, rolling her bright blue eyes. "Not impressive. More like amateur hour. You should see my sister dance. She's amazing. Growing up, whenever she wanted to practice with someone, I was her conscripted partner. I picked up a few things, but if this were a musical, she's the one who'd be the star. And she'd dance right on by your Bing Crosby, since I'm sure she has no idea who he is. I certainly don't."

Amusement warmed his chest. "Were you raised by wolves? How do you not know Bing Crosby?"

"If he's some 1940s musical star, I feel like I should be asking you why you know who he is."

He felt a grin stretch his cheeks and raised his hands in mock surrender. "Okay. That's fair. Maybe I shouldn't expect everyone to have a mom who is an old musical buff. You have no idea how many Bing Crosby movies I've seen and how many times I've watched them. If you ever need somebody for Boomer trivia, entertainment category, I'm your man."

Her laughter was like tinkling bells. "I'll keep that in mind. I think it's really sweet that you have that connection with your mom." Her smile dimmed. "Time like that is precious."

He would've known her mother, or someone else important to her, was deceased even if he hadn't read it in the file. Her wistful tone, the reflexive clench of her hands, the protective inward shrug—they were all easy tells. But having that inside knowledge of her mom's passing and not being able to acknowledge it gave him an oily, smarmy feeling, like when he was in eighth grade and had gotten caught passing a nasty note about sweet Ms. Butler. As an awkward preteen, he'd written the note to try to fit in with the cool kids, but seeing Ms. Butler's hurt expression was ten times worse than being one of the nerds.

Seeing a look like that on Rosemary's face would be devastating.

And where the hell had that thought come from?

He couldn't afford to think like that. Rosemary was important because she might be the key to bringing Phillipe's killer to justice, the key to assuaging the guilt that constantly gnawed at his intestines, the key to bringing some closure for Phillipe's wife, Samantha. Aleksei had been the one to tell her. Gone in person to the quaint Cape Cod with an actual white picket fence. She knew the minute she saw his face. She'd collapsed, screaming and sobbing in his arms, demanding to know what happened.

And he'd had no answers.

So yeah, it might feel like crap to have to play this seemingly sweet woman who could be just one more of Moresco's innocent victims, but if it meant bringing Moresco down, if it meant getting answers for Samantha and answers for himself, if it meant bringing Phillipe's killer to justice, he couldn't worry about whether Rosemary ended up with a hurt expression on her face like Ms. Butler. Even though it turned his stomach, he played his next card.

"I know exactly what you mean. Time with loved ones is precious. My dad died a few years ago. It was about a month after we got back from a fishing trip we'd put off for too long. There was always some reason why it wasn't a good time to go. I'm so glad we went on that trip. I'd hate myself if he passed and we never went."

Rosemary laid a hand lightly on his elbow. A slow, gentle warmth flowed up his arm.

"I'm sorry for your loss. I know how you feel. I lost my mom a couple of years ago, and I'm so grateful for all the good times we had together." She lifted her hand from his arm and stretched it out in front of her. "I'm Rosemary Cashman."

He engulfed her smaller hand in his own, and that same soothing heat that had flowed up his arm now filled his palm. He stared into her shining eyes. The sound of passing cars faded, and suddenly, it felt like they were the only two people on the sidewalk. He'd meant for their initial meeting to be a quick touch and go, but their joined hands lingered, as if she, like him, had some deep-seated need to hold on.

"I'm Aleksei. Aleksei Thompson. I know this might seem presumptuous, but would you like to have dinner with me?"

Chapter Four

Her breath whooshed out of her lungs, leaving her slightly lightheaded. Thoughts skittered through her shocked brain.

A handsome stranger had just invited her to dinner. One with the slightest hint of a mysterious accent. One who made sure trash got into the trashcan and who watched musicals because his mother liked them.

Things like this happened to Sage, not her.

Plus, he was a dog lover. From inside the door, she'd watched him offering tastes of his gelato to his dog from a spoon. She loved Thor, but she wouldn't share her ice cream with him. Well, unless he did the sad-eyed paw lift to shake when she hadn't even asked him to thing. Then she would probably be offering him tastes from a little spoon too.

Thor was an expert manipulator—or, maybe, she was just soft. It seemed like Mr. Tall, Lean, and Handsome had the same soft spot she did. At least on the inside. On the outside, there didn't seem to be one soft thing about his body or the strong, calloused fingers that still held her hand.

Ugh! Her palms were a sweaty mess. How completely unattractive.

She tugged her arm back, instantly missing the warmth of his palm. "I don't usually go to dinner with strangers."

She *didn't* usually go to dinner with anyone other than Sage and Ryker and, occasionally, Davis when he guilted her into it. And Sage would be upset if she went.

No. That was unfair.

Sage would want her to go. Sage wanted her to be happy. Wanted her to experience all the amazing things she'd missed for so many years when she was sick. But Sage would want it done on her terms. Her sister would demand a photograph of Aleksei's driver's license so she could have Ryker's PI run a background check, stalk him on social media, insist on knowing the exact time and location of the dinner, and require numerous check-in texts during the event.

It wouldn't be an impromptu date. It would be a well-orchestrated military operation.

She got it. Sage loved her. Sage wanted her safe. She was the best sister anyone could ask for. Sage had sacrificed so much for her, even leaving Juilliard and dancing in a gentlemen's club to keep them both safe. But truth be told, sometimes her sister's love, no matter how deep, sincere, and well-intended, was suffocating. Rosemary was done with being smothered and confined.

She'd given up so much freedom during her cancer treatments. She did exactly what the doctors told her. She spent years barely leaving the house. She ate what they said to eat, took pills when they said to take them, slept the exact number of hours they demanded, and avoided doing anything fun and exciting for fear of germs. She'd lived a life dictated by others.

But not anymore.

Since starting with Pannetone & Associates, she'd turned over a new leaf. She made her own choices based on what *she* wanted. She stopped at her favorite coffee shop every day on her way to work for a blueberry muffin and cinnamon latte. Damn the caffeine and damn the carbs.

She went to hot yoga and the rock-climbing gym—previously

forbidden places the doctors had labeled "germ factories." On weekends, she went to the art museum, concerts, and crystal shops. She purchased fresh vegetables in the Italian market, never worrying about getting overtired or being in a crowd.

She could do it all now without considering the impact on a battered, immuno-compromised body because, thanks to the experimental medicine that had saved her life, she was finally healthy and strong. She was twenty-seven years old and had barely scratched the surface of what life had to offer. If an attractive, charming man wanted to take her out for dinner, she would damn well go if she wanted to, regardless of what her sister would think.

"But in your case, I'll make an exception," she finally answered.

His smile broadened, showing straight, white teeth. "Great! With the way you hesitated, I thought you were going to turn me down."

"I considered it, but then I reminded myself I'm supposed to be living life adventurously."

"Living life adventurously. I like the sound of that. I could use a little adventure."

There was that touch of an accent again, like Alexander Skarsgård in that *Legend of Tarzan* movie Sage had loved when they were teenagers.

Despite the chill in the air, warmth curled through Rosemary's stomach. "Maybe we can help each other. But food first. In a public place. I may be embracing adventure, but I'm going to be smart about it."

"Yes, ma'am." He straightened his back and gave her a sharp salute. Really sharp. Like it was a reflex. "Any suggestions on where we should go?"

She crouched down, her briefcase banging against her leg, and extended her hand slowly so Aleksei's dog could sniff and lick it. The dog's nose was cold, and her tongue was wet and rough on Rosemary's fingers. She shifted her hands to pet the thick, soft, brown and white fur at the dog's neck as she said, "We need to go somewhere pet-friendly. Right, girl?"

Aleksei's large hand encircled her arm, his grip strong yet gentle, as he helped her stand back up. "Her name's Jaka. I was so focused on you, I almost forgot she was with me."

She dropped her gaze to her navy pumps. She'd been so flustered by her encounter with Lily that she'd forgotten to change into her sneakers. The pavement was chilling her feet through the thin soles. Aleksei's words made that same cold snake into her belly, dimming the glow of their encounter.

"Don't do that," she said.

"Do what?" he asked.

"The fake flattery. You don't need to use it. I already said I would go to dinner with you."

He moved closer. Dark gray leather sneakers with gray laces and white soles appeared in front of her own shoes. One firm, rough-skinned finger slid under her chin and eased her head slowly upward. The sneakers turned into dark wash jeans, then a black zip-front jacket, then a chiseled jawline with a sprinkling of stubble, full lips, a strong straight nose, and finally, intense, gray-blue eyes. Eyes like the sky on the cusp of a storm.

He lowered his head.

She smelled mint and fresh pine.

Warm breath brushed her ear. "I don't use fake flattery. It's not my style."

And just like that, the cold was gone, replaced by a sharp, intense, poker-hot heat racing up her thighs.

She stepped aside, allowing the evening breeze to cool her burning body. "I know a place we can go. A place we can go to eat. To eat dinner. A place to go eat dinner."

Aleksei's smile turned wolfish.

"What else would we eat?"

* * *

The white strands in Rosemary's arrow-straight hair looked like flames in the red and yellow light of the heat lamps and decorative string lights on the small patio. Something about the way the color reflected the light nipped at the edges of his mind.

"Is something wrong with my hair?" Rosemary's question came out tight.

He turned his gaze to her face. "No. Sorry I was staring. That was rude. Your hair...it looks bright and radiant in this light. Like a halo. You look like an angel."

She rolled her eyes. "You don't mean that."

Annoyance flashed through him. "Why do you do that?"

"Do what?"

"Assume a compliment isn't sincere. Are you always negative about yourself, or do you doubt me in particular?"

Rosemary's pretty pink lips gaped open, and she blinked a few times. She looked cute when she was taken off guard.

"What I should say is, it's completely rational for me to be cautious about trusting a random man who conveniently bumped into me on the street and charmed me into going out to dinner. A smart person might say that's suspicious behavior, so it's wise to be wary of compliments."

His hand froze on his water glass. Had he been that obvious? He was better than that. Or at least he was supposed to be. Had he blown it already?

Gentle fingers grazed the back of his hand. "That's what I should say, but it isn't true. I'm sorry. I'm not used to compliments. My sister is usually the one people notice. Attention makes me uncomfortable, so I deflect. But it's still wrong of me to undercut your words that way."

He leaned back in his chair.

Who the hell was this woman? Most people weren't self-aware enough to recognize their behaviors and the reasons behind them. Even fewer people would openly admit they were wrong—and do it sitting on an outdoor patio in 40-degree weather after shifting away from the heat lamp so someone else's dog could lay directly under it. She had even convinced the host to give them a few tablecloths and fashioned a makeshift bed so Jaka didn't need to lie on the cold ground.

So far, nothing about her was setting off any alarm bells. He couldn't see this woman as being involved with the mob and certainly not as Moresco's girlfriend, so lying to her felt like chewing nails. On the other hand, she could be really good at keeping secrets. His instincts were excellent, but they weren't perfect.

Phillipe had been keeping secrets, and he hadn't had a fucking clue.

Regardless, if Moresco was having her followed, there was a reason. She was either on Moresco's payroll and an excellent actress, or she was an innocent who had inadvertently attracted the attention of the mob. Either way, he couldn't risk playing it straight with her. If she was on Moresco's side, it was dangerous to ask direct questions. It might tip her off and blow the whole operation. If she was one more innocent in Moresco's oily web, she'd be safer not knowing who he was or what Sal had done. She might panic or slip up and end up in even more danger. Keeping up the façade was the best option for both of them—and the surest way to keep her safe.

"So, you don't get along with your sister?" he asked.

"What?" The word came out as a gasp. "Sage is my best friend."

"Your best friend who gets all the compliments."

Rosemary shook her head, the long blonde strands flicking over her shoulder. "No. It's not like that. I love my sister."

"But?" He knew there was a *but*. Her downcast eyes and flushed cheeks were a dead giveaway.

"My sister is amazing."

"But?"

She crinkled her nose. "Are you always this pushy?"

"Yes. And I'm not going to let you change the subject. What's the *but*?"

She sighed, a huffy, irritated breath. Heat coiled low in his stomach. He knew she didn't intend it to be, but the sound was soft and sexy.

"She tends to hover."

He lifted a questioning eyebrow. "Hover?"

"I was sick when I was a teenager."

She pushed at her silverware until each piece was perfectly straight, then repositioned her bread plate, water glass, and wineglass.

He waited. Undercover work had taught him the value of silence. Human nature inclined people to fill the void.

He ticked off the seconds. She lasted a lot longer than most. People generally felt the need to fill the silence after about five or ten seconds. He counted to thirty-four before she released a slow breath and lifted her bright blue eyes with a stare so direct, he felt like she could see straight through him. She looked...*pissed.*

"I had cancer."

"Cancer?"

There hadn't been anything about cancer in the file. He knew Kemper hadn't used FBI resources to run a full background check on Rosemary to keep his side mission off their radar, so he shouldn't be surprised that her medical history hadn't made it into the file. Still, he felt like he'd been hit by a Humvee.

And she backed up and ran him down all over again.

"Yes. A rare type of bone cancer. They found it when I was twelve. It came back when I was seventeen, and then it came back again a few years ago. I'm fully cured now, but it was pretty rough." She took a breath, then continued to force her words out through gritted teeth. "My mom and Sage did everything they could to help me make the best of a hard situation. My sister was always protective, but after Mom died...things got a little nuts."

"I'm sorry." The words felt small, but he was too stunned to think of anything else to say.

"I don't know why I told you that." She went back to fiddling with her silverware. "I had a crazy day at work today, and you kept pushing about my sister." She waved her hand toward the sparkling patio lights. "And it feels like we're in another world here."

He got it. He'd felt like he was in another world since the first moment he laid eyes on her.

"I know what you mean. It feels like we're on our own little island out here. Now dare I ask what you meant by 'a little nuts'?"

She arched a meticulously sculpted eyebrow. "Are you a professional interrogator?"

A laugh burst from his throat, popping the vestiges of the tension that had sprung up between them. "Something like that."

Rosemary glanced around, perhaps absorbing the ambiance of the outdoor patio before returning her gaze to meet his. Her pink lips scrunched as she considered her next words.

"Nuts is my sister accusing my stepdad of killing our mom. Nuts is my stepdad threatening my sister and kicking us out of the house. Nuts is us going into hiding, and my sister working as a stripper to support us. Nuts is my cancer coming back, and Sage seducing the owner of a pharmaceutical company so he would give me the experimental medicine that cured me. So, yeah. Things got a little nuts."

The water he'd just sipped caught in his throat. Hard coughs ripped through his chest, making his eyes water and his nose run. When he finally caught his breath, lowered the napkin he'd been hacking into, and met Rosemary's gaze, her bright eyes sparkled like the Caribbean Sea at noon.

She was laughing at him.

The file had mentioned her mother was deceased, and her stepfather had been convicted of fraud, but hadn't said anything about cancer, murder accusations, or seduction. Apparently, Kemper couldn't even run a goddamn Google search.

"Are you serious?"

She nodded, grinning like the proverbial Cheshire cat. She seemed to be enjoying seeing him dumbfounded.

"You said it like that on purpose to shock me," he accused.

"You were peppering me with questions. Plus, you kept steering the conversation to me, and you've barely told me anything about yourself. I figured if I got all the scandalous stuff out hard and fast, maybe you'd get flustered enough to start talking about yourself."

Now he was the one smiling.

"Your manipulation skills are terrible. If you lay out your plan like that, it's not going to work."

"Why would I want to manipulate you?"

The sincerity of her question was almost more shocking than her previous disclosure. There weren't many truly straight shooters in the world. And the more she spoke, the more he believed that Rosemary was one of them. Just like Phillipe had been. Not when they were undercover, of course, but in real life, Phillipe believed in honesty. *Real friends, real truth* had been one of his many mottos.

If Rosemary was as good a person as she seemed, and this ruse ended up hurting her, Phillipe would find a way to haunt him for the rest of his goddamn life.

The waiter arrived with their entrées, saving him from explaining to her all the ways he'd seen people manipulate each other and all the reasons they'd given for doing it. It also provided a distraction so he could study the couple standing in the middle of the restaurant. He and Rosemary were the only diners on the patio, as it technically wasn't open. Rosemary knew the host and had convinced him to let them sit outside since Jaka was with them. With the dim patio light and the bright restaurant interior, he could see clearly into the restaurant, and the couple's odd behavior had grabbed his attention.

A tall, dark-haired, broad-shouldered man in a suit that, from a distance, looked like it cost more than most folks' rent, was scanning the room like he owned it. His hand rested on the waist of a short, curvy woman with wide eyes, full lips, and a mass of dark, wavy hair that reached the bottom of her back. She wore black, flared yoga pants, a tight, black, long-sleeved crop top, and bright white platform sneakers. One long-nailed finger rested worriedly between her teeth as she frantically surveyed the diners.

He had an odd hunch they were looking for Rosemary.

"Why do women wear half shirts when it's cold outside?" he asked. "I get that it's spring, but it's still too damn cold for bare skin."

Rosemary's laugh was like delicate chimes.

"Don't let my sister hear you say that. She lives in them. But she likes them for dancing and exercise. She always has a sweatshirt with her, so she's practical."

"Is your sister petite with a hell of a lot of hair and keeps company with a well-dressed guy who looks like he's better suited for an alley fight than an office?"

He pointed to the couple making their way to the patio. The short woman was trying to rush, but the man had positioned himself in front of her, taking the lead. Protective, Aleksei noted.

"That's... that's...Sage...and her fiancé, Ryker," Rosemary sputtered. "What on earth are they doing here?"

Despite her assurance that she knew the couple, Aleksei eased his chair back from the table so he had room to react if needed.

As soon as Sage reached their table, she said, "Oh my gosh. I'm so glad you're okay. I was so worried."

Rosemary's cheeks flamed pink. She opened her mouth, closed it, closed her eyes, pressed her fingers into her hair, and blew air audibly from her full, rosy lips. She reopened her eyes, stood, pulled her hands from her hair, and carefully folded her napkin, neatly placing it on the seat of her chair.

"Aleksei. Go ahead and start eating. I don't want your dinner to get cold. I'll just be a minute."

He didn't attempt to contain his smirk as Rosemary gave the couple a look that would have cowed a seasoned criminal and then dragged them to the corner of the patio. The low music prevented their words from carrying, but body language didn't lie.

Scallops perfectly seasoned with lemon, garlic, and something delightfully bitter melted in his mouth as he watched frustration shift to concern, then to friendly ease, then back to frustration. In the end, Sage stomped out, the tall man gave Rosemary a quick hug before dashing after his woman, and Rosemary returned to their table.

"Everything all right?" he asked.

"My sister has to go to DC with her fiancé. His brother's in the ER with stomach pains. They think it's appendicitis. She was texting and calling me to let me know she was going out of town, and I wasn't answering because my phone is in my purse, and I've been"—she waved her hand in his direction and took a long sip of her wine—"distracted. So, she used Life 360—which I didn't want, but she bullied me into getting—to stalk me. Who does that, I ask you? Who the hell actually does that?"

Her cheeks had shifted from pink to red, and her blue eyes sparked and flashed while she spoke. He wouldn't tell her because she'd probably toss her water at him, but feisty looked adorable on her.

"Apparently, your sister does," he teased. "She should be happy she found you safe and sound. Why did she storm off like that?"

Her eyes flicked upward, as if she were searching for patience, and she took another deep drink of her Pinot Grigio. "We're supposed to go to the theater tomorrow. Sage bought me a subscription to the Walnut Street Theater for my birthday. I couldn't go to movies or plays when I was younger because I was sick so much, so she's trying to make up for that. Now, she's in a tizzy because she can't come to the play since she's going to DC with Ryker."

He refilled Rosemary's glass of wine and then slid the bottle back into the ice bucket. The temperature was low enough that the wine probably would have stayed cold without it.

"Why is she upset? You two can go to the next one."

"That what I said!" she exclaimed, her bright blue eyes flashing again. "She's mad because I told her I still plan to go. She's so ridiculously overprotective that she thinks I can't go to the theater without her."

He was starting to think Rosemary's sister was a little melodramatic.

"She's mad because you want to go to the theater alone?"

She smirked. "Not quite. She's angry because I told her that, since she's dead set against me going alone, I'm asking you to come with me."

Chapter Five

Mist tickled Rosemary's nose as she looked left, then right. It wasn't raining hard enough to warrant the umbrella that hung from her wrist, but if she lingered outside too long, she'd be a bedraggled mess. She glanced over her shoulder at the warm yellow light shining through the doors to the lobby. It was only 6:25, but the entryway was already bustling. If she waited inside, she and Aleksei would be stuck trying to find each other in a sea of people. They hadn't set an exact time or place to meet, and now it felt overeager to start texting about details.

She should have pinned down meeting details when he'd texted her this morning to confirm the time of the show instead of just writing, "Perfect. See you there." Or, she could have texted him one of the two hundred times he'd popped into her mind today, but she'd been so busy. Plus, she didn't want to be the woman who starts blast texting after only one date. She wanted to be low-key.

And that brilliant approach had left her standing in the almost rain, getting soggier by the second.

She brushed the dampness from her nose and tried to ignore the hummingbird wings of her pulse. As soon as she'd left work, nervous thoughts had been skittering through her mind. How would Aleksei react to her wig? He was bound to find out about it if they engaged in any level of intimacy. And what about the rest of her body? She hadn't dated since recovering from Remiza. Would all her female parts still respond the same way they used to?

She glanced at her watch: 6:28. The three minutes she'd been waiting felt longer than her entire workday. She'd spent the whole morning laser-focused on finishing the Girard financials. As soon as she'd triple-checked the last number, Armando had rushed in with an emergency assignment for another client. She'd gotten out of work late, rushed home, taken Thor on a measly 10-minute walk, showered, and dressed faster than a middle school boy.

Somehow, she'd still managed to get here before Aleksei. Hopefully, he was on his way. She looked at her watch again: 6:29.

She hated being late. Of course, late for her was probably early for most. The play started at 7:00, which, on her normal schedule, meant walking into the theater by 6:30 for a quick—or not so quick, since there was generally a line—trip to the restroom. That way, she could get to her seat by 6:45. She hated rushing and climbing over random people.

Sage always managed to slide in next to her as the lights were going down. That would never work for Rosemary. It made her uncomfortable to cut it that close. She just wished she'd mentioned that to Aleksei.

"Hey!" Aleksei appeared next to her, laying a hand on her shoulder. She'd been so lost in thought, she nearly jumped out of her flats.

His lips parted in a grin. "Sorry for startling you."

She felt her own lips widen in return. "If you were really sorry, you wouldn't be laughing."

"I'm not laughing. I'm smiling because your surprised expression is so cute."

Her chest and cheeks warmed at the compliment.

He stepped toward her, sliding his palms down the sleeves of her jacket. Her tense muscles instantly relaxed under the weight of his hands. He was so close, her nose almost touched his jacket. His spiced pine scent and proximity sent a wave of heat to her thighs.

"You should have waited inside. You're getting wet."

Yep. She was. Just not in the way he meant.

"It's okay. It's a rain jacket. All the wet is on the outside," she said, grateful for the cool drizzle on her flaming cheeks.

Aleksei pulled his phone out, glanced down at the screen, then slid it back into his jacket pocket. "We'd better get inside," he said, closing his warm, calloused hand over her wet, chilly one. "I want to hit the restroom and get to our seats. I hate rushing in at the last minute."

The heat that had ignited in her thighs curled up higher, inching toward her heart as she added "punctual" to her mental list of Aleksei's positive attributes.

He kept hold of her hand, using his body to carve a path through the crowded lobby. He was tall but lean, more tennis player than football player, yet he navigated the theatergoers with ease. She'd taken up hiking and rock-climbing when she'd started taking Remiza. She loved nature, and if the drug didn't work, she wanted to spend every minute of the life she had left doing what she enjoyed. As a result, she'd grown strong and was perfectly capable of making her own way to the ladies' room, but there was something bone-meltingly sexy in the way his bearing made folks step out of his way.

As she emerged from the restroom, her eyes feasted on the delectable sight that was Aleksei. His face had strong Eastern European features, with high cheekbones and a chiseled jaw that looked like they were carved from granite. His feet were covered with the same gray dress sneakers he'd worn yesterday. Today, instead of jeans and a Henley, he wore khakis and an untucked, fitted, white dress shirt.

A cozy, hot-chocolate feeling filled her chest. He'd gotten dressed up for her.

That warmth snaked through her abdomen as he guided her into the theater with a firm hand resting on her lower back. Once they were settled in their seats, she shifted her attention to the playbill the friendly usher had handed her.

"Oh." The sound escaped her lips before she could censor herself.

"What's the matter?" Aleksei asked, his accent changing the "a" in *matter* to more of an "ah" sound.

She hesitated, letting her teeth sink into her bottom lip. If she answered honestly, he would think she was uncultured and overly sensitive. The theater subscription had been Sage's idea. They'd already seen *Matilda* and *Beauty and the Beast*, so she'd assumed all the plays in the package were upbeat musicals. Now, she regretted coming at all.

She shook her head, irritated by her own insecurity. She wasn't going to pretend to be something she wasn't, no matter what Aleksei might think of her.

"I've been so busy that I didn't have a chance to look at what tonight's play is. It was probably on the sign outside, but somehow, I didn't see it."

She hadn't seen it because she'd been savoring Aleksei's lean height and square shoulders.

"I didn't even look at my phone when the usher scanned the QR code. So here we are"—she raised her playbill toward him—"getting ready to see *Of Mice and Men*."

"You're not a fan of Steinbeck?"

She huffed out a breath. "I'm not a fan of miserable, tragic stories."

The edge of his lips twitched, and a twinkle of amusement lightened his gray-blue eyes, like sun rays through clouds.

His smile encouraged her to continue. "It was required reading in ninth grade at my high school. I hated Mr. Hoffstetler for it. I woke up with nightmares for weeks. How can teachers do that to kids?"

His hand covered her forearm, and the sunbeams disappeared from his eyes. "Do what?"

"Traumatize kids with horrible stories. I get that somebody decided to call it literature, but I was fifteen and just getting back to school after years of home tutors because of my wrecked immune system. I was desperate for joy and normalcy, and Mr. Hoffstetler rolls out goddamn *Of Mice and Men*."

The white-haired woman in front of them whirled around and shot Rosemary a disapproving glare.

The amused gleam returned to Aleksei's eyes.

She dropped her voice to a whisper. "And now, twelve years later, he's getting me dirty looks for cursing in the theater when he never should have made us read that terrible book in the first place. There's plenty of hate and misunderstanding floating around in the world—especially in high school. Shouldn't kids be reading books with happy endings? Or at least ones where good things come from pain and suffering? There's way too much tragedy in real life. Kids don't need it in books."

* * *

This was personal for Rosemary. Deeply personal. He saw it in the sorrow in her eyes and heard it in her ever-rising tone. Well, rising until the senior citizen in front of them had given them the evil eye. Aleksei was grateful to her for it. It had brought a bit of levity to Rosemary's dark mood.

He hated seeing her so agitated, but hell, she was beautiful. She looked like an avenging angel. Even damp, her white-gold hair sparkled in the chandelier light. Bright pink circles stained her pale cheeks, and her bright blue eyes flashed with an intoxicating blend of heartache and passion. Even her basic, navy-blue jacket contributed to the image, providing the perfect blank backdrop for her luminescence.

It was a good thing Mr. Hoffstetler wasn't here, or Aleksei would tell him just what he thought of him. Yeah, school districts set curricula, not individual teachers, and the guy was just doing his job. But that job had left Rosemary with trauma that lasted a decade. She was chewing her lip and twisting her hands, and the play hadn't even started. Staying here was only going to make her miserable.

The lights began to rise and fall. The show was imminent.

"Let's make a run for it."

The audience had quieted, so his voice was louder than he intended, earning them another glare from the woman in front of them.

Rosemary's hand flew to her mouth, covering a giggle. Illogical joy filled him at the transformation of her pinched lips to a full-on grin, but then the theater grew dark. The deep voice of the narrator boomed through the theater, setting the scene. He didn't know her well, but from what he'd gleaned during their short acquaintance, Rosemary wouldn't be comfortable disrupting the play. If they were going to leave, he had to push her to do it now.

"Stand up, say excuse me, and dash up the aisle. I'll meet you on the sidewalk out front."

"We can't," she protested.

He put the no-nonsense edge in his voice that he used when teaching new recruits how to go through a door. The tone he used when hesitation could get someone killed.

"Do it now," he ordered.

And she did.

He left the theater a few minutes later at the sensible, concerned pace one would use when checking on an ill friend. He found her outside, hunched over, arms wrapped around herself, shoulders slightly shaking.

Panic squeezed his chest. Was she crying?

He stepped toward her, slid a hand under her already damp chin, and lifted her face. Her eyes were watering, and a lone tear slipped down her cheek.

She gulped in a breath and squeezed his elbow. "Did you see the look on that usher's face when I ran by him?" Full-body laughter shook her, and she wiped another tear from her eye. "He was horrified! He couldn't even get a word out. He just sputtered and waved his flashlight at me."

Her delight was infectious, and amusement welled up from his gut. For a few seconds, they were both shaking and gripping their sides, roaring with laughter.

"We have to stop," she said. "People are staring, and we're getting soaked."

She was right. The windbreaker he'd worn for the trip wasn't waterproof, and cold rain was seeping through, dampening his arms. Plus, his hair was so closely cut that raindrops were sliding down his head and into the neckline of his shirt.

He reached out, pulled the umbrella from her wrist, popped it open, and slipped his arm around her waist, pulling her soft curves against his side. Her shoulder slid perfectly under his arm as if they were pieces of the jigsaw puzzles his father had liked so much.

"Let's go get a drink," he suggested.

He guided her through the damp streets, chatting and dodging puddles, his body moving without thought, like driving to work. You did it so frequently that some days you left the house and then parked and didn't remember the drive. That same feeling struck him when he realized they were at McGillin's.

Shit.

He hadn't meant to bring her here.

"You okay?" she asked, rubbing his biceps.

He was not okay. They were at fucking McGillin's.

He and Phillipe would come here whenever they needed a break. Half the time, Samantha would leave the kids with her mom and meet them. The three of them would spend the night drinking beer, eating wings, playing pool, and laughing their asses off.

Aleksei hadn't set foot in the place since Phillipe was murdered. Trapped grief pressed against his ribs, making his chest feel like it might burst. His heartbreak was fighting to get free, and for the first time in years, he wanted to let it out, wanted to lighten his burden, wanted to talk about his pain and loss. He wanted to share it with Rosemary.

She rubbed his arm again, and he pushed memory and heartache away. His feelings weren't relevant. He had a job to do.

"Sorry. My mind wandered for a minute."

She tugged the umbrella from his hand and splashed water toward him as she lowered it. Icy wet droplets bombarded his face.

"What was that for?" he demanded.

The exterior lights illuminated her teasing smile. "You looked sad. You needed a distraction."

She was perceptive. Years of covert ops and undercover work had made his impassive mask a second skin, yet she'd seen his pain and acted to pull him back from that dangerous edge of guilt and despair. This was only their second date, and already, she was reading him better than the bureau-assigned psychologist ever had.

He was going to have to be careful around her if he didn't want to blow his cover.

He pushed open the door, and the sound of Noah Kahan singing about dialing drunk poured out. A smile tugged at his lips, lightening his thoughts. Some things never changed. You never knew what you'd hear at McGillin's. Sinatra, Nirvana, Post Malone, Morgan Wallen, Arrowsmith, The Cure, Dua Lipa, The Weekend. It was a total crapshoot. Now, Noah Kahan was in the mix.

Rosemary sang along as they wound their way through the crowd. It was one more thing they had in common. They both hated *Of Mice and Men* and liked Noah Kahan. It was as good a place to start as any.

A burly man in a flannel shirt bumped into them and murmured apologies. The place was packed. The crowd ran from college students to boomers, with everything in between, and way more off-duty cops than anyone other than the cops and bartenders realized. When you did undercover work, no place was completely safe, but Moresco's crew never strayed far from their south Philly stomping grounds, so for Phillipe and him, McGillin's had felt like another planet. A planet where they could relax and blow off steam.

Aleksei searched for the clearest path to the bar, and his gaze found the easy warmth of Samuel's smile. Samuel nodded at him and crooked a finger to call them forward, ignoring the sea of patrons jostling to order drinks. Aleksei put his palm on the small of Rosemary's back. She'd slipped off her jacket, and the heat of her body warmed his cold hand. He fought the desire to slide his fingers into the waistband of her dark jeans. Instead, he kept his hand where it was and guided her to the side of the bar reserved for the waitstaff.

Samuel leaned across the bar and clenched his hand like a sailor pulling a shipmate into a lifeboat. "Hey, man. It's good to see you. It's been too long."

It had been too long, and not long enough. Memories were deep here. Too deep for tonight. He couldn't afford to be distracted when he was running the most important op of his life.

"Sorry I haven't been back. I wanted to come, but I wasn't ready. I didn't even mean to come tonight. I just"—he shrugged—"ended up here." He cocked his head to the side. "This is my friend, Rosemary."

Samuel understood the words he hadn't spoken. There would be no talk of Phillipe tonight.

Samuel greeted Rosemary, took their drink order, and told Aleksei he could pull the *Reserved* sign off one of the pool tables upstairs. As Samuel laid on his full bartender charm, the light from a hanging pendant caught a scar on Rosemary's neck, making it shimmer in rosy contrast to her pale skin.

It was probably from one of her cancer treatments.

She had battled cancer three times, and he hadn't even had the guts to talk to Samuel after the funeral. Samuel was good people, and Aleksei had been a flaming shit. He was going to stop back later this week and catch up with the guy. Even if the memories killed him.

He passed Rosemary her fruited sour. Then, he took his chilly Guinness in one hand and her soft, now-warm hand in the other, guiding her upstairs to the pool tables. The music was quieter on the second floor, so they didn't need to shout to hear each other.

"That was an interesting conversation you had with the bartender," she commented as she racked the balls. "What's the story there?"

Her question wasn't surprising. She was smart, and with his hesitation at the door, his conversation with Samuel, and the mutterings of "sorry" and backslaps he'd received as they'd made their way upstairs, it didn't take a genius to know there was a story. It had been stupid to come inside.

"Samuel's a friend of mine. I haven't seen him in a while."

It was a non-answer. The question was, how would she respond to his obvious avoidance? Would she be hurt? Angry? Irritated enough to decide she had way too much going for her to spend time with a guy who couldn't answer a simple question—a guy who wasn't willing to open up a little after she'd spoken so freely about her cancer, her family, and even her high school *Of Mice and Men* trauma?

He had to give her something. Not just because he was afraid she'd bolt if he didn't. He needed to release a little of his pain, or he might make a mistake. Until now, he'd rebuffed every opportunity to share his heartache, because that meant facing it. He thought ignoring it was the only way to survive, but it was impossible to hunt Phillipe's killer and suppress the pain. Philly held too many memories. If he didn't find a way to control his grief, he risked it controlling him—just like it had brought him here tonight.

The crack of pool balls cut through his thoughts. The three hit the side pocket, and the seven hovered on the edge of the top right pocket before falling in.

"I'll take solids. And for every ball I drop, you tell me something about yourself," she said.

He arched a questioning brow at the command in her voice.

"I'm an open book, and every time I ask you a question, you give a non-answer or deflect with a question back to me. Wasn't it Ghandi who said, 'All compromise is give and take'?"

Rosemary quoting Ghandi in Phillipe's favorite bar was a message from the universe.

Aleksei was a practical person. Years of military training and FBI work demanded it, but his mom was Romani. His father's Nordic genes dominated his appearance, but his mother always insisted that magic lived in his blood. Right now, that magic was telling him that when the universe spoke, a practical man listened.

Phillipe had been on a mission to make it through the one hundred volumes of the *Collected Works of Mahatma Gandhi* and was always dropping some random fact or quote from whatever current volume he was reading. Aleksei wasn't so naïve to think that one quote meant he could trust her—but he would take it as a message that he was on the right track. That this might be the road to bringing Phillipe's killer to justice. That Rosemary might be his path to atonement.

She leaned against the table, hand gripping the cue that now stood vertical to the floor, eyes daring him to agree to her proposition. Her jeans were snug but not overly tight. Her emerald-green blouse was plain but pretty, and her flat shoes were cute and sensible. There were gorgeous, glossy women here tonight showing more skin than his sister showed at the beach, but they didn't interest him. Rosemary's blend of easy prettiness and her feisty challenge absorbed every bit of his attention.

His gaze settled on her pert pink lips, hunger rising within him. He didn't know if it was the Guinness, being back in McGillin's, the message from the universe, or just Rosemary herself, but he'd never found a woman more compelling. The need to know how those soft, perfect lips would feel crushed beneath his own raged through him.

Just one kiss. He hadn't had any intimate contact in more than two years. He could let himself have just one kiss.

He set the beer on the table's edge and closed the distance between them in two long strides. He slid his hands up the warm, silky skin of her neck into her soft hair. He lowered his head toward those luscious pink lips, eager for the feel of her tongue in his mouth.

And she kneed him in the nuts.

Chapter Six

What the hell had she been thinking? She hadn't thought. Her body had just reacted. One second, she was falling into the sexy heat of Aleksei's dusk-colored eyes, reveling in the fact that in a crowded, noisy bar, the intensity of his gaze made her feel like they were the only two people in the room. Warm, calloused fingers stroked her neck, and her thighs had weakened in anticipation. Then those tantalizing fingers slid up into her wig, and fear had overwhelmed her.

Fear that his fingers would recognize the slightly raised border at the edge of the wig. Fear that he'd grip too tightly, and her wig would shift. Fear that the unspeakable would happen—that he'd accidentally pull the wig right off her head. Her stomach lurched at the thought, but she wasn't sure which would have been more catastrophic: the fact that a bar full of people would have seen her ghost-white scalp or that she would have been left standing bare in front of Aleksei.

He had convinced her to flee the theater instead of sitting there watching a terrible play that would have made her miserable. He'd laughed with her, held the umbrella while they walked in the rain, took her to a place that was special to him, bought her a beer, and was getting ready to kiss her. And what had she done? She'd lashed out like a caged animal. He'd been sweet, funny, and charming, and she'd kneed him in the goddamn balls.

No wonder he had nothing to say to her.

They stopped in front of the fifth house in the block-long row of attached, red brick homes. A few concrete steps led up to an arched doorway framing a Columbia-blue door. They'd walked the fifteen or so blocks in silence. Right after they left the bar, she tried to apologize for the third time, but Aleksei had interrupted her, saying he needed a few minutes. The few minutes had turned into twenty.

Tense silence added to the weight of the misty air. She liked Aleksei. She barely knew him, but she felt drawn to him. Was it like a bee to honey? Or like a moth to a flame? She'd never know if they didn't get past tonight. She'd spent way too much time caged by illness. She was stronger than fear. Strong enough to live a life instead of just surviving it. Strong enough to admit to him why she'd reacted the way she did.

"There's something I need to tell you."

She met his gaze, expecting anger, but his eyes held something else. Sorrow? Regret? Embarrassment? She couldn't quite put her finger on it, which confused her. Her cancer had made her an expert at reading masked emotions.

It had started with her family. They always put on a cheerful face and seemed joyfully agreeable to whatever she wanted. It took a while for her to realize they were acting—acting because they thought she was dying.

With time, she'd learned to see past the feigned cheer. To notice tense shoulders, a smile that was a touch too wide, a laugh that was a few seconds too long, and the vast range of emotions that could be conveyed with only the eyes. After that, she'd been able to read the doctors and nurses, giving her a few precious seconds to compose herself before a seemingly expressionless face gave devastating news.

Aleksei's gray eyes deepened, and his pupils grew.

Shame. He was feeling shame.

Just like she was.

But that made no sense. She was the one who'd acted like a cornered cat. All he had done was try to kiss her.

"Let me go first." His voice was deep and slightly rough, again with that hint of an Eastern European accent. If they made it to a third date, she was going to ask him about his heritage.

A car swooshed by, splashing water on their feet, but neither of them glanced toward the street. Their eyes were locked. He held the umbrella over their heads, but it was too small to cover them both fully, causing raindrops to pelt her back. He lifted his free hand as if to touch her arm and then changed his mind and slid his palm across his close-cropped, blond hair.

"I owe you an apology. I shouldn't have tried to kiss you without your permission. I'm sorry." His lips quirked. "Of course, I would have preferred a good old-fashioned slap in the face, but since you didn't want me to kiss you, you had every right to react how you wanted." He shifted his weight from one foot to the other. "Even if I'm still feeling the effects."

Confusion washed over her. He hadn't seemed sorry. He'd seemed royally pissed.

"But you were so angry. You told me you didn't want to talk to me."

He barked out a wry laugh. "No. I told you I *couldn't* talk to you. I could barely stand or breathe, let alone talk. And yes, I was angry. But not at you. Just angry in general because I was in pain."

"You mean the kind of mad you feel when you stub your toe on the dresser on the way to the bathroom in the middle of the night?"

He smirked. "Yeah. Like that. But about fifty times worse."

"Ouch," she said.

"Ouch," he repeated.

She glanced toward the door. "Is this your place? Should we go in before we're both completely soaked?"

Sage would have her head if she knew Rosemary was suggesting hanging out in the apartment of a man she barely knew. But she was in DC with Ryker and his brother, and Rosemary was over playing things safely. It was their second date. She had friends who swiped right and met up with total strangers. She could damn well go into Aleksei's apartment.

Besides, Sage was probably tracking her every step on Life360.

Sliding a strong lean arm around her waist, he pulled her against his side. Despite the chilly rain, his body was warm and hard against her hip and thigh. Heat curled through her abdomen, and she shivered. It had been far too long since she'd been with a man, and this man was temptation incarnate. Maybe he'd try to kiss her again once they were upstairs. This time, she'd be ready.

He pressed the umbrella into her hand, pulling her back to the present. "Let's get inside. You're shivering. Hold this while I unlock the door."

He punched numbers into a keycode, guided her through the entryway, then took the umbrella and shook it dry, his long fingers quick and competent. He gripped her hand with chilly, wet fingers and led her up three flights of stairs to the doorway of the apartment.

"You're not even winded," he commented.

"Backpacking. I do a lot of backpacking and hiking," Rosemary said. "Those stairs are nothing compared to the hills at Valley Forge."

"I'm a big hiker too."

Of course he was. Because why wouldn't he be more perfect?

He used another keycode to unlock the apartment door. His movements were met with excited barking and scratching at the door. That was one of the wonderful things about dogs. They were always happy to see you.

He wrestled Jaka back from the door so she could shimmy in behind him. Jaka jumped at her legs.

"Down, girl. Down." Aleksei's voice was firm, but his hands were full of love as he stroked Jaka's fur with one hand while holding her collar with the other.

She dropped down in front of Jaka, the wood floor hard under her knees. The dog lunged forward, gracing her with a wet, rough-tongued lick up her cheek. She wiped the drool from her face, laughing.

She rubbed Jaka's soft fur as the dog quivered with excitement. "You're a good girl. You just want to say hi, don't you?"

Aleksei grabbed a blue leash from a set of hooks by the door. "I'm going to run her out quickly and then settle her in her crate. She and I went for a long jog today, so it's bedtime for her anyway. Hang up your coat, grab a beer from the fridge, and have a seat. I'll just be a few minutes."

The front door shut with a hard thud, and she was left in eerie silence. It felt odd to be alone in someone else's apartment.

She shrugged out of her jacket and hung it up, grateful to have the damp material away from her body. The jacket wasn't quite as waterproof as she'd thought. She opened the refrigerator. It was sparkling clean with none of the chocolate syrup spills or grape stems she always seemed to be wiping up in hers. Its limited contents consisted of beer, water bottles, a Brita, and eggs, with everything lined up neatly. She'd wait for him to hand out the beers. She shut the door and ran her hand along the round white kitchen table as she walked the few steps from the kitchen to the living area.

Oversized chocolate-brown leather chairs sat at soft angles at either side of a matching couch, forming a U around a rustic-looking wood and metal coffee table. IKEA-esque side tables stood on either side of the couch, and a tan braided carpet covered the weathered, large-plank hardwood floor. The opposite wall featured a fireplace, flanked by floor-to-ceiling bookcases. A television was perched atop a steamer trunk, angled in the corner of the room. Moss-green walls, earth-toned pillows, and Philadelphia themed artwork brought color and interest to the space. The overall effect was cozy and welcoming.

The bookcases held a small globe, a decorative tile from the Moravian tileworks, a framed copy of the Declaration of Independence, a replica Liberty Bell, and a few other innocuous knick-knacks, most of which continued the Philly theme. The books were a mix of tourist guides, local histories, and popular fiction—the kind they had in the B&B her mom took her to in Cape May the few times she'd been well enough to go to the beach.

The front door banged open. Her head snapped up at the sound, her eyes meeting Aleksei's inquisitive gaze. She dropped her hand from the book she'd been about to pluck from the shelf. She hadn't been doing anything wrong, but for some reason, she felt like she'd been caught snooping.

"Did you find the beer?" he asked as he hung up his coat and returned Jaka's leash to its hook.

"I figured I'd wait for you."

He smiled broadly, transforming the hard angles of his face into something softer and warmer. He lifted his hand, his middle and pointer fingers raised.

"Give me two minutes to get Jaka in her crate."

She closed her eyes, took a deep breath, and let it out slowly. Anticipation was making her jittery, and her scalp was starting to sweat. She should sit. If she sat, she might feel more relaxed. She'd definitely look more relaxed than she did fidgeting with the stuff on his shelves. She eased onto the leather couch and thrust her nails under the edges of her wig for a quick scratch. If she scratched now, hopefully her head wouldn't itch for a while.

The sound of footsteps, the refrigerator door, and the pop of cans opening heralded Aleksei's arrival. He strode into the room, two tall silver-and-brown cans in hands, his long lean legs eating up the space between them. He was so striking, she almost forgot to breathe. His face was sharp angles and ocean-storm eyes. His movements hinted at the hard muscles she felt each time their bodies touched.

Her thighs tingled. Her core clenched. This was the time to say something coy and flirty. Something funny and suggestive.

Instead, she blurted out the thought dancing on the edges of her mind. "You don't actually live here, do you?"

He paused, gray eyes wide, beer partially raised. Then he smiled widely and pushed the icy can into her hand. "I do live here. Just not often."

His answer was so quick. Had she imagined the hesitation?

"I changed jobs a couple of years ago and work in DC now. I have an apartment down there and rent this place out on VRBO. I'm off for a couple of weeks and decided to spend the time in Philly since I haven't been back in a while."

She took a sip of the crisp, citrusy, slightly bitter liquid and then set it on a pewter coaster with stars and the year 1776 circling the edges. "I'm going to use the restroom. It's just back there, right?"

He lifted his beer toward the hall at the far end of the kitchen. "Up those two stairs. It's the first door on the right."

As soon as she got inside the bathroom, she collapsed against the door, snippets of her various conversations with Aleksei whirling in her mind. She'd been sure he lived in Philly, but had he ever actually said that? Why hadn't he told her he lived in DC? He'd said he was a consultant, but she didn't know where he worked or what he consulted on. Did she really know anything about him?

Her heart was beating too fast. Her breathing was erratic.

And she was being ridiculous.

She kicked her flats off, the tile cold on her bare feet. She envisioned roots extending from her toes and heels down through the floors, through the concrete foundation, and into the earth. Calm flowed through her. Her heart rate and breathing settled. Logic returned.

She was being paranoid.

They'd had two dates. He'd directed a lot of the conversation toward her, which was polite and showed he was interested in her. He was smart, witty, and handsome. No. Not just handsome. His face could launch ships...but her ship wasn't going to even get out of the harbor if she didn't stop freaking out over nonsense.

Her illnesses had kept her isolated so frequently that her meter for normal social interaction was skewed. She was panicking over nothing. If she wanted to know more about Aleksei, she needed to get her ass back out there and ask. And if she wanted him to be honest about himself, she was going to have to be honest about herself, too.

* * *

Aleksei pulled some junk mail from the basket next to the fireplace, crumpled it, then used a poker to push it under the logs, ramping up the flames. He added kindling and paper until he was satisfied with the burn. As he rose from his crouched position, Rosemary returned to the living room. He'd dimmed the lights, and the white strands that punctuated her blonde hair flashed in the firelight.

She grabbed her beer and settled on the couch, angling her back to the armrest and curling her legs up under her. She pulled the green knit throw his mom had given him off the back of the couch and smoothed it over her lap. As he watched Rosemary's pale hands, with their short, unadorned nails, arrange the blanket, the image of her sister's long, red nails flashed through his mind. He preferred Rosemary's simple, subtle sexuality. Maybe it was the outdoorsman in him. Long nails weren't practical when fishing and camping.

She took a healthy swig of her IPA, closed her eyes, and released a satisfied "mmm." The beer left her full pink lips wet and shiny. There was nothing simple or subtle about her lips. Her mouth was the stuff teenage boys dreamed about. Obviously, grown men did too since he'd been thinking about that mouth on him since the first time he laid eyes on her.

He'd smiled more in the hours he'd spent with Rosemary than he had in the past year. How could he not? The joy with which she embraced life was infectious. She was a woman who made the most of every moment. He liked how she settled in and made herself at home on his couch. He liked that she ate and drank with gusto. He liked how she savored his favorite beer like it was a fine wine. He liked how she'd leaned into his musical comment that very first night and danced on the stairs in public. He liked that she openly shared whatever was on her mind. He liked that she had strong muscles and soft curves and the most compelling lips he'd ever laid eyes on.

"Chain Reaction," she said, reading the beer label aloud. "This is awesome." She looked at the label again. "Thin Man Brewery. Is that around here? I'd like to check it out."

Of course, she would. Just one more thing to like about her.

He confirmed that the fire was in good shape, then walked over and sat down next to her on the couch, picking up and taking a long drink of his own beer. He loved the hints of pineapple, passionfruit, and berry that balanced the dankness of the IPA.

"The brewery is in Buffalo, so it'd have to be a road trip. Luckily, a local place carries the brand, so I can get it here."

He lifted the part of the blanket pooled between them, spreading it over his own lap. "Mind if I share?"

Pink tinged her cheeks and neck as she nodded affirmatively.

Did she blush everywhere? Would her breasts and thighs turn that bright, rosy pink when she came?

His cock instantly responded to the thought, and he shifted on the couch, trying to get comfortable in pants that suddenly felt too tight.

"Am I crowding you?" she asked.

"No. All good. Just still recovering a bit from that strong right knee of yours."

"I'm sorry..." she started.

"Don't say it. There's no need to apologize. Like I said, if anyone should be apologizing, it's me. I shouldn't have assumed it was okay to kiss you."

"Does that mean you owe me?" she asked.

Owe her. That was an intriguing thought. If he said yes, how would she want to collect?

"I guess I do."

She set her can on a coaster and clapped her hands together like an excited child. "That means I can get you to answer my questions."

What the hell was she talking about?

"What questions?"

"Remember when I said at the bar that you had to tell me one thing about yourself for every solid I dropped? Since I never got my Aleksei facts, I'm going to get them now."

He groaned. Partly because he didn't want to spend the night playing improv and partly because he knew she would think his sour reaction was funny, and he loved the chime-like sound of her laugh.

"I don't like talking about myself," he said.

"No one does."

"Actually, almost everyone does," he retorted.

She rewarded him with more tinkling laughter and an even deeper flush of the portion of her chest the few open buttons of her blouse exposed. Again, the image of her soft skin, pinkened with arousal, flashed through his mind. The blanket covering his lap was a godsend.

"We've been out twice, and I feel like I don't really know anything about you. I thought you lived in Philly, but you live in DC, and I don't even know what you do for a living."

"I never said I lived in Philly."

She scrunched her pert nose and rolled her eyes, making him laugh. If she kept making him smile, his jaw might actually hurt.

"You never said you didn't, and that's a big omission. When you meet someone walking a dog down the street, a normal person would assume they live in the area."

So, it was going to be improv after all. The more time he spent with her, the harder it was to imagine her being in thick with Moresco, but he still needed to hold his cards close to his vest. If there was accounting fraud, maybe she didn't realize what she was doing was a crime. Or maybe she knew the numbers were phony but felt loyal to Pannetone & Associates and didn't view fiddling with some numbers for an important client as a big deal. He'd seen how she was about her sister. Her loyalty ran deep.

To him, right was right, and wrong was wrong, but he knew lots of people didn't view crime that way. Not that the police were always right and criminals were always wrong. He'd known plenty of bad cops. It was just that sometimes people thought certain crimes were victimless. He knew better. Behind the scenes, when crime was involved, people always suffered.

People like his mom.

People like Phillipe.

And for Phillipe, he was going to lead this bright, shining woman through a game of question and answer. He would give her a mix of truth and lies, because her reactions to his quasi-truthful answers would probably reveal more about her than his answers would reveal about him. He would just have to be very careful—she was clever.

And that cleverness showed in her first question.

"So, what exactly is your job? And don't give me that consultant nonsense. What company do you work for and what, specifically, do you do?"

Shit. This might be harder than he thought.

Chapter Seven

T*hen you will know the truth, and the truth will set you free.*

That's what Nana Thompson used to say. John 8:32 was one of her favorite Bible verses, maybe due to Grandpa Bill's penchant for stretching the truth. When Aleksei was young, Grandpa Bill told him about the three-foot tiger trout he had caught in the Loyalsock, about the bear who'd rear up on his hind legs and tap on their window, looking for honey biscuits whenever Nana baked them, and about Grandpa and his brothers using a spudzooka—their homemade potato launcher—to scare off a mountain lion.

That was probably why, when Grandpa first told him about his dad talking to his mom through a crack in a boarded-up window, planning her escape, and freeing her and the other princesses from the evil lord who'd captured them and forced them to labor in his castle, he'd thought the story was fiction. He'd thought it was a tall tale to make his dad seem larger than life.

But it wasn't.

The story was true, with details changed because you didn't tell an eight-year-old about sex trafficking. His tall, broad-shouldered father—who carried lumber with ease, who taught him how to camp, fish, and hunt, who was loving and kind but stern when he needed to be—had always been his hero. But after Aleksei learned the truth of how his mother and father met, his image of his father shifted from hero to superhero.

So, he'd followed in his father's footsteps, joining the military, getting a job in law enforcement, and working to protect the innocent people criminals preyed upon. But where Dad had succeeded, he had failed.

His mother had been on a path to certain death. It was only a matter of time. She was already bloody and beaten, concussed, and with a broken arm when Dad had gotten her out—but he *had* gotten her out. His father had saved his mother's life.

He had let Phillipe die.

"What are you thinking about? Your eyes have gone sad again."

His undercover training included learning to control his features so they didn't show his thoughts, and he'd been told he was damned good at it. Apparently not. At least not when it came to Rosemary and what she could see in his eyes.

Nana Thompson's voice reappeared at the edges of his mind. *And the truth will set you free.* Maybe it was time to see if the truth *would* set him free. Silence sure as fuck hadn't done him any good these past couple of years.

"I was thinking. About my partner. I used to...I was...an FBI agent. Based here in Philly." The words were sticky and too big in his throat, so they came out stilted with odd pauses. It was so goddamn hard to talk about.

"My partner was killed. Murdered. During our last assignment. It's been just over two years, but...." He pressed a balled fist to the gaping hole in his chest. "I can't get past it. The pain, the guilt, the emptiness. They're like teeth, constantly gnawing at me. I wasn't enough. I didn't do enough. And my best friend is dead because of it."

He'd intended to share the facts, but these words were too stark. Too real. Too bare. He'd always thought the truth of his failure was unspeakable.

But he had just spoken it.

"Do you want to tell me what happened? Would that ease your burden?"

He didn't detect that undercurrent of morbid curiosity that so frequently crept into questions about Phillipe's passing, but old suspicions stuck with him. What if Rosemary was like everyone else?

People always wanted the details.

His superiors wanted them for their reports. The psychologists so they could assess his fitness for duty. The press so they could skewer Phillipe's good name. His colleagues so they could assure themselves they wouldn't make the same mistakes. Random friends and neighbors because they were sickeningly entranced by tragedy. Everyone said talking about it would make him feel better, but those comments were always laced with a dark hunger for gossip that infuriated him and stretched his self-control to the breaking point. Talking about it had never made him feel better.

The truth wasn't going to set him free. It was going to kill him.

"You wouldn't understand. When someone dies, everyone's obsessed with their death. No one thinks about who they were when they were alive. No one wants to talk about the good times."

A sarcastic *hmmph* flew from Rosemary's lips.

"You don't believe me? Do you think anyone wants to hear about what a great guy Phillipe was? How he always had your back? How he was the first person to offer to help you move, to let you borrow his truck, to buy you a beer when you had a shit day? No one talks about how he coached Little League, volunteered at the homeless shelter, and spent hours playing in the yard with his kids. All anyone cares about is how he was murdered. They fucking shot him in the back of the head. They cut off his goddamn hands and shoved hundred-dollar bills down his throat. It was a fucking mob-style execution for a thief."

His eyes were hot and stinging. Emotion kept finding crack after crack to break through, and he couldn't stop it.

"All anyone wants to talk about are those fucking horrid details. Or if they get past that, it's how much money they found in his jacket.

How his suits and cars were always just a bit too nice. How they froze his assets. How they tried to kick Samantha and the kids out of their own goddamn house, saying Phillipe bought it with mob money."

He sucked in a ragged breath. "He was like a brother to me. I feel like a piece of me was hacked away. Like there's a jagged hole in my flesh. Every second of every day, I wish he were still alive. I remember all the good times, but all anyone else remembers is the way he died."

He'd looked at the fire while speaking, the heat of the flames matching the heat of his emotions. Now, he lifted his head and met Rosemary's gaze. Her cheeks were flushed a bright cherry pink. The contrast of her pale skin and red cheeks reminded him of the angry cartoon characters from his youth, the ones who jumped up and down and had steam pouring from their ears.

"Imagine living through it." Her voice quivered with a rage that mirrored his own.

What the hell was she talking about?

"I did live through it. I'm still living through it! I live every day without him, and now, I don't even get to see Samantha and the kids. She won't see me or talk to me because I remind her too much of Phillipe. I have nothing left of him but his death. You have no idea what that's like."

"My mother's dead. Of course I know what it's like!" she shot back.

His training was screaming that he was out of control. That his anger was misdirected. That he needed to calm down and shut up. But his body wouldn't listen. His rage was a bullet train with no brakes.

Being back in Philly, going to McGillin's, seeing Samuel, working with Kemper again. They had all battered at the dam he'd built around his emotions. Sitting here, sharing with Rosemary, thinking she might be different, that she might understand, and then having her respond like that was just too much.

He didn't know how to stop the deluge of rage and despair pouring out of him.

"Your mother is dead. My father is dead. Parents die. It's sad and heartbreaking, but it's normal. What happened to Phillipe was *not* normal. Having your best friend murdered and his good name dragged through the mud in the news, on social media, and around the goddamn coffee machine in the office is *not* normal!"

Rosemary's blue eyes sparked like fireworks. "Fine. Let's play it your way, Mr. So-wrapped-up-in-yourself-you-don't-think-anyone-else-can-suffer. My mother was murdered. Did you know that? Murdered by my best friend. My best friend is sitting in prison for killing my mother. So don't tell me I have no idea what it's like. I know all about headlines and betrayal."

Jesus Christ.

Her mother had been murdered? Kemper's report noted Carolyn Cashman as deceased, but the detail was limited to her age and date of death. Most of the information about her parents in the report focused on her stepfather. Kemper had included Davis's criminal record, employment history, financial information, and speculation about his involvement with Moresco, but nothing about how Carolyn had died.

An image flashed through his mind of Rosemary telling him during their impromptu dinner that Sage had accused their stepfather of murdering their mother. Why hadn't he focused on that? During that dinner, his concentration had bounced between his attraction to Rosemary and his determination to avenge Phillipe. Her comment wasn't relevant to either, so he'd let it fly right by. He was a better agent than that.

Or he used to be.

"I'm sorry." The words felt meager, but he wouldn't insult her further by offering excuses.

"You should be!" she said, poking his thigh with enough force to sting. "You're mad at the world and taking it out on me."

She poked his thigh again, but more softly this time. "I *understand.* Your best friend died a horrific death, and instead of celebrating his life, the people around you gawked and gossiped. It's terrible, but you should give them some grace. People fixate on the details because they're scared the same thing will happen to them. Death is terrifying to most people, and it's human nature to focus on what we fear most.

Some people just do it in a horrible way. Some because they're shitty people. Others because they're scared and they don't understand the impact their words can have. They can't understand. They haven't lived it."

Her words were ice water, cooling the fire within him.

"How can you be so reasonable?"

She shifted closer so her knees pressed against the side of his thigh, took a swig of her beer, and set it on her lap, fiddling with the pop top as if searching for words.

"It's terrible listening to people spread rumors about someone you love. Listening to them speculate about what happened, how they died, whether they were having an affair." She waved a hand in the air. "It goes on and on. But my mom and Phillipe, at least they didn't have to hear it and see it. They aren't here to read what people are posting on social media. To feel the weight of eyes when they walk into a room. To overhear people speculating about their life and death as if they don't have feelings, as if they didn't exist."

Rosemary's pain emanated from her in waves. His chest ached with empathy, but he didn't agree with her logic.

"I'd rather have Phillipe alive, even if it meant public embarrassment."

"Of course. I didn't mean that. What I meant was..." She hesitated, the sound of her flicking the pop top loud in the quiet room. "Imagine being the one dying but not being dead. Imagine having a terminal illness and people you barely know thinking it's perfectly acceptable to grill you about your doctors, your treatments, and your prognosis. Asking you if cancer runs in your family. Asking you what your symptoms are. Asking how you realized you were sick. Having the nerve to ask you, to your face, how long you have to live."

She released a long, slow breath and lifted her gaze. Her eyes had grown dim and somber.

"They looked at me as if I was already dead. As if I wasn't a person anymore. I was a curiosity. An interesting, gruesome topic of conversation that, somehow, they couldn't let go. Most people, even my friends, stopped seeing *me*. They only saw the cancer that was killing me. How I can be so reasonable? I had to be. I had to find a way to understand the obsession with death or hate was going to destroy me. I think that's where you are now. If you don't find a way to process your grief and anger, it's going to consume you. I know. I've lived it."

Her strength and compassion tugged on the knot of torment and outrage that was tangled tightly in his chest. She was right. His grief and anger were slowly burning him alive, but after talking to her tonight, the jagged edges of his pain had softened a bit. For the first time in two years, he'd spoken about Phillipe and felt better, not worse. Maybe Rosemary could be the key to helping him heal.

But for her to help him heal, he was going to have to tell her the whole truth of his pain. The cold facts he'd provided his superiors, the one-word answers he'd offered the psychologists, the icy stares he'd given his colleagues—they weren't going to cut it.

Phillipe's memory deserved more.

Rosemary deserved more.

* * *

Rosemary took another drink of her fruity, bitter beer while she waited. Aleksei's face was impassive, but his eyes churned. What had begun as a predictable evening of theater had morphed into laughter, rain, anger, sadness, and souls laid bare.

The night was as crooked as her stepfather, but she wouldn't have it any other way.

She wanted to know Aleksei. Really know him. In her opinion, a relationship wasn't real if it wasn't completely honest. The question was, now that he'd gotten a handle on his emotions, would he still be open with her?

He reached out, resting his long, lean fingers on her bent knee. She could feel the warmth of his hand through her jeans and the blanket.

"You're right. I've been completely wrapped up in myself. My mom told me the same thing, but I didn't listen."

"I guess she's not one for gentle parenting?" she asked, trying to lighten the moment.

A chuckle rumbled in Aleksei's chest, erasing some of the pain in his expression. "My mom is a determined woman. She doesn't mince words or hold her tongue. She told me I was wallowing in self-pity, and it was time to get over myself. I think her exact words were, 'Get your head out of your ass and see a therapist. The wounded, distant, tough guy thing is getting old fast.'"

Rosemary giggled. She'd probably really like his mother.

She shifted her legs closer to him and relaxed into the quiet. When she was sick, she'd learned to listen. Really listen. The tension in the room had eased, but it was going to be incredibly hard for Aleksei to keep talking about Phillipe. Hopefully, her silence would give him the space and time he needed to find the words he wanted to use. After a few minutes of listening to the sounds of the crackling flames, he finally spoke.

"Phillipe was my best friend. We started at Quantico on the same day. We were both Special Forces. He was a Green Beret, and I was a Marine Raider. We'd both been through some real shit and had an instant connection. After training, we were both assigned to work out of DC. They normally pair new agents with more experienced ones, but a few months in, my partner blew out his knee playing softball the same week Phillipe's partner announced his retirement, so they put us together."

It was as if he'd flipped the off switch on his anger and was retelling a story he'd heard second-hand. His demeanor appeared calm, but his muscles were rigid against her legs. He was as taut as an overstretched elastic wrapped around a too-large ponytail. So tight that it might snap free at any moment.

"And then you moved to Philly?" she prompted. He would feel better if he kept talking.

"Samantha, Phillipe's wife, wanted to move to this area to be closer to family, so they transferred us. I moved here, and they bought a house in Abington. Things were great. Sometimes we'd hang out in town. I went to their place for barbeques, Sunday dinners, the kids' birthday parties, all that kind of stuff. We played in a softball league. Sometimes Samantha would bring the kids to watch our games."

He ran his free hand through his close-cropped hair and then grabbed his beer from the coffee table and drained it. "I loved being an honorary uncle. I thought we were so fucking lucky. And then the shit hit the fan."

Aleksei's tension emanated from his body in such forceful waves that it was like sitting next to a furnace. The heat of his stress combined with the heat from the fireplace made sweat bead along the edges of her wig. She pressed her hands to her thighs, trying to draw her mind away from the itchy feeling building along the edges of her scalp. He deserved her full attention.

"What happened?"

He ran his long fingers over his hair again, his head slowly shaking back and forth. "The worst thing is, I don't really know. We had an apartment in Northern Liberties that we used for our cover. It was a quiet night, and I was tired as shit. I had a beer with Phillipe and went to bed. When I woke up in the morning, he was gone. His bed hadn't been slept in. And I knew. Right then, I knew something terrible had happened. We found him later that day. It was...difficult."

He closed his eyes for a few seconds, then reopened them. "It's crazy the things you focus on. When the ME flipped him over, he had some kind of dirt on his face. I remember wishing I could just clean his face. There was nothing I could do about the bullet wound or his missing hands, but the least I could do was wipe his face. And they wouldn't let me. They wouldn't let me."

Her lungs felt weighted down, like they were full of rocks. She would give anything to ease his pain.

"Did they find the person who killed him?" She had to ask even though, in her heart, she knew the answer.

He shook his head again. "No. There were no fingerprints. No physical evidence. I think it was someone from the case we were working on, but there was no proof. Somehow, it got leaked that he might have been an undercover cop. He was never linked to the FBI, and Philly PD denied he was one of theirs, but the murder was all over the news. The FBI closed down the op and shut down the investigation into the murder. They didn't want any bad press. They wanted it to all blow over."

He shrugged. "They moved on to the next thing and expected me to do the same, but I couldn't. I couldn't work every day with people who were willing to sweep Phillipe's murder under the rug. People who could just go on with their lives and ignore his death."

She hated the contrast of the pain in his eyes and the neutrality of his voice, the forced calm that masked his sorrow. She knew all about survivor's guilt. She'd waited months for her mother's murderer to be brought to justice. Aleksei was still waiting.

"So, you quit the FBI and started working as a consultant?"

He nodded. "We were supposed to have each other's backs, but he chose to go out alone that night. In the weeks before his murder, he seemed quieter than usual. He blamed his mood on being separated from his family for too long, and I believed him. He was my best friend. I should have known there was more to it."

Aleksei's voice cracked, a small fissure in his composure. "He didn't trust me enough to tell me what was going on. He didn't wake me up to go with him. He never should have been out there alone. I should have asked more questions. I should have pushed harder. If I had been a better partner, been a better friend, if Phillipe had trusted me...maybe I could have saved him."

"And if you couldn't?" Rosemary asked.

"At least he wouldn't have died alone."

Chapter Eight

The words hung in the air, creating distance while at the same time forging an unbreakable connection. He had just told her he would have preferred to die with Phillipe rather than let him die alone.

Was that love? Loyalty? Insanity?

He'd been an FBI agent. He'd been a Marine. His best friend had died a brutal death. Was his sense of duty misplaced, or was it exactly where it should be?

His words warmed her heart and spoke to her soul, so what did that say about her? What kind of person empathized with that sentiment?

One who had visited death's doorstep. One who had lain awake too many nights, terrified of dying alone. One whose life consisted of years of illness-imposed solitude. One who was desperate for the type of true, deep friendship Aleksei shared with Phillipe.

At least she was self-aware.

"One time, when I was in an argument with Sage, she told me something profound. It was the second time my cancer came back, and the treatments were brutal. The doctors weren't even sure they would work. My labs kept getting worse instead of better. One of the doctors suggested I stop treatment so I could have more quality of life during my last few months, and I told him I would think about it." A wry laugh escaped her lips. "Sage was livid. Absolutely livid. I told her it was my life and my choice, and she said she couldn't live without me. That sometimes it's harder to be the one who lives."

Aleksei lifted his hand to her cheek. His fingers were warm and rough with calluses.

"Your bravery shames me."

He couldn't be serious.

"You were in the Marines and the FBI," Rosemary said. "I think everyone you know is brave."

He leaned toward her until their faces were inches apart. His warm breath danced over her lips, and the sweet scent of beer filled her nostrils.

"You. Are. Brave." He spoke slowly, enunciating each word.

This fierce, strong, loyal, hot-as-the-sun man thought *she* was brave. His lips were so close. All she had to do was lean forward a little, and they would touch her own. If she'd been brave enough to battle cancer, then closing the gap between them should be no big deal. But his hand was still on her cheek, the tip of his pointer finger resting on her earlobe. Leaning forward might shift his hand into her hair. She couldn't lose herself in a kiss if she was worried about her wig.

"If I kiss you, will you promise not to touch my hair?"

He didn't pull back, but she felt him startle. She'd had far too few nights like this one. She didn't want to ruin this moment.

Firm fingers trailed down her jawline, grazed the side of her neck, then gently gripped her shoulder.

"Is this better?" he asked, his voice husky.

His fingers on her knee and shoulder were hot pokers on her skin. Her breasts felt heavy, her nipples tingled, and her core clenched with desire. The temperature in the already warm room seemed to jump even higher. The itchy sensation prickled her scalp, but this time, the itch was like distant music—her body's arousal muting the sensation.

She swayed forward, erasing the space between them.

The instant their lips touched, electricity arced through her. His tongue slid into her mouth. He tasted of mint and the spicy sweetness of lager. He kept their mouths together as he caught her legs in his hand and slid her down the leather couch until they were both prone. The arm of the couch supported her head, while his lean, muscled body pressed tightly against her. He was all hard heat, like lying on a hot sidewalk in the summer.

He nibbled her lips, sucking the lower one into his mouth. Then he returned to exploring her mouth with his tongue. His kisses were a drug, stripping her of the ability to think of anything other than the force of his tongue and the steel of his body.

She curved toward him, stroking his back and shoulder muscles. Then she trailed lower. His ass was nearly as muscular as the rest of him. As she squeezed, she pulled him into her, his erection creating a delicious pressure against her stomach, making her ache to be even closer.

His teeth nipped her chin and neck. He alternated languorous licks with gentle bites. Softness mixed with intensity.

Her thigh muscles tightened.

Hot, firm fingers slid under her shirt, up over her ribs, and closed over her breast. He squeezed her nipple through her bra. The rough lace edge rubbing across such delicate skin, combined with the pressure of his fingers, was exquisite. He released her nipple and then tugged again, this time adding a flick of his finger. Liquid rushed to her core. A moan escaped her lips. Her breasts felt weighty and needy. The muscles in her thighs grew tighter.

Her body was on fire. He was barely touching her, and she felt like she could come from one stroke of his hand. God, how she wanted that stroke. Needed it. With each brush of his lips, each scrape of his teeth, each press of his erection, each tug on her nipple, tension built.

She was one of those little race cars where you kept pulling the wheels backward until they were wound so tight, the car practically jumped when you let go. She wanted to let go, needed to let go. She needed Aleksei to wind and wind and wind until she raced off into oblivion.

She gripped his wrist. He stilled and lifted his head from her neck.

No, no, no. She didn't want him to stop. Not now. She shifted so she lay flat on her back. With her free hand, she grabbed his head and pulled it back down, but lower this time, so his face was at her breast. He exhaled, and his breath on her skin made her back arch. Her nails were digging into his wrist, but she didn't release her grip. Instead, she pushed his hand down her body.

"You want me to touch you?"

"Yes." The word was almost a moan.

His voice was deeper, his accent thicker. "That's good, because I want to touch you. I want to feel you hot and slick under my fingers. I want to feel you come on my hand."

His words were like a lightning strike. Muscles she thought couldn't get any tighter contracted further. Her body arched. The universe had shrunk to the space between her thighs.

"Please."

Her plea seemed to strike him like a match. His teeth sank into her breast. Deft fingers had her jeans unbuttoned and halfway down her thighs before it occurred to her to help him with her clothes. The idea was a flash, replaced by the divine sensation of her thong pressing against her clit. He'd slid the thin fabric between her folds and was tugging it slowly back and forth. But the pressure was too light, too teasing.

"Please."

She didn't care that she was begging. She was consumed by the need to feel his hand on her bare flesh.

As if he knew she couldn't take one more second of his exquisite torture, he slipped his hand under her thong, replacing the material with rough-skinned fingertips. Liquid heat soaked her core. A long finger slid inside her, twisting and pushing gently against her wall.

His nearly buzzed hair pricked her palm as she pushed his head harder into her chest, wishing she possessed magical powers to make the fabric between his mouth and her breast disappear. Still, each suck and nip sent pulses of heat directly to her clit. It throbbed against his thumb as he continued to swirl his finger inside her.

She arched her hips again, shaking them. "Please."

It seemed to be the only word her lust-hazed brain could produce.

Keeping his finger inside her, he pressed his thumb harder into her flesh, separating her folds, bringing his calloused thumb in direct contact with her epicenter of sensation. Each stroke of his thumb fueled the storm raging within her.

"Oh yes. Oh yes. Oh yes." The words tumbled from her mouth in mindless encouragement.

She held his wrist, her grip growing tighter and tighter with each brush of his hand. Suddenly, the warmth on her breast vanished, and the spicy-sweet scent of beer filled her nose—he'd lifted his head. She opened her eyes, meeting a gaze that reminded her of a thunderstorm cracking with lightning.

"Come for me, Rose. I want to watch your face when you come."

He quickened his pace as he spoke, sliding his finger expertly in and out of her.

She closed her eyes again, losing herself in the ever-increasing tension rising within her.

He squeezed her breast with his free hand while increasing the pressure on her hot, swollen clit.

It was too much. It was just enough. It was perfect.

She flew over the edge with one long, jagged scream.

* * *

Rosemary's core pulsing around his finger had nearly sent him over the edge. His dick was wedged so tightly against her hip, each squirm made him harder and harder. He felt like a teenager, ready to erupt from fully clothed contact. At least her writhing had stopped, giving him a minute to gather himself.

Her sumptuous body was now limp against his, and her rapid

breathing was beginning to slow. Rosemary, in her afterglow, was beautiful, but lying next to her while she orgasmed had been stunning. Watching her skin turn pinker and pinker as her excitement grew, feeling her buck and squirm, hearing her soft gasps and pleas, seeing her face transform from tightly closed eyes and clenched lips to the lax features of pure bliss—it didn't get any better than that.

Her eyes fluttered open. She lifted a hand and laid it gently on the side of his face. "That was amazing. My bones have gone liquid."

Her voice was still husky, and his dick responded with another jerk against her thigh. She wiggled a bit in response, and his balls tightened.

"I aim to please." His throat was dry, and his voice sounded hoarse to his own ears.

Her responding laugh was like bells. "Or maybe they melted. It's a thousand degrees in here."

He'd been so focused on her, he hadn't noticed the heat. Now that she mentioned it, he could see sweat beading along her hairline and realized his undershirt was damp and clinging to his back.

"Maybe we're just wearing too many clothes."

She bit her lower lip and peered up at him, blue eyes sparkling under hooded lids. "I think that's a pretty easy fix."

He pushed up to a sitting position. His right leg tingled from lying too long in the same position. He rose, shaking his sleeping leg and extended his hands. "Let's go back to my bedroom. It will be cooler there, and we'll have more room."

She tugged her jeans back up over her glorious skin and grasped his hand, her grip strong and firm. She let him pull her up. No questions. No hesitation. Just straight trust and determination. A sharp pang of guilt cut through his lust.

What the fuck was he doing?

Rosemary trusted him. What would she think of him if he took her to bed while she was the subject of his investigation? If their relationship continued, he'd have to confess that he'd orchestrated their meeting. Would she think he'd pursued her only to get to Moresco? Was that what he was doing?

She squeezed his hands. "Is everything all right?"

He had to tell her the truth before things went any further. But loyalty to Phillipe warred with the need to treat her fairly. It was hard to think with his dick raging. The room was too fucking hot. Rosemary was too fucking hot. He needed to think clearly, and to do that, he needed to put some space between them.

He released her hands, turned, and took a step away. Stabbing pain shot through his foot.

"Fuck, fuck, fuck!"

He'd stubbed his toes on the goddamn coffee table.

He flopped back on the couch and pulled his foot up over his knee, rubbing his toes.

"Are you OK?"

He lifted his gaze. Rosemary's lips were pressed tightly together but tilted up at the ends, and her eyes had a mischievous glint. Her expression was infectious. He felt the corners of his own mouth lift despite the ache in his toes.

"Are you laughing at me? You know, stubbing a toe is more painful than surgery. It's a little-known fact."

She sat down next to him, her weight shifting his cushion. "What made you change your mind?"

He respected her too much to pretend he didn't understand her question.

And the truth will set you free.

"There are things you don't know about me."

She tilted her head to the side, her white-blonde hair glinting in the firelight. "We just met. There are a lot of things we don't know about each other."

"These are important things. Things about my job. Things I'm afraid you won't like."

She lowered her eyes. "There are important things you don't know about me, either. Things I'm worried *you* won't like."

Her secrets couldn't be at the same level as his. Unless she really was in league with Moresco. But it was hard to believe *that* could be her secret. It didn't fit with the glimpse of her soul he'd seen tonight. He couldn't imagine her involved with a cold-blooded killer. Still, his training wouldn't let him discard the possibility without firm proof.

She lifted her gaze, features fierce with determination. "I don't want whatever this is between us to wither and die because of fear. Something good is growing here, but it needs water and light. And part of that water and light is honesty. Nothing real is going to grow if we aren't real with each other. I'm done being afraid."

She inhaled a deep breath, as if bracing herself, her gaze never leaving his. "This isn't my real hair."

Confusion hit him like Thor's hammer.

"You dye your hair? Or is your hair short and you do that thing where they add hair to make it long?"

Now she was the one who looked confused. "You mean extensions?"

"I guess. My sister does that sometimes. One minute her hair is short, and the next minute it's long. She complains about how expensive it is, and I tell her that's the price she pays for cutting her hair every time she sees a pic she likes on Instagram."

Rosemary released a heavy sigh and shook her head from side to side.

A full belly laugh burst from his mouth.

"What are you laughing at?" she asked.

"You're giving me the same look my sister does when I'm clueless about something she thinks every other person on earth would know."

"Most people do know about extensions," Rosemary joked, but her smile was tight, and her pink cheeks had gone pale.

Silence settled over them. The lust was gone. The romance was gone. The laughter was gone. The air was heavy with unspoken words.

He folded his hands over hers. Her skin was sweaty, her fingers rigid.

"What is it?" he asked.

Tension vibrated between them. A tear slid down her cheek.

"It's not mine."

"What's not yours?"

"My hair. It's not my hair." A quavering breath left her lips. "My last cancer treatment was a drug called Remiza. It saved my life, but it took every bit of hair on my body. It will never grow back. I'm bald. And I always will be."

Chapter Nine

"Your bravery shames me."

Aleksei's words brushed against her mind, but she couldn't process them. Her heart was as loud in her ears as the walk-through heart at the Franklin Institute, but beating a hell of a lot faster.

Cancer had taken her hair, but without cancer, she wouldn't be the person she was. She wouldn't embrace the joy in the little things like taking Thor for a walk, watching the leaves turn, sipping the first pumpkin latte of the fall season, or skipping the theater to spend a crazy night with one of the sexiest men she'd ever laid eyes on. A man whom she'd just told that she was bald. A man who was sitting next to her, looking at her like she was a teacup being juggled over a concrete patio—ready to fall and shatter at any moment.

She'd been forged by fire. She would not shatter.

"I'm sorry. What did you say?"

"Your bravery shames me," he repeated.

"I'm not sure it counts as bravery since I didn't really have a choice."

"Most people in difficult situations don't choose to be in them. It's how they respond to that situation that shows their character. You. Are. Brave."

Silence settled between them. Slightly awkward. Slightly expectant. She knew it was better to wait for him to speak, but fear of rejection sat in her stomach like a greasy meal. She hated the idea of him sitting next to her, trying to think of how to let her down gently. Trying to find the nicest way to tell her that he thought she was a great person, but that the bald thing was too much to handle. Admiring her didn't mean he would accept her. She came with baggage. It might be too heavy for him to help carry.

"It's okay if you want to stop seeing me."

Lightning flashed in his eyes. "If I were the kind of guy who would walk away because you wear a wig, then *you* should want to stop seeing *me*. You're way too good for someone who thinks like that."

"But you haven't seen me without the wig. Not even my sister has."

The storm clouds in his eyes became a tornado. "I like you, Rosemary. You. Yes, I think you're beautiful and sexy as hell, but if I were only attracted to your looks, I wouldn't be sitting here. So, you wear a wig. Lots of women wear wigs."

Damn him. Sage had tried this same argument on her.

"This isn't a fashion thing. I am *completely* bald. I had to have a treatment to replace my goddamn eyebrows!"

His hand settled on her shoulder. The fire was dying down, and although her head was still prickling, her body had cooled. The weight of his palm was soothing.

"I'm not saying you shouldn't feel nervous or worried about me knowing you're bald. You've been through hell and survived. You deserve to feel however you want to feel. What I'm saying is, I can't imagine thinking you're anything other than perfect with or without hair. You're a warrior. Any man should be honored to be with you."

This man was going to be her undoing. His kindness. His sensitivity. His honesty. And then there was the way he spoke. Part cop, part old-fashioned gentleman, and part motivational speaker. It was probably a mix of his job and all those old movies his mom made him watch. It didn't matter. The substance of his words spoken in that deep, sexy, slightly accented voice made her skin tingle.

"You'd make a great narrator for spicy romance."

"What?"

Her neck heated. Why had she said that out loud? Now he knew she read spicy romance.

"You have a great voice. I sometimes listen to novels when I'm walking or biking at the gym."

Novels. That made her sound well-read and intelligent.

"Got it. So, if I need some extra cash, I'll give Audible a call."

He slid the hand that had been resting on her shoulder down her arm to her wrist, where he started making circles with his thumb. How could such a small motion be so soothing and distracting?

"So, are we good? Do you believe that I'm okay with you being bald?"

He'd used the word *bald* intentionally. She was sure of it. Who knew what would happen when he saw her without her wig? But right now, he wasn't mincing words. He was facing the fact of her hair loss head-on. She couldn't ask for more than that.

"I think the only other thing is that you know how important it is for me to keep my wig on. I don't want you accidentally pulling it off, which is why I asked you not to touch my hair."

He lifted his hand from her wrist and saluted. "Yes, ma'am. Remember, I was in the Marines. You won't find anyone better at following orders."

"Good. Do you still want to show me your bedroom?" she asked, butterflies dancing in her stomach.

Aleksei's eyes became hooded, and he leaned toward her, so close that his lips brushed hers as he spoke. "Do you still want to see it?"

Desire snaked through her belly. Instead of answering, she closed the distance between them, pressing her lips against his warm, firm ones. His tongue pushed against her mouth, and she opened for him, savoring his sweet, spicy, minty taste. She dropped her hands to his thighs. His pants were smooth, but the muscle beneath was hard. An image of him using those muscles to thrust deeply inside her flashed through her mind. Heat swirled in her stomach and thighs. She needed to touch him.

She inched her hands higher and higher, circling the tips of her fingers in exploration until she found what she was looking for—his erection. He was rock hard, and she could feel the heat of his skin even through his pants. She closed her hand around his cock, squeezing.

He groaned and thrust his tongue deeper into her mouth, sending electric waves through her. She found his waistband, tugged his undershirt free, and let her fingers roam, finding firm muscle and fiery skin. His coarse chest hair contrasted with the smooth planes of his sides and back. The need to feel him under her tongue rode her.

She jerked his shirt upward and bent her head to bite the flesh just above his waist. Hard fingers dug into her shoulders as his hips jerked forward, making liquid heat rush to her core. His cock was rigid against her cheek, warm even through the layers of material separating them. She fumbled at the button of his pants, the metal cool under her fingers.

Buzz. Buzz. Buzz.

Buzz. Buzz. Buzz.

Buzz. Buzz. Buzz.

His hand left her shoulder, and she peered up just as he glanced at the vibrating smart watch on his wrist.

"Shit. Shit. Shit."

She eased back, disappointment mixing with concern.

His mouth was set in a grim line. "I'm sorry. I have to take this call."

He leapt off the coach, agile as a cat, grabbed his phone from the coffee table, and answered the call as he headed toward the hall. She leaned in his direction, straining to hear.

She heard Alexsie ask, "What's wrong?" Then, the click of his bedroom door cut him off from her hearing.

The concern in his voice sent a chill down her spine.

* * *

Aleksei's eyes adjusted quickly to the darkened bedroom. The room faced the road, so streetlights and headlights always provided bands of light around the blinds, no matter how late it was. Jaka lifted her head in her crate, but she didn't bark. As he waited for Kemper's response, he peered carefully through the narrow opening between the blind and the edge of a window that flanked his bed, scanning the street. If Kemper called late on a Friday night when he knew Aleksei was supposed to be out with Rosemary, shit was brewing. If Moresco was somehow on to him, he'd be easy enough to find. He owned the apartment. A quick search of real estate records and he'd be a sitting duck.

The hiss of Kemper blowing out cigarette smoke filled the line. "Why do you always think something's wrong?"

"You're calling me when I'm with Rosemary," he said through clenched teeth. "I told your we were going to the theater and that I was going to try to find out more about her work. So, it's reasonable to assume you wouldn't fucking call unless something was wrong."

"It's past midnight. You said you'd be home around 10."

He glanced at his watch: 00:37. The theater. The bar. The walk back to his apartment. Talking outside, then inside. Watching Rosemary come while lying in his arms. It felt like days, and it felt like seconds. Too much and too little at the same time.

"Shit."

Kemper barked out a laugh. "That's what you always say. You gotta get a new line."

"She's still here."

"You brought her back to your place? What the hell are you doing, Thompson? You know better than that. This op isn't going to be worth shit if you blow your cover."

He fought to keep his voice quiet. "This is no op, and you fucking know it. It's me, solo, trying to catch Phillipe's killer with an occasional bone from you."

Another hiss from the cigarette. "All right. All right."

Aleksei could almost see Kemper raising his hands in surrender.

"You're right. You're in there solo, doing the best you can."

His temper settled. They'd both lost Phillipe. Kemper was doing everything he could. He was risking his job by having Aleksei pursue this lead. Giving him a hard time was a dick move.

"Sorry. I'm on edge. I lost track of time, and your call was unexpected. It put me on high alert."

"No problem," Kemper responded. "I just called to ask if you had Phillipe's last notebook. You know how he was always scribbling shit in one of those mini composition books he kept in his back pocket? Evidence had a few from his desk and the ones they seized from his house, but I remember his last one was blue. The blue one wasn't there."

Caged memories broke free. Phillipe, looking like a strung-out truck driver or a nineties grunge star, with his greasy long hair, beard, flannel shirt, and shit-kickers, writing in a little notebook with a chewed-up pencil that spent more time in his mouth than in his pocket. The savory aroma of eggs, bacon, onion, and sausage mixed with the sweet smell of pancakes and that nutty coffee aroma that seemed ever-present in every diner. Aleksei had lost the coin flip, so they'd gone to the Oregon Diner instead of the Trolley Car.

When they were in deep cover, they were always "on," but this was downtime. Aleksei preferred to stay farther away from their marks when they weren't active, but Phillipe loved the creamed chipped beef at the Oregon Diner, so there they sat, on circular stools that had no back support, eating breakfast at the cracked, shiny counter.

"What's in the notebook?" Aleksei had asked the same question so often that it had become a running joke between them.

I'm writing a novel.

My request for a new partner.

Guidance for your dumb ass when you finally land a nice woman, so you don't fuck it up.

Phillipe's answers were always snarky and flip, but not that time.

Aleksei squeezed his eyes shut, trying to make the fuzzy image sharper. Kemper's request made it imperative that he recall Phillipe's exact words. He was trained to remember details. This would be a walk in the park if thinking about the last breakfast he'd had with Phillipe didn't feel like taking a machine gun to the gut.

He forced his shoulders and the muscles in his face to relax. The soft chatter of diners filled his ears. Their server, whose nametag read "Emily," was brewing a fresh pot of coffee behind the counter. Phillipe's clean plate was pushed back, and his head was bent over the small navy-blue notebook. The jagged scar from the alligator gar bite at the base of his thumb was shiny and white-pink on his tan hand.

He'd lifted his head, his eyes alert and serious. "It's all the facts. Everywhere I go. Everything I do. Everything I think. It's my secret code."

Aleksei's stomach dipped with the same nauseous feeling he got every time he had to jump out of a plane. He'd thought it was just one more joke. He'd fucking laughed. Had this been the one time Phillipe told the truth? Had his best friend been trying to tell him something important?

"So, do you have it? The last notebook?" Kemper demanded.

Yeah, he had it. It had been sitting on the kitchen table that hellish morning he'd woken up and realized Phillipe was gone. Phillipe always had that goddamn notebook in his back pocket. Of course he'd looked at it. It was half food diary and half doodle pad, with random notes mixed in. He'd figured it had been a fucking prank.

Phillipe had always complained about his reflux. So he tracked what he ate, doodled to chill out, and pretended the notebook was more than it was. He surely got a kick out of Aleksei trying to guess what the hell he was doing.

Aleksei hadn't given the notebook to Internal Affairs because it felt too special. It was one of the few things he had that was personal to Phillipe, and there was no reason for some random suit with a stick up his ass to know that the Reuben at the Trolley Car Diner gave Phillipe heartburn.

And Kemper wasn't getting his hands on it without a damn good reason. If he gave it to Kemper, he might never see it again. This wasn't an official op, so Kemper couldn't give it to the code crackers. That would raise too many questions. The notebook would have to be evaluated on the down-low. Kemper could give it to anyone, and who knew when, or if, Aleksei would get it back. Plus, Aleksei knew Phillipe better than anyone. If that notebook held something important, he had a way better chance of figuring it out than Kemper did.

"I don't think so, but I'm not sure. I've got a couple of boxes of stuff in the crawl space here. I'll look when I get a chance."

"What about in DC?" Another puff of smoke filled the line. "You got anything there? I could grab it if you give me the alarm code."

"Nope. What little I have is here."

That was a half-truth. He did have precious little left of Phillipe. Samantha had given him Phillipe's medals. She'd want them back one day—or the boys would. So, he was keeping them safe for them. Other than the medals, the two file boxes held photos he couldn't bear to look at, the books Phillipe had thrust on him so he could "expand his minuscule brain a bit," and that one little blue mini composition book full of Phillipe's pencil scratches.

The stuff wasn't here, though. Out of sight wasn't out of mind. The boxes hadn't lasted a week in the crawl space. They'd haunted him. He couldn't bear to have those remnants of Phillipe so close, so he'd moved them to his mom's attic in Virginia. He'd have to get his ass there ASAP.

"All right. Let me know if you find it. The other notebooks were full of nonsense, so I think it's a long shot, but I figured I'd ask."

"Good idea," Aleksei said. "I have to go. I need to get back to Rosemary."

"One more thing. Did Phillipe ever talk to you about the deliveries he did for Moresco?"

He glanced toward the closed door. Rosemary was going to be wondering what was taking him so long.

"We did most of the deliveries together, you know that. Lots of cash. Some drugs. All little shit, and all through go-betweens. If we'd done a bust, some low-level criminal would have gotten probation, maybe done a year at most, and we'd have been blown. We weren't under long enough for them to trust us with anything real."

"What about the deliveries he did with Frankie? The ones to the gelato store?"

Footsteps sounded. He recognized the click of the bathroom door and the loud whir of the fan. If he didn't get back out there soon, Rosemary would probably come check on him.

"I assumed they were the same. Phillipe never said anything different. If you know something, spill it."

"Cool your jets, kid. I don't know shit. I was just going over the op files and thought about those deliveries and how that gelato place is in the same building as Pannetone & Associates. Just seemed interesting."

Yeah. It seemed really fucking interesting.

The toilet flushed.

"I have to go. I have to take Rosemary home."

"All right, let me know if you find that notebook."

"Get some sleep, Gary. And lay off the cigarettes. That shit will kill you."

"Something kills everyone, my friend. Something kills everyone."

Kemper's response stuck with him long after he'd disconnected the line.

Chapter Ten

This had to be her ten of swords moment.

Rosemary sat in the same conference room she'd been in with Armando and Mr. Moresco last week, and just like last time, her armpits and head were sweating.

The low cabinets that ran the length of one side of the room were covered with Redwelds. The labels reflected the organizational system Armando required for all Pannetone & Associates files. The first label was always the name of the client. The second label was always the name of the project. The third and final label was a barcode.

Rosemary's gaze darted back and forth from the glass wall in front of her that provided a clear view of the hallway and the files to her right. The files were separated into two groups. The first label on all the files read Moresco, Salvatore. The second label on one group of files read Girard Warehouse, while the second label on the other set read Penrose Warehouse.

She wiped a bead of sweat from her forehead. When she'd started at the firm, Armando had emphasized that she shouldn't access any Moresco files without his permission. The fact that she was sitting here in this room—summoned to this meeting with a red exclamation point

Outlook invitation that contained no information other than the subject line "Girard and Penrose Files"—seemed pretty good evidence that she'd been caught violating that edict. Still, she was holding on to a sliver of hope. Maybe Armando wanted to review her work and had asked Lily to bring up the files in case they wanted to delve into more detail.

She could only hope.

Muted voices filled her ears. Her gaze shot up. Armando and Lily were heading down the hall. Armando's arm was curled around Lily's shoulder in what appeared to be a comforting gesture, and Lily's eyes were red and swollen. They looked like old-fashioned typecasts: Lily, the pretty, picture-perfect receptionist in a pencil skirt, blouse, sweater, and heels. Today, the hair she normally wore free was pinned up, adding to the effect. Armando was the distinguished Italian lawyer: deeply tanned skin, slicked-back salt-and-pepper hair, dark pinstriped suit, and imported leather loafers.

Lily turned down the corridor that would take her back to her desk. Their eyes met as Lily rounded the corner, and Rosemary watched her sadness twist into a sharp glare. It looked like their brief truce was over.

She shifted her gaze toward the opening conference room door. Armando's lips were thin and tight, his expression grave.

The sprig of hope she'd been clinging to dissipated.

She'd definitely been caught. She should have never asked Lily for help. Lily was an unhappy, dissatisfied person. She should have known she would rat her out. Sage always told her that she put way too much stock in "positive thinking, idealist, glass is half full crap." Sage was way too pragmatic for Rosemary's liking, but in this instance, her sister was right. Sage would never have trusted Lily, and it appeared that Rosemary shouldn't have either.

A bead of sweat dripped down the side of her face. She could feel hair sticking to her face and neck. She rubbed the back of her neck, and her hand met hot, slick skin. Her body's sweat response to stress was the absolute worst. Perspiration had probably already darkened the armpits of her baby-blue top. White and dark colors were safer for work, but Aleksei's cute, flirty, good morning text had put her in such a good mood that she'd gone with a new, fun, fitted turtleneck. Another mistake.

Thump.

Armando's hands thudded on the wooden conference room table as he took his seat. Her body jerked to attention, all thoughts of sweat and blue shirts fleeing like birds startled from a tree.

"I am a firm believer in keeping an open mind. I pride myself on not prejudging people or situations, but I'm having a difficult time doing that right now." The hard lines of Armando's face softened, and his shoulders slumped. "I'm also incredibly disappointed. I was extremely impressed by you, Rosemary. Not just your mind and the quality of your work, but also your enthusiasm and spirit, and what I perceived as true integrity. I thought you were trustworthy."

She glanced down at her lap. Armando was talking about her in the past tense, as if he'd already written her off. Her morning coffee and muffin threatened to make a second appearance. She hated disappointing people she cared about. Absolutely hated it.

Yep. Definitely her ten of swords moment.

The only good thing about the ten of swords was that, once you were down, there was really only one way to go. Another good thing about tarot was that it was just information from the universe. Fate brought what it would, but the cards didn't dictate a person's response. Each person owned that. In her view, when facing a bull, it was always better to grab it by its horns. Yes, it was dangerous, but she'd rather face trouble head-on than run and get stabbed in the back.

But that didn't make grabbing the bull easy.

Her heartbeat filled her ears. The room seemed to fall away, and it was just her, perspiration pooling on her neck, legs sweaty and sticking to her pants, wig scratchy on her head, blood rushing in her ears. The table was cool and smooth under her elbows as excuses flitted through her mind. She could tell Armando she hadn't understood his instructions about not viewing the Moresco files, but he'd been pretty goddamn clear. If she hadn't understood, she deserved to be fired for sheer stupidity. She could say she'd picked up the files by accident. She had multiple projects, and she was allowed access to the files for other clients. Just not Moresco.

Her mom's voice shimmered in her mind.

A lie is a weed. If you don't nip it in the bud, it'll take over the whole garden.

She'd seen how lies had almost ruined her sister's relationship with Ryker. The lies had torn them apart and put their lives at risk. The lies hadn't just taken over Sage's garden—they'd nearly destroyed it.

Armando had taken her under his wing, welcomed her with open arms, and treated her with kindness. If there was a chance she could keep her job, she wanted a good relationship with him, and any relationship without honesty would be shallow at best. If she didn't tell Armando the truth, she would lose all his trust, and more importantly, her own self-respect.

She forced her head back up so she could look at Armando directly. "You're wondering why I was looking at the Penrose paper files when I was supposed to be working on the Girard project, particularly after you specifically told me not to go through any Moresco paper files without your permission."

She hated the quiver in her voice. Armando had a soft heart. He couldn't bear tears. They needed to have a professional, direct conversation. She wanted Armando to speak his true mind, not thoughts skewed by a reaction to her distress.

"I was."

"I guess Lily told you I had the files?"

If Rosemary was lucky enough to keep her job, she was going to have to work with Lily going forward. She needed to know if her suspicions were correct.

Armando plucked a red paisley handkerchief from the outer breast pocket of his suit coat. "Here. Use this for your forehead."

She'd always assumed colorful handkerchiefs were for decorative purposes only, and the silk felt way too fine to use to mop up the sweat dripping down the sides of her face, but it seemed rude to refuse

Armando's kind offer. Plus, what had started in her scalp as an occasional twitch had turned into a full-blown itch. She dabbed at her forehead and face with the cool material, using the opportunity to scratch along the edges of the wig. When she was done, she tucked the damp cloth into her pants pocket.

"Thank you. I'll get this cleaned and return it to you."

Armando waved a tanned hand in a dismissive gesture. "The handkerchief is the least of our worries. Don't you agree?"

She'd rather discuss the handkerchief, but there was no point in delaying the inevitable. She nodded.

"You can't blame Lily," Armando said. "The girl is what she is."

The "girl" was in her early thirties, but Rosemary didn't think this was the time to point out the societal and psychological impacts on gender equality of using childlike terms to refer to grown women.

"She didn't betray your trust," Armando continued. "She simply scanned the files."

"What do you mean?" she asked.

Armando's heavy ring flashed in the light as he gestured toward the credenza. "All the files have barcodes. As you also know, Lily is supposed to be the only one removing files from or putting files into the file room. She uses a scanner to scan each file and key in the location. So, if Lily were to give you a file, she would scan it and note that it's in your office. That way, we always know where the files are."

Realization dawned. "When Lily returned the files I'd taken, she scanned them back in."

"Like I said. You can't blame the girl. She is what she is. A creature of habit who can be counted on to follow procedure and scan files back into the file room, which, based on the system, had never left. Our computer systems are set up to detect anomalies. When I confronted Lily, she told me you'd asked her to do you a favor and return the files to the file room. She said she was just doing her job."

Well, that settled a few of her jangled nerves. Lily hadn't betrayed her trust after all. Yet, on the shit side, Dante must have been the one who'd reported the anomaly.

Armando was a keen accountant, but technology was not his friend. He was competent with Word, Excel, and the accounting program they used for financials, but creating a program for tracking and reporting file movement was light-years beyond him. Dante was the only one in their small office who had the skill set to do it. And he knew she was the one working on the current Moresco matter.

The betrayal stung, but she understood it. Dante's primary loyalty was to his family.

Armando sighed. "Lily is a known factor. She follows the rules, does what she's told, and doesn't think outside the box. She's loyal and predictable. That's why she works here and will continue to work here. Mr. Moresco is an exacting individual. He—and his father before him—have used this firm for more than forty years. I've assured him complete privacy and discretion. My word is my pride. I simply cannot and will not have an employee I don't trust. An employee who could ruin what I've spent my life building because she won't do her job within the perfectly reasonable parameters I've set."

"Do you want an explanation, or do you just want me to pack up my office and go?"

She hadn't meant to sound so curt, but her patience was waning. Yes, she appreciated this job. Yes, Armando had been wonderful to her. But his rules were *not* perfectly reasonable. Her other job had no restrictions on accessing paper copies. Review of original records and a certain amount of confirmatory checking of reported numbers against invoices and other original source documents was actually required when preparing audited financial statements or conducting a forensic accounting analysis. Prohibiting that practice was *not* reasonable.

She was a hard-working, intelligent, thorough accountant. She was always on time, worked late when needed, and never complained. Armando was acting like he'd caught her stealing from the sunshine fund Lily used to pay for birthday cakes and holiday parties instead of treating her like a valued employee who had simply been trying to do the best job she could. Yes, she hadn't followed his silly rule about not reviewing paper files without permission, but she thought the rule was in place to avoid billing clients for busy work.

Armando's eyes narrowed. "I expected you to be more remorseful."

"And I expected you to trust me and raise any questions or concerns with an open mind. Instead, you set this meeting with the clear intention of intimidating me and came in here playing judge, jury, and executioner."

Annoyance laced her voice, but she didn't care. The meeting was pointless. She was covered in sweat, and her wig felt like scratchy wool. At this point, she wished he'd just hurry up and fire her so she could go to the bathroom, put a cool, wet towel on her face and neck, and scratch every inch of her irritating scalp.

An odd sense of calm settled around her, and the room suddenly felt a bit cooler. If Armando wanted to hear her perspective, he'd ask. If he didn't, he'd fire her. She'd be embarrassed. Davis would be pissed. But life would go on. This wasn't life or death. She'd been there and done that. This was just a job.

As minutes passed in silence, Armando's expression slowly shifted from indignation to professorial contemplation. Finally, he broke the silence.

"All right, explain it to me."

This would be her only chance to convince Armando she hadn't been trying to do anything wrong. That her intentions were pure. That she had only been trying to do the best work she could.

"You're always saying Mr. Moresco is the firm's most important client. I was super nervous. I really love working here. You've been so good to me."

This was not a good start. Nerves sent her thoughts jumping all over the place. She closed her eyes and pressed her fingers to her temples, letting her nails scratch at the edges of her wig just a bit. For some reason, scratching her infernally itchy head always calmed her. She started over, trying to present a more linear sequence of events.

"When you told me you were giving me the Girard warehouse to work on, I knew it was a show of faith on your part. I was excited but apprehensive. I didn't want to disappoint you, so I wanted everything to be perfect. I couldn't start working on the project until Lily scanned all the invoices into the system. While I was waiting, I thought it would make sense to review the Penrose warehouse financials since it's the most recent Moresco project that's similar. I thought taking a quick look at the invoices, payables list, and financials would get me acquainted with how you do things. That way, I'd be able to hit the ground running as soon as Lily finished. But then..."

"But then what?"

How did she explain without sounding ridiculous?

She released a long, settling breath. "My brain works in an odd way. Sometimes, it will notice something, but the observation sits in the back of my mind instead of coming to the front. Almost like when you wake up, and you know you were dreaming, but you can't remember what the dream was about. The images are there, but you just can't reach them."

Armando was looking at her like she was an alien.

Just stick to the facts.

"When I started work on the Girard warehouse financials, my mind kept turning to the Penrose numbers, like it was telling me that there was some important piece of information in there that I had seen and not processed. Like something was wrong."

"Are you saying you thought I made a mistake on the Penrose financials?" Armando's tone was more confused than offended.

She shook her head, frustrated that she wasn't being clear. "No. No. I didn't think you made a mistake. I just had this sensation that something was off with the Girard numbers, and that something I'd seen in the Penrose financials was the key to figuring it out. It was a gut instinct that wouldn't go away. I should have forced myself to ignore it."

"But you didn't ignore it. You tried to figure out what was bothering you," Armando finished her thought for her.

She nodded. "I couldn't shake the feeling that there was some crucial piece of information in the Penrose files that was relevant to the Girard warehouse financials."

Armando closed his eyes, slid his glasses down, and pressed his hand to his forehead. He looked like he wanted to be anywhere but in the conference room with her.

Maybe she should suggest an espresso. With a touch of brandy.

After a moment, he opened his eyes and readjusted his glasses. "That doesn't make any sense. The projects are completely independent. They have nothing to do with each other."

"Exactly!"

Again, he looked at her as if she'd just emerged from a spaceship. "Did it?"

She was baffled. "Did what do what?"

"Did looking at the paper files for the Penrose warehouse and Girard warehouse, both of which you weren't supposed to have access to, help you figure out the problem?

"I think so." She could barely hear her own words over the sound of her heart, which was as loud as a teenager blasting rap.

"And?" That one word was needle-sharp.

In for a penny, in for a pound.

"Have you been to both warehouses?" she asked.

"Yes. I make it a point to visit every construction project when it's completed. Sal is quite proud of his accomplishments. Visiting the completed buildings is good for client relations."

"Are there any elevators in the Penrose warehouse or the Girard warehouse?"

His eyebrows winged up. "Elevators?"

"Yes. Elevators."

"No. They are standard single-story warehouses. I've been inside both of them multiple times. I assure you, there is no elevator in either."

Weary irritation laced his tone. She needed to get to the punchline.

"When I decided to give up trying to figure out what was stuck in the back of my brain, I thought about using the elevator to return the files." She fought to keep her hands in her lap. "And I had the 'aha' moment. I remembered seeing an invoice in the Penrose files for an elevator. I hunted through the files and found it. It was for almost $600,000."

"Are you certain?" he asked.

She was a hundred percent certain.

"Absolutely." She paused. "I'm pretty sure there's an elevator invoice in the Girard files, too. I never got to look for it, because I bumped into Lily. I didn't want to get in trouble, so I decided to stop looking."

Color leached from Armando's burnished skin. He angled his head toward the files on the credenza.

"Show me."

Chapter Eleven

The cool air in the attic above his mother's garage chilled his fingers as Aleksei stared at the little blue notebook, the cardboard cover firm against his palm. It was a miniature version of the marble-style composition books he'd used in elementary school. He fingered the edge of the cover, bracing himself against what he knew he would see when he opened it: Phillipe's barely discernible scrawl and intricate doodles.

"Your boss was here yesterday."

Even after nearly forty years in the US, his mother's speech retained the long vowels of her first language. Hearing her voice usually warmed his belly like a cup of hot chocolate after a long snowball fight, but now, her words stiffened his spine.

He was a consultant. An independent contractor. He didn't have a boss. Anyone claiming otherwise was full of shit.

And probably dangerous.

He should have come earlier. He hadn't thought there was a need to rush. His mom was allergic to dogs, so he'd dropped Jaka off at his sister's place and stayed longer than he intended. Kids changed so fast when they were young, and hers had grown like weeds. They'd climbed him like a tree, demanded he play basketball on the new hoop they'd gotten for Christmas, and then his sister had brought out his old bow and arrow.

What he thought would be an hour stop turned into a two-night stay. It had been too long since he'd visited Zina. Far too long. After Phillipe died, spending time with the people he loved was terrifying. Bone-bendingly, heartbreakingly terrifying. All he could think about was how it would slice up what was left of his heart if he lost them.

He was a fool. And a fucking hypocrite.

He'd sat talking to Rosemary in his apartment in Philly, judging all the people who'd been laser-focused on Phillipe's death, holding onto the holier-than-thou attitude that had smoldered in his gut for the past two years. Yet he, too, had allowed his loss to control his actions every day. He'd been doing the same goddamn thing as the people he criticized, just in different packaging.

Now it seemed his obsession with Phillipe's death might have put his mother at risk.

"Who was here? What did they want? What did you tell them?" he demanded.

His mother narrowed her dark eyes and clicked her tongue. "Do not speak to me like that. I am no fool. Do not insult me by suggesting otherwise."

His mother had always been fierce. A strong wind that pushed obstacles out of its way by sheer force of will. He'd teased her, calling her RBG after she'd told him she was in the running for a federal judgeship—until she'd given him one of her lethal stares and said, "Enough of that. Do not joke about Justice Ginsburg. She is too good for that."

He'd never used the nickname again.

Still, his throat went thick. His mom was a force to be reckoned with in the courtroom, but the size and strength of her personality seemed to make her forget she was a 5'3", 115-pound woman in her early sixties. She'd have no chance against a grown man, especially a professional. What if Moresco had sent someone impersonating an FBI agent to his mother's home? To get close to her. To send him a message.

His pulse quickened, and then reason kicked in. It didn't add up. Didn't quite fit. For Moresco to send a man, it would mean he knew exactly who Aleksei was, who his mother was, and where she lived. It was a big stretch to think that Moresco knew he had been part of the FBI investigation three years ago. And an even bigger stretch for Moresco to know he was now back on the case—solo and off the books. Phillipe's murder screamed thief, not a blown cover. And it was hard as hell to get the home address of a federal judge. That information was buried deep in the federal cyber abyss. It would take a lot of time and effort, or a lot of money.

And for what? For someone to visit his mother and pretend they were an FBI agent? That was risky and inefficient. If Moresco had someone who could access federal records, it was a hell of a lot more likely Moresco would use that access to get his details and take him out.

Logic said something else was going on.

Hopefully, his mother could provide a good description of whoever had shown up here yesterday. She was leaning against the rectangular opening in the attic floor, arms folded over her chest. She looked serious in a gray blouse and black suit jacket, with her black hair pulled back tightly in the twist she always wore when she was on the bench. He didn't know if her legs were covered with pants or a skirt, but either way, she'd have on low, sensible heels. Mila Stanković was a creature of habit.

His mom was in great shape, speed walking five miles a day and taking toning classes at the YMCA twice a week, but that didn't mean he liked her climbing the attic ladder. If she fell, she could break her hip or leg. Yet expressing his concern would only make her climb up the rest of the way. Determination was her strength, but the flip side of that attribute was stubbornness. And that stubbornness meant she would be distant and aloof until he apologized for the insult.

"I'm sorry. I know you would never betray my confidence."

Lawyers knew how to keep secrets, and a lawyer who'd spent forty years married to a cop was doubly good at keeping them.

Aleksei slipped the notebook back into its box and pushed the box toward the hole in the floor. He left the second box sitting on the shelf behind him. He didn't need the pictures and medals. They held only pain and nothing valuable for the op. That box was for later. After he'd avenged Phillipe. If then. Maybe never.

"I'll bring this down. We can talk in the kitchen over tea if you have a few minutes."

His mom gave him the same look she'd given him in middle school when he told her his homework was done so he could go outside and shoot hoops before it got dark. She knew he was bullshitting her. She knew her presence on the ladder made him nervous. Knew he wanted her in the safety of the kitchen.

She sighed and waved a thin hand in the air. "Fine. I will go make us tea. Not because I am too old to climb into the attic, but because you will feel better when we are settled at the kitchen table. And then you will tell me what is bothering you. My first hearing isn't until 10:30, so I have some time."

His mother was, as she was most times, correct. He did feel better once they were settled at the kitchen table. Her homemade oatmeal cookies and lemon ginger tea always soothed him. She made the tea from scratch. Lemons, grated ginger, a dash of turmeric, and a squeeze of honey.

"Remember when I bought you that box of lemon ginger tea?" he asked.

She grimaced. "Poison."

He laughed, which he was sure was her intent. "Would you tell me about the man who came here yesterday?"

"He came in the afternoon. He flashed an FBI badge. I didn't need to study it to know it was real. Everything about him was government. Dark, mid-priced suit. Dark, mid-priced car. Cagey but very polite. Serious, placid face but sharp eyes. He told me twice that he was your supervisor but never gave me his name." She rolled her eyes. "These men always think I am stupid because I am a small woman and have an accent."

"Only a fool would think you're stupid. What did he want?"

She gestured toward the little notebook he had placed to the right of his placemat. "He said he was looking for Phillipe's personal effects. He said there were some missing items that needed to be returned to his family. He said that Phillipe had worked for him, and he was trying to do his best by him. He seemed genuinely distressed."

She squirted a bit more honey into her tea and stirred, the spoon clinking. Both of their cups were porcelain, white with blue imagery. He looked at his cup more closely, seeing dragons in the sky, lightning bolts, shipwrecks, falling towers, and so much more.

"What are these mugs?"

She sipped her tea and released a satisfied sigh. "Perfect. The mugs are catastrophe mugs. I use them when there is a bad omen. I sensed something unpleasant was brewing, and then that man came yesterday, and you visit unexpectedly today. If we drink from these mugs, the catastrophe will stay on the cups and out of our lives."

"What would your colleagues think if they knew their esteemed judge seasoned her daily life with a good shake of Romani superstition?" he teased.

"They would know why I have been so lucky." She waved at his tea. "Drink. I put ginseng and rosemary in your tea. For strength and luck. And a touch of lavender to open your heart."

The strength and luck he'd take. The heart opening he could do without. He'd already opened his heart way too far to Rose.

He turned the conversation back to the visitor. "He didn't give his name?"

"No."

"What did he look like?"

She sipped her tea thoughtfully. "He was handsome. Around fifty, I think. Maybe younger, maybe older. Not short, not tall. Maybe five foot ten. Brown hair. A bit of middle-aged paunch but otherwise in decent shape."

His mom's description sounded like half the guys he saw every time he went to Home Depot.

"Any defining features? Scars? Tattoos?"

She shook her head, but then her eyes took on a bird-like intensity. "He smoked."

"Smoked?"

"Cigarettes." Her gaze grew distant, and her voice took on a wistful note. "When I was a teenager, everyone smoked. No matter where we traveled, people smoked. Even I smoked. I know it is a terrible habit, but I miss it."

Vapes were more common now, but smoking was still a multibillion-dollar industry.

"A lot of people still smoke."

"I guess. But the way he smoked was distinctive. He asked if I minded if he had a cigarette before he left. He was outside, so I didn't care. He had the oddest look on his face when he inhaled. It was as if the cigarette was a religious experience. And every exhale was like a hiss. I remember thinking he sounded like a snake."

Aleksei knew that look, and he knew that sound. He'd seen and heard it hundreds of times.

Gary fucking Kemper.

Chapter Twelve

I'm going to be stiff for days.

The thought flashed through Rosemary's mind as she leaned back, gingerly stretching out one cramped leg and then the other. Thank goodness she'd worn pants today, or her frequent shifting and stretching would be showing parts that were not work-appropriate. Not that Armando or Dante would even notice. Dante only tore his eyes away from his laptop when he went to the basement to bring up more files, and like her, Armando's head was buried in paper.

Paper was everywhere.

She had claimed a small piece of real estate in the corner of Armando's office when they'd carried in all the files from the conference room. He'd said he wanted more privacy while discussing what she'd found. He went positively gray when she showed him the invoice for the elevator at the Penrose warehouse. That had kicked off the whirlwind of figuring out how deep the hole went.

Armando had called Dante in to conduct some electronic sleuthing. Rosemary's computer skills were good, but Dante was a wizard. Since the scanned invoices were PDFs, and the various programs for payables contained limited data points, it was a coin toss as to what results the electronic records would yield. Tackling the paper files with Armando while Dante handled the electronic ones seemed like the most efficient approach.

Clear space had consistently dwindled as Dante brought in additional files throughout the day. Now, every inch of Armando's boat-sized desk, guest chairs, black leather couch, and glass-and-chrome coffee table were covered in a sea of creamy yellow manilla folders, stark white invoices, with some blue and green ones mixed in, and burgundy Redweld file folders.

Her stomach growled, the sound loud in the pin-drop quiet room. They'd worked through lunch, grabbing drinks and snacks from the gelateria. The sky had transitioned from bright blue to rose to the bluish purple of springtime dusk.

Armando dropped his forearms onto his desk with a thud. "It's time we called it a day. My eyes are going blurry. Dante and I will pick this back up tomorrow."

"I can help too," she quickly offered. She didn't want Armando battling the paper stacks solo.

"You won't be here. You're on vacation."

She blinked a few times, eyes gritty from hours of names, numbers, and spreadsheets.

Vacation. The day had taken such a crazy turn that she'd completely forgotten she was supposed to be leaving for vacation today. A few weeks ago, Armando had insisted she schedule her carryover vacation days from last year before they expired at the end of the month. She couldn't even remember if she'd put the time off in their work system. She'd figure that out later. Right now, there were more important matters at hand.

"I can't leave you with this mess."

"You most certainly can." As if sensing the argument on the tip of her tongue, Armando added, "This isn't open to discussion. You're going on your vacation. I insist."

Armando's reminder about her trip immediately turned her thoughts to Sage's texts last night. They were branded into her brain.

What the hell were you thinking inviting a complete stranger on vacation?

You barely know this guy. What if he's a serial killer? Or a rapist?

You're taking this live life to the fullest shit too far. Living fully doesn't mean being stupid!

Do you want to die?

After the last one, she'd set her phone on Do Not Disturb.

She was done being micromanaged by her sister. Yes, Sage had lived and worked in France, while Rosemary had never left the tri-state area. Yes, Sage had gone away to college and worked in gritty strip clubs, while she had attended all her university classes virtually and had only one brief job before this one. There was no arguing that Sage had more life experience, but that didn't give her sister the right to run her life.

But really, what the hell had Rosemary been thinking? Or had she even been thinking at all?

She'd invited Aleksei on impulse last night after Sage called, apologizing, saying she and Ryker wouldn't be back for a few more days. She'd been disappointed but not surprised. There had been complications with Christian's appendectomy, so the doctors had to do it the old-fashioned way instead of laparoscopically. Ryker was a lot like Sage when it came to his sibling—way overprotective. Even though Christian was a grown man who worked in the FBI cybersecurity division, Ryker wouldn't leave his brother's side until he was fully recovered.

Rosemary would feel the same way if their roles were reversed, but that didn't mean she was canceling her vacation. Sage said it wasn't safe for her to be alone in the woods for five days. Easy fix. Invite Aleksei. But instead of being content, Sage had lost her goddamn mind.

Do you want to die?

She knew her sister hadn't meant it. Sage was low on sleep and high on stress, worried sick about Christian, and freaked out about the possibility of Rosemary traveling with a man she barely knew. Still, her sister's text had cut deep.

She did not want to die. Had never wanted to die. It was hard for her to believe anybody would *want* to die. But she knew what it was like to be given a death sentence. When she was diagnosed, there was no cure for her cancer, so the goal had never been her recovery. It had been to use every treatment possible to extend her life as long as possible.

Remiza had cured her cancer, but her cancer had taught her to accept the reality of death. Death would come for her eventually. Death was inevitable. It was what she did in the time she had that mattered. That was why she had invited Aleksei.

She wanted this time with him, but now Sage's words had planted a seed of doubt in her mind. She wasn't worried about rape or murder, but her sister was right. She'd known Aleksei for barely a week and had dumped a lot on him in a short period of time. Doubt nipped at her mind, flipping her empty stomach. What if he was having second thoughts about her being bald?

He'd said he didn't care, but he'd had a few days to process her confession, and their texts had been sporadic over the weekend. He was visiting his sister and busy with her kids, but maybe that was an excuse. What if he had changed his mind? What if he said he would come to Ricketts Glen because he didn't know how to nicely refuse? What if he ghosted her? Or worse. What if he was doing the mature thing and coming on the trip so he could tell her in person that he didn't want to pursue a romantic relationship with her? What if he gave her the dreaded "I'd like to be friends" talk?

Maybe she should tell him not to come. Five days alone hiking and fishing would be great. Just great.

"Did you find any more elevator invoices?" Armando interrupted her reverie.

Heat flushed her cheeks. She had the feeling it wasn't the first time he had asked the question.

"No, and I don't think I will. Whoever's doing this is smart."

Armando grimaced. "I agree. We've run company names, addresses, and deposit instructions for invoices we pay via ACH, and every duplicate has checked out. We've had three people working for close to seven hours, and other than the elevator invoices you identified for Penrose and Girard, we've only found what we think might be a duplicate sprinkler invoice on one property and duplicate lighting expenses on another."

"Or maybe they actually needed two different companies to work on the sprinklers and the lighting for those buildings?" Rosemary lifted her palms and shrugged. "That doesn't make sense to me, but I'm no construction expert. Of course, I'm not a fraud expert either."

She let her words hang in the air. They were looking for needles in haystacks without the personnel or expertise to find them. What they really needed was a team of forensic accountants to go over each of the Moresco company files, line by line. Armando had to know that, but for some reason, he hadn't suggested it. Maybe he was worried Sal would judge him. Or maybe pride was holding him back.

Maybe he'd feel better if she suggested it.

"Should we call a few experts and see if there's fraud detection software we could use? There are more than one hundred separate Moresco businesses. It will take us months to review all those files in enough detail to see signs of fraud. Maybe longer. And there's still a chance we would miss something because this isn't our area of expertise."

"You know we can't do that."

"Why not?"

Armando peered over the reading glasses perched at the tip of his nose. "You know why."

Embarrassment warmed her skin.

"I don't think she does," Dante offered, looking up from his laptop and meeting Armando's stern stare with one of his own.

"She has to." Armando's tone was implacable.

"Only if Davis told her, and I don't think he did. Would you trust that bastard to tell anyone the truth? Think about it. Think about her. Who would choose this?"

"He's her father," Armando responded in a tone that sent a shiver down Rosemary's spine.

It didn't seem to faze Dante. "Stepfather. He's her stepfather. And a pretty shitty one, I think. He threw her to the wolves and didn't tell her a fucking thing."

"Wolves?" Armando scoffed. "We are not wolves. And watch your language. You know I don't permit foul language in my office."

Rosemary looked from Armando to Dante and back to Armando again. They were talking about her as if she weren't there.

"What am I supposed to know?" she demanded. "What was Davis supposed to tell me?"

Two sharp raps on Armando's office door broke the uncomfortable silence that had enveloped the room, leaving her questions shimmering in the air, unanswered.

Armando shot to his feet. "Yes?"

Lily appeared in the open door. "I'm headed out for..." Her words shifted into a shocked intake of breath.

"My f-f-f-files," she sputtered. "What have you done?" The volume of her speech increased as her tone shifted from shock to outrage. "This is a disaster! It will take me hours to organize this mess! How could you do this to my files?"

Armando's brown eyes blackened, and his expression hardened. The avuncular gentleman was gone, replaced with someone fiercely serious, almost deadly.

"This is *my* office, and these are *my* files. I will do whatever I want with them. You work for me. If you would like to continue doing so, you will go back to your desk, pack up, and go home."

Lily backed away from the door, eyes wide, hands trembling.

Armando called after her. "Mr. Moresco will be stopping by during our staff meeting tomorrow. Make sure you pick up the cinnamon buns he likes from Giovanni's on your way into the office."

Lily nodded, then dashed away.

Armando whirled to face Rosemary, pointing. "And you. Pack up and leave for your vacation. Now."

What the hell was happening? She'd never seen Armando this angry, and there was no reason she could think of as to why he should be mad at her. He couldn't still be upset about her reviewing the Penrose warehouse files. If she hadn't done that, she wouldn't have discovered the invoice issue. Mr. Moresco would be thrilled they'd identified the problem. Armando would look like a hero. Yet instead of being grateful, he seemed furious and was arguing with Dante about some secret Davis knew but had certainly never shared with her.

Her eyes were blurry, and she had a pounding headache. The fuel from the lunchtime snacks had run out hours ago. If Armando wanted her gone, she was more than happy to oblige.

She rose, legs achy from nerves and too many hours on the hard floor. Dante sprang up from the couch and slid a firm, supportive hand under her forearm, grounding her. The energy in the room had turned cold, so Dante's warm, friendly hand was most welcome.

He guided her into the hallway toward the metal door that led to the basement. "Come downstairs with me. I want to refresh your computer while you're gone, so I'm going to give you a loaner laptop to take with you. It'll just take me a few minutes to set up. Let's swing by my desk and grab it."

She hadn't planned on bringing a computer with her. On a good day, cell service and Wi-Fi were spotty at Ricketts Glen. On a bad day, they were nonexistent, but she didn't have the energy to argue. She'd keep an eye on her email from her phone the best she could, and if she needed to log on for something, she'd cross that bridge then.

She glanced down at her smartwatch. *Ugh.* It was already after 6:00 p.m. She and Aleksei had agreed to meet at the park office at 9:00 p.m. If he was really planning on meeting her, he'd have already left. If she didn't get her ass in gear, he'd get there before her. She still needed to go home to pack the car and get Thor. If Thor didn't take to Aleksei, or if Thor and Jaka didn't get along, she'd take it as a sign from the universe that she'd been meant to take the trip alone. But if she didn't grab dinner first, she was going to faint.

Relax, my little one. Just relax. Her mother's voice lilted through her overtired mind.

She closed her eyes, visualized the tranquil sandy beach at the lake at Ricketts Glen, then released a long, slow, cleansing breath. She'd get there when she'd get there, and Aleksei's choices were his own. She'd leave her vacation in the hands of the Fates.

They would spin, measure, and cut as they pleased.

Chapter Thirteen

Melancholy guitar notes and Zach Bryan's deep twang filled his ears as Aleksei flipped a perfectly browned blueberry pancake. Rosemary was going to be impressed. When he'd packed the pancake mix, he'd assumed his frying pan would be sitting atop his cast-iron over-fire grill, but Rosemary had rented one of the few modern cabins at the state park.

Cabin E. You'd think all the natural beauty of the park would inspire something a little more creative in terms of a cabin name. Despite its drab name, the cabin was beautiful. All wood planks, furnished with a stove, sink, and refrigerator. It even had a bathroom and a shower. Even though it had two bedrooms, he'd insisted on pitching his tent out front. Rosemary had seemed nervous last night, twisting her hands and looking at the ground instead of meeting his gaze as they'd chatted briefly. Then she'd pleaded exhaustion and retired for the night.

She'd offered multiple times for him to stay in the second bedroom but had seemed relieved when he insisted on sleeping in his tent. He told himself he shouldn't be disappointed. He'd been thrilled but also surprised that she'd asked him to join her on this trip. Camping was a close-quarters kind of activity, and they hadn't known each other very long. He was taking the fact that she had given him the extra cabin key as a sign that, despite her nerves, they were still in a good place.

Maybe she was just tired. She'd worked all day, and it was a long drive from Philly to Ricketts Glen. Or maybe her reticence was because they'd barely spoken over the weekend. Barely texted.

That was his fault. Zina's house had been nuts. Good nuts. But still nuts. He didn't remember having that many lessons, practices, and games when he was young. And the kids wanted him to go to everything. Everything. It wasn't fair of him to assume that he and Rose would slip right back into familiar comfort and easy rapport.

You slipped into it pretty quickly on your first two dates.

And the calls and texts they had exchanged had been like those he'd had with his family and Phillipe. Easy. Even when they talked about hard things.

Her reticence could be due to Thor's tepid response to his presence. The giant that looked more like a deer in a cow costume than a dog had taken to Jaka right away. The two dogs had immediately started chasing each other and wrestling. Thor seemed to know he was more than twice Jaka's weight and was gentle in his play. Rosemary had explained that Thor was a Great Dane Dalmatian, a gentle and affectionate breed, but Thor had no interest in him. Every time he approached, the dog would turn his head and walk away. No barks or growls, just extreme indifference.

He hadn't wanted to push his luck with a dog that, on his hind legs, was taller than Rosemary, so the tent was the best choice. Rosemary had promised to keep Thor in her room so he could use the cabin restroom if needed. Hopefully, Thor would warm up to him today. He had a feeling that, if the dog didn't accept him, Rose would send him packing. Her love for the animal was evident. If Thor didn't trust him, she wouldn't either.

He slipped a pancake onto the pile he'd started on a platter and ladled more batter onto the frying pan. He hadn't woken until after ten. Then, he'd showered at the shower house, dressed, and packed his backpack for their planned hike. At this point, the pancakes were going to be more lunch than breakfast. He was exhausted. He'd slept poorly the past few nights and had the same recurring nightmare. Even now, hours after he'd woken up in a cold sweat with Jaka licking his hand, the images still haunted him.

He'd dreamed of Phillipe. The night was dark and eerie. The wind whipped as he stood at the edge of the walkway where Phillipe had been found dead on the cold, hard ground. Then Phillipe's eyes jumped open, and he rose, the bullet's exit wound round and bloody on his forehead. Phillipe's arms ended in gory stumps where his hands had been hacked off.

Phillipe had Frankenstein-walked toward him, repeating the same thing over and over. "It's all right there. Why can't you see it? It's all right there. Why can't you see it?"

A hand touched his back. His heart jumped into his throat. He squealed. Both the pancake he'd been flipping and his spatula went soaring through the air. He pulled the earbud out of his ear just in time to hear the pancake land on the wood floor with a squishy thump. Both Thor and Jaka skittered around the kitchen, barking.

"Shit."

Bell-like laughter filled the air.

Rosemary's pale fingers stroked both dogs' heads as they butted up against her legs, nearly knocking her off balance. "Settle down, guys. Settle down. Shh. Aleksei's just a scaredy cat. He didn't mean to startle you with that yelp."

Her teasing tone pulled his lips into a smile. She looked radiant and ready for action in leggings that were already covered with dog hair, hiking boots, and a forest-green long-sleeved shirt. Her hair—well, her wig—was pulled back into a low ponytail.

She must have noticed the direction of his stare, because she ran long, pale fingers down her ponytail, pulling it over her right shoulder, the white-blonde contrasting sharply against the dark shirt.

Her fingers twirled the ends of the ponytail, and she shifted her weight from foot to foot. "It's the most practical for hiking."

"The ponytail looks great."

"You won't tell anyone this isn't my real hair?" she asked.

He didn't care about her hair. Truly. And he would never betray her confidence.

"I'll take your secret to my grave," he said with the same solemnity he'd used when reciting his Oath of Enlistment. The heaviness of the vow and his reference to death seemed to suck the air from the room, so he shifted to humor to lighten the mood.

"Now you better swear to me that you won't tell anyone about that ridiculous sound I made when you spooked me." He pointed to the pancake on the floor, smushed by dog feet and half eaten before Rosemary had nudged Jaka and Thor out of the way. "And if you don't promise, that one's yours."

He was rewarded by more tinkling laughter and a relaxation that continued to grow as they ate breakfast, cleaned up—him washing and her drying as if they'd lived together for years—grabbed the dogs' leashes, and headed out for the Falls Trail.

They hiked together like longtime partners, with similar speed and caution. The dogs continually darted ahead and circled back, spryer and more sure-footed than their humans. Like him, Rosemary hiked with a fully stocked pack. It didn't matter that it was just a day hike and that, even with stopping to take pictures and have a snack, the 7.2-mile in and out trail should only take a few hours. She had several protein bars, a few bottles of water, Aquatabs, a couple of emergency blankets, and a first aid kit.

He liked that she was as prepared as he was, that she was smart enough to know that people got lost and accidents happened. He'd had friends grouse at him over safety gear, telling him that he was a pessimist or that they didn't need another grandmother, but he didn't believe in taking chances. Not with the health and safety of people he cared about.

"Did you grow up hiking?" he asked as they approached Wyandot Falls.

At fifteen feet, it was one of the smaller falls on the trail, but

Rosemary exuded the same blissful wonder she'd shown when they'd stopped in front of Ozone. At sixty feet, Ozone's crash of rushing water had been nearly deafening. Despite being petite by comparison, Rosemary gazed at the rocks and rushing water of Wyandot with an expression that mixed elation with reverence. She took a few steps closer and raised her hands, letting the spray sprinkle her palms and face. Just as he'd begun to wonder if she'd heard his question, she answered.

"No. I remember going to the beach and Disney when I was young but never hiking or camping. My dad committed suicide when I was in middle school, and for a while, money was too tight for travel. When my mom remarried, our finances improved, but then I got sick. So, it was lots of rest and indoor time for me." She waved her hand, encompassing the rocks, falling water, and woods surrounding them. "Now, I hike and camp whenever I'm able. I try to spend as much time as I can doing the things I love."

"I'm sorry." The words felt trite. Her life had been a series of tragedies. It was no wonder she tried to bring as much joy as she could into every day. With so much shit in her life, she must always be waiting for the other shoe to drop.

Or maybe she was trying to experience as much as she could before it did. Maybe too many brushes with death had given her a "life is short" attitude, so she threw caution to the wind and did whatever she had to in order to live life fully before tragedy struck again. Maybe she was working for Moresco to fund the lifestyle she'd never been able to have. Money laundering was lucrative and could seem victimless. Kemper hadn't found any anomalies in her financials, but he'd done only a quick search. He easily could have missed it.

Rosemary shrugged. "It's OK. If life weren't hard, how would we know to appreciate what we have? If we didn't know loss, we wouldn't know joy."

Her words only reinforced the worm of doubt that continued to wriggle in his thoughts.

She turned from the waterfall, her face slightly damp. "I feel my parents with me in places like this. In the rocks, the trees, the water, the ferns, and the flowers. I know they're watching me from above. I know they're with me."

He wished he felt Phillipe the same way Rosemary felt her mother and father. Or maybe he did but had never realized it. Maybe he felt Phillipe in the space next to him he had never filled. He and Phillipe had hiked and camped together for years. After Phillipe died, Aleksei hadn't wanted anyone with him. Hadn't wanted the intimate closeness created by sharing nature, by sharing resources and space. Hikers took care of each other. He hadn't wanted the responsibility of another person. Not again.

"You're quiet. What are you thinking about?"

He pasted an easy smile on his face. One he'd spent months practicing before his first undercover op. "I'm wondering how experienced a hiker you are."

It wasn't a complete lie. Her pack, pace, and ease on the trail made him think she'd been hiking for years, but that didn't gel with her earlier comments.

She whistled and then scanned the area around them, turning her head to answer him only after Thor and Jaka trotted out of the woods and onto the trail. "I've been hiking for about eighteen months. I started as soon as I began taking Remiza. The drug performed well in trials, but I wasn't sure if it was going to work for me. If it didn't, I wouldn't have had much time left. I love nature, and I didn't want to die without spending more time in it, so I started hiking and figured what would happen would happen."

The calm acknowledgement of her potential death was like a physical blow. He tried to ignore it. "You pack like an expert."

"I pack like someone who knows how to take care of herself," she retorted. "My mom and sister wasted years of their lives taking care of me. Years. I swore to myself that if Remiza cured me, I was taking care of myself going forward. I hate that I was a burden on them for so long. I promised myself I was never going to be a burden on anyone else ever again."

He reached out and rested a hand on her shoulder. The spray from the waterfall that had beaded on her lightweight jacket was cool and wet under his palm. He'd seen the deep affection in Sage's eyes when worry drove her to track Rosemary down at the restaurant. She'd come to check on her sister out of love, not a sense of obligation. He hated the thought of Rosemary separating herself from her family because she felt like a burden.

The thought of her standing alone unsettled him.

The fact that she saw herself as an obligation rather than a gift made his heart ache, but his body reacted with an odd sense of ease, a softening of muscle and bone. As Phillipe's partner, he'd taken on the same responsibility Rosemary's family had accepted. The responsibility to do everything in their power to protect a life. Rosemary's family had succeeded, and he had failed. But instead of that contrast making him rigid with guilt, his body had relaxed.

Rosemary didn't want anyone taking responsibility for her life. The weight of that sat too heavily on her shoulders. For him, bearing that responsibility was something he could never do again. He'd learned that the cost of failing was just too high.

Shame washed over him as he recognized the warm ease that had settled into his bones. It was the emotion of a coward.

It was relief.

* * *

Hiking with Aleksei was easy. Almost too easy.

He was in better shape than she was—not surprising considering his military background and job—but he didn't rush her. She spent more time at each waterfall than the few other hikers they crossed paths with on the trail, but he seemed just as content to watch the crashing, swirling water as she was. At every fall, while the dogs splashed and played or explored the nearby woods, they would choose fallen leaves and place them in the stream to race. She'd won more races, but maybe he was letting her win.

Before the hike, she'd have said it was impossible to "fix" a race based on purely natural elements, but now that they'd been out several hours and she'd discovered just how vast his knowledge of the outdoors was, she wasn't so sure. The nature Rosemary had learned about was a different kind of nature. No. Not a different kind of nature. She'd just learned different things.

Her mother had focused on the rhythm of life, as expressed in the seasons and the cycles of the sun and the moon. She'd taught Rosemary how to meditate to foster a deep connection with the earth. So, with each stop at each waterfall, Rosemary would touch the water and feel the falls as if they were rushing through her veins. When they stopped for a snack, the tree she rested against shared its life with her, entering her bones, warming her back and shoulders.

This was the knowledge of nature her mother had passed to her.

Aleksei's knowledge was all practical. He pointed out slippery spots on the trail that she didn't notice. He identified various plants and trees, pointing out some mushrooms and leaves that were edible in a pinch. Not tasty, he said, but edible. He knew what kind of rock surrounded them. Apparently, there was sandstone, shale, and siltstone. They saw some fish in a deep, clear pool, and he told her they were brown trout. They both laughed when the dogs jumped in, and the fish scattered. When a bird cawed loudly in the trees, he told her it was a blue jay. Of course, she'd already known that one.

She wasn't completely clueless.

Despite offering information and insight from time to time, Aleksei didn't fill the silent spaces with idle talk. They hiked most of the time in the same kind of companionable silence she shared with Sage during long car rides or when they did a jigsaw puzzle. Each was comfortable focusing on their own thoughts, chiming in only if they found a missing puzzle piece, saw something exciting out the window, or some interesting or funny thought popped into their minds.

But this hike was punctuated by strong hands holding her steady when the trail turned steep, a firm chest and hips pressed against her back when they squeezed against the rockface to allow other hikers to pass on narrow sections of the trail, and soft touches on her back and shoulders to get her attention.

Quiet time with Sage was, well, sisterly. The thoughts that crossed her mind with each graze of Aleksei's hand across her back or shoulder, each brush of his thigh when they sat together on rocks, each puff of warm breath when he leaned close to say something in her ear so he could be heard over the cacophonic music of the falls—those thoughts were not familial.

She wanted him to press her against a rock, wrap her legs around his waist, and kiss her senseless. If there were fewer hikers on the trail and the weather were warmer, they could risk making love in one of the frigid pools formed by the falls. She imagined him lying her next to one of those pools. She could almost feel the cold rock against her back, smoothed by years of flowing water, and the chilly water that would swirl around her calves as she lay back, her legs dangling in the water. The early spring air was not much warmer than the water. His tongue would be deliciously hot on her icy skin.

She shivered.

"Are you cold?" He glanced skyward. "We should get moving. It's getting late."

They'd hiked longer than expected, covering the entire Falls Trail and exploring some side trails as well, taking their time at each waterfall, letting the dogs run and play. The sky was beginning to gray. The hours had passed like a gentle flowing stream.

Was it normal to feel this comfortable this soon? Was the thing budding between them a pile of kindling? Something that would burn fiery hot, but die out quickly? Or was it something that would last?

She was reluctant to move. They sat side by side, backs propped against a sun-warmed boulder, their feet cooling in the water. Her feet had gone numb in the icy cold. The swirling water tugged on her buoyant feet. This was a perfect moment in a perfect day. But Aleksei was right. The spring equinox had not yet come, and sunset still came early. Dark would come fast on the wooded trail, and temperatures dropped quickly at this altitude. It was time to head back.

She watched him don his socks and boots, his long fingers quick and efficient. A curl of jealousy snaked through her. All his movements were expertly fluid. Thor had even seemed to recognize his skill, accepting him as the leader of their little hiking group, responding quickly when he called. After her feet were snuggled back in her padded socks and cushioned boots, he pulled her up with one rough-skinned hand.

"We probably have only ninety minutes of good light left," he said.

"I know. And at least forty-five minutes of straight hiking to get back to the cabin."

Her tone was sharper than she'd intended. Much sharper. Embarrassed, she dropped the calloused fingers that still gripped her own.

"What's wrong?" he asked.

She forced a smile. "Nothing. Let's go."

"Sit," Aleksei commanded the dogs as his pack hit the ground with a thud.

Of course, both dogs immediately sat. The claws of jealousy dug in a little deeper. She'd have to give the command three times before they'd listen to her.

Cool, roughened fingers cradled her cheeks, lifted her head. "I've done something to hurt you. I'm sorry."

"It's not you."

"Then what is it?"

Words clogged her throat. Too many at once. But none of them were the ones she was looking for. They would all make her sound petty, but truth was truth. She was not going to degrade this amazing day with dishonesty. She stepped out of his grasp, kicking a stray pebble into the stream while she mentally sorted out the uncomfortable bitterness squeezing her spine. The words wouldn't be perfect, but they would be out.

"Sage was supposed to come on this trip with me. When I was sick, there were so many things we wanted to do together but couldn't, so we've been trying to make up for lost time. She and Ryker are still in DC with Christian. Ryker wanted to stay with his brother until he fully recovered from the appendectomy."

Aleksei's storm-colored eyes darkened, his eyebrows coming together. "Do you wish your sister were here instead of me?"

That wasn't it at all. She was thrilled to have Aleksei here, but this was supposed to be her chance to show Sage how far she'd come. Her chance to show her sister that she could stand on her own now. That she was independent. That Sage didn't have to worry about taking care of her anymore, because she could take care of herself.

"No. No. No. I'm glad you're here. It's just that Sage doesn't know anything about hiking. I worked really hard to make myself an expert. I took safety classes, researched equipment, watched videos, and spent months going on solo hikes to build up my stamina and learn as much as I could. Sage is a control freak, but she asked me to help her buy the right clothes and equipment for this trip. She trusted me to make all the arrangements."

She crouched down, allowing a large ant to crawl over her hand, its small legs tickling her skin. After it was safely back on the ground, she rose.

"Sage could never do that. She's afraid of bugs. We went into a butterfly house at the zoo, and she freaked out when one flew into her hair. That's why I rented the cabin. We had originally planned on tent camping, but I knew she wouldn't make it. Sage relied on me to make all the plans and decisions. I was the one in charge. This trip was supposed to be me showing her that I'm a competent, capable adult. That I don't need her hovering over me anymore. For once, I was supposed to be taking care of her."

She waved a hand toward his lean, athletic physique. "I was supposed to be the expert on this trip, and here I am with a goddamn Marine who could probably win *Naked and Afraid* with his hands tied behind his back."

She clasped a hand over her mouth, mortified. "I'm sorry. I asked you to come with me at the last minute, and you dropped everything and came. We had such a great day, and now I sound like an ungrateful ass."

He closed the gap she'd intentionally created between them. Strong hands slid from her wrists to her elbows, finally resting on her shoulders. The scent of spiced pine replaced the mossy, musky smell of the stream.

"Once again, you're apologizing to me when I should be apologizing to you."

Her reaction was instantaneous. "You have nothing to apologize for."

He shook his head, the late afternoon sun catching a strip of reflective material at the neckline of his jacket. His pale coloring, combined with the glint of the sun, had images of Edward Cullen lying sparkling in a field dancing through her head. She was glad Aleksei didn't seem to have the same no-sex-before-marriage rule that Edward did. Being this close to him for five days with no sex, and she'd be the 996th recorded victim of spontaneous human combustion.

"I'm the ass. This is your vacation, and I took charge. I didn't even ask you what you wanted for breakfast or if you even wanted me to cook. Then I took the lead on the trail and just expected you to follow."

"You're the more experienced hiker, and I get the sense you're used to taking the lead."

He glanced to the right as if checking the trail, but she saw a barely perceptibly cloud darken his expression.

"I used to hike a lot with my former partner. The one who died. He was always content to follow. I teased him about it once. Do you know what he said?"

"What?" she asked.

"That if he took the lead, there'd be no one to watch my back."

He waved in the direction of the trail.

"Lead us back to the cabin. I've got your back."

Chapter Fourteen

Aleksei told himself that he was getting Rosemary's back by asking her about her job as they followed the trail toward the campsite. He couldn't see her face because they were hiking single file. Everyone had little tells when they lied. Not being able to see her expressions was a disadvantage, but he focused on other signs. Her body didn't tense. There were no sudden shifts in her stance. The volume and tenor of her voice didn't change.

There were no obvious signs of subterfuge. She seemed like any other working professional, except with more gratitude. Illness had delayed her college graduation, and she'd had to quit her first accounting job because of the ghastly situation with her stepfather. Still, she'd forgiven him, and he'd helped her get her current job. Aleksei tucked that fact away to delve into later when he had time.

Otherwise, everything she said about work seemed normal. She'd worked at Pannetone & Associates for less than a year. She liked being able to walk to work. There was an amazing coffee shop on the way. The hours were good. She liked her coworkers, although Lily—the receptionist and file clerk—could sometimes be annoying. He was glad to hear her complain about Lily. It would be suspicious if everything were perfect.

Just when he'd started to feel confident that Rosemary didn't know anything about Salvatore Moresco, her voice took on a worried edge that fired up his instincts.

"Something happened at work the other day. I almost canceled this trip because of it."

"What happened?" he asked, keeping his tone easy and mildly curious.

She gave him a quick backward glance but kept pushing forward on the trail. "I found an issue with one of our client's files right before I left. I feel like I dropped a giant jar of jelly and left my boss to clean up the sticky, glass-covered mess."

"I don't know much about accounting. What kind of issue can cause such a big problem?"

Long seconds passed, filled only with the distant sound of rushing water, the rhythmic crunch of their boots, the padding feet of the dogs, and the occasional rustle of leaves.

"I found a couple of odd invoices for work that didn't really make sense. They could be perfectly legitimate, but if they're not..." Her pace slowed.

"If they're not?" he prompted.

She shook her head and resumed her quick pace. "Listen to me droning on about work. You don't care about strange invoices. Could I be any more boring?"

He did care. He cared a hell of a lot. It sounded like she might be an innocent bystander who had inadvertently stumbled onto evidence of Moresco's criminal activity. Double books? Fraud? Money laundering? Who knew? But if she'd discovered something she wasn't supposed to, Kemper was right. She was in danger.

He'd have to get more details from her, but he couldn't push right now. Not when he couldn't see her face and hold her hands while telling her exactly who he was and why he'd orchestrated a way to meet her. Not before he had a chance to tell her that she wasn't just a job to him. To tell her that even though he wasn't ready to accept responsibility for another person in his life—and didn't know if he ever would be—that he still cared for her. A lot.

The quickening of Rosemary's steps interrupted his thoughts. They were at the cabin. She shuttled the dogs inside and then locked the door and pressed forward, gesturing for him to follow. He didn't know where they were headed, but he was happy to trail behind her, admiring the sway of her hips. Within minutes, they broke through the trees, and the blue expanse of Lake Jean lay in front of them.

"Last one in the lake is a rotten egg," she yelled as she raced up toward the bathroom.

He'd shoved a swimsuit in his backpack at her insistence, but he was sure there was no way he'd use it. Rosemary had set a rigorous pace on the way back, and he was covered in sweat despite stripping down to a T-shirt. Still, swimming was a bold move. He'd hiked here once before, and the lake water was damn cold, even during the summer.

When he emerged from the changing room in his swimsuit, he barely processed the chill. Rosemary was resplendent. Fucking resplendent.

He'd seen her in jeans. He'd seen her in a tank top. He'd felt her full curves and soft skin under his hands, but he hadn't seen much of her bare skin. Now she stood before him in a combination of strings and triangles the color of the Caribbean Sea, with her lush, athletic shape on full display. She had the build of a curvy volleyball player. Strong shoulders, full breasts, a slightly tucked waist, and lusciously curved hips and thighs. She'd donned a swim cap over her wig, but her hair lay in blonde sheets over her shoulders, giving it that cute look like when women wore beanies.

She was perfection.

"I've never worn this suit before," she said shyly. "Sage talked me into it. It's ridiculously impractical, but we won't be swimming for long. It's too cold for anything more than a quick dip."

His skin was so hot, he didn't think he'd notice how cold the water was, but maybe it would help with the quickly changing situation in his swim trunks. At least they were the only ones in the beach area, so there was no one to see him pitching a tent.

The water was chilly, but it felt amazing. It was like an ice bath on his aching legs and shoulders. They swam in the same direction, in unspoken agreement that their destination was the line of rope and buoys that identified the end of the designated swim area. When they reached the barrier, Rosemary turned her back to it, wrapped her arms around the ropes, leaned back, and closed her eyes. The position propped her round breasts above the water. He treaded water a few feet in front of her, admiring the view. The urge to slide his tongue along the edges of the scant triangles of her bikini top was nearly overwhelming.

He glanced back toward the beach. Still empty. The sun was approaching the horizon, and the sky was turning gray. Even if someone did happen upon the beach, their distance from the shore, combined with the waning light, would make it difficult for anyone to see them. Aleksei swam forward, gripping the rope on either side of her shoulders and sliding his hips between her parted legs.

She giggled, opening eyes that instantly hooded as he closed one hand over her shoulder and used his thumb to draw circles on the soft skin above her breast. She wrapped her legs around the back of his, pulling him in until his already throbbing dick pressed against the enticing heat between her thighs.

"We should head back to shore," she said, her voice low and sultry. "This is dangerous."

"Are you worried we might get hypothermia?" he teased.

"I think we might heat up this entire lake."

"What an interesting experiment that would be. Maybe we should try for the sake of science," he said as he pushed her chin back gently with the tip of his thumb. The small motion eased her slightly backward, flattening her back and causing her chest to lift farther out of the water. Her nipples were like pebbles pushing against the blue triangles that barely covered her breasts. He'd intended to nibble on the sweet pale expanse of her neck, but primal need hijacked his thoughts, drawing his mouth lower.

The lake water was earthy and fresh on his tongue with an almost metallic undertone as he found her breast. The material of her swimsuit was thin but still too thick to get the response he wanted with only his lips. He nipped at the hard, taut bud straining against her bikini top. His cock jerked at the feel of her Lycra-covered nipple between his teeth. She bucked in response, her legs squeezing his hips. Her heels pressed into his hamstrings, pushing his hammer-hard dick even tighter against the blissful warmth of her core.

He released her breast, shifting upward on soft skin in search of her mouth. The pulse in her neck was like his early morning sprints. Hard and fast under his lips. He nipped her chin, then found those full, firm lips he'd been seeking. Her mouth was even more perfect than he remembered. Sweet, hot, and feisty. Rosemary kissed with ferocity, with a darting tongue, nibbling teeth, and roaming lips. She kissed with her entire body, too, her legs shifting and gripping, hips grinding, and hands traveling over his arms and back, alternating between squeezing and caressing.

He moved one hand from the scratchy rope to the smooth skin of her neck. Something soft flickered across his arm. He opened his eyes. Her hair floated like ribbons near her shoulders.

"Is your hair okay in the water?"

"What?" Her voice was dazed and languid.

"Your wig. Is it okay?"

"Ignore the wig and kiss me."

That small intrusion of reality allowed sense to creep back in. They needed to talk. He shouldn't let things go further between them until he'd told her the entire truth of who he was.

Teeth nipped at his jaw, then his earlobe, sending a rush of heat to his already raging cock. His body and mind were at war.

He spoke before his body could win. "I need you to know that I'm not ready for a relationship. I can't lose someone again like I lost Phillipe. I have feelings for you, but before we do this, you need to know that I'm not ready to care deeply again. I'm not ready to take responsibility for someone else. I don't know if I ever will be."

Their bodies remained intertwined. Her strong legs wound tightly around him.

"I'm not asking for a commitment. I'm not asking you to be responsible for me. I had to rely on other people for too many years. I want to take care of myself now. I want to be responsible for myself. This is my time. My time to make up for every minute I lost being sick. My time to do what makes me happy. My time to live every moment like it might be my last. In this moment, I want you. Let's enjoy the time we have now and worry about the rest later."

"There are things we should talk about. Things you don't know about me."

The firm legs wrapped around him loosened, and her lush body slid against his, her tongue tracing down his neck to the center of his chest, where she pressed a kiss.

"I know who you are in here. That's all that matters. There will be plenty of time to talk later. I promise. I've missed so much. You've lost so much. We both need this. We both deserve it. Just let us have it."

She was right. He did need this. She was like the sand his dad packed between the stones of the patio every few years. She filled in the cracks, repairing the damage that, if left alone, would cause him to break and crumble. He didn't know if he deserved this time with her, but he needed it. And he could see she needed it too. Her gaze held a bone-deep longing he couldn't ignore. She wasn't asking for a commitment. She was only asking for this moment. They were here for four more days. There'd be plenty of time to talk, to tell her the whole story.

Right now, they both needed the other to fill the holes in their hearts.

Even if it was just for this moment.

Chapter Fifteen

Aleksei pulled back, removing his hand from her neck. She loosened her legs. Icy water replaced the warmth of his skin. Lust shifted to disappointment. She knew that he wanted her. She had felt it in the hot, hard length pressed against her. This moment was perfect. She wanted to seize it here and now. Impromptu sex in the middle of the lake would be a perfect ending to their day.

"We can't do this here," he said. "It's not safe."

His voice was firm, but she saw his eyes flick to her breasts. He wasn't as resolute as he was pretending to be. Maybe he thought she wasn't a strong enough swimmer to manage intimacy in the lake. She let go of the rope with one hand and tugged the wet string of her bikini top. As soon as she pulled, the knot released, and the scant material fell away. The chilly water lapped at her nipples, sending flames racing through her. She reached for his hand, pulling it to her exposed breast.

As his rough palm skimmed the soft skin of her breast, a flash of heat coursed through her, and she arched toward him. "I won't drown."

"It's not that." His voice came out as a croak.

Hard muscles pressed against her legs as he reached behind her, bracing his free hand on the rope. The thumb of his other hand circled her nipple in teasing swirls, then he squeezed the pebbled bud, sending a bolt of heat to her core. Warm breath and sharp teeth grazed and nipped at her neck and earlobe, making her shiver.

Her hands found the lean muscles of his shoulders, chest, and stomach, exploring bare skin, coarse hair, and then bare skin again. His waistband was as cold as the water, but when she slipped her fingers inside, they grazed hot, rigid flesh.

He groaned, and his fingers tightened on her breast. She pulled one hand from his waist and slid a finger along the line where his leg met his body, her knuckles brushing against the tight skin of his balls. He bucked and gripped her flesh even harder.

She smiled. She liked that her roaming fingers made him jerk and moan. She liked that his hand was rough and firm, that he treated her like a healthy woman, not a porcelain statue that might break.

She shifted her hand higher. His swim trunks had no liner, so nothing stopped her fingers from finding his cock. Long, thick heat filled her palm as she grasped and squeezed, moving her hand in a slow stroking motion. She watched Aleksei's hooded eyes, heard his heaving breaths, and listened to his deep groans of encouragement.

She wanted to make this pensive, careful man lose control. She wanted his emotions to flare in passion rather than grief and sorrow. She closed the few inches between them, sliding her tongue between his minty, firm lips. His cock twitched beneath her hand. Calloused fingers squeezed both of her breasts, and her thoughts scattered.

One part of her mind processed that he was no longer holding onto the rope, that his legs were moving, kicking, holding them afloat, but her attention was focused on the tongue exploring her mouth and his fingers that sent bolts of electricity straight to her core.

She pulled her mouth away from his. She needed to see the nipples that had become the center of her world. Her breasts were pulled taut, each nipple extended, pinched like a rosebud being plucked. Her core was hot as lava. Her clit tingled. He lowered his head, catching her gaze with a wicked glint in his eye. Holding the stare, he grazed his teeth along the tip of one nipple. The sensation was almost too much. He was balancing her expertly on a blade of pleasure and pain.

And it was fucking perfect.

Without warning, the pressure disappeared, replaced by chilly air. Her breasts were hot, achy, and desperate for his mouth. She opened her lips to plead for him to suck on them, but icy lake water splashed over her skin, shocking her already taut nipples into pebbles of pleasure.

"I love seeing your nipples so fucking tight and hard," he rasped as he squeezed them again between strong fingers.

Her eyes snapped shut. Lights danced behind her lids. Liquid heat engulfed her.

"I need you inside me." She barely recognized her own voice in that whimpering, husky plea.

"It's not safe," he repeated.

His words cut through some of her lusty haze. She didn't understand his hesitation. She knew he wanted her. The proof was in his groans, in the thunderstorm swirling in his gray-blue eyes, and in the searing, rigid heat straining against her fingers.

"The water isn't that cold, and it's almost dark. No one will see us." She gave his lower lip a hard bite. His hips thrust forward, seeming to operate on a different agenda than the one he was vocalizing. Maybe he was concerned about them spending too much time in the cold lake under the quickly darkening sky. "We can be quick here and then take our time back at the cabin."

"I'm not worried about the cold. I don't have a condom with me."

Now she understood.

"Oh. That kind of safe."

"Yes, that kind of safe." He smiled. "Unfortunately, my military training didn't cover carrying condoms in the event of spontaneous water sex."

A full laugh erupted from her stomach, and she had to tread water faster to stay afloat. The cool water circulating around her body did nothing to slake the fire raging within her.

"I haven't been with anyone since I was tested, so I'm all good there, and I'm on the pill," she offered.

He closed the space that had opened between them, pushing them backward until the bristly rope of the buoy line pressed into her back. He ran a wet, water-wrinkled fingertip down the side of her face.

"Same here. About the testing. Not the pill."

She laughed and settled one hand on his shoulder, relishing the feel of his cool, lean muscles under her hand. She slid her other hand over the hard lines of his abs and under the edge of his waistband, curling lazy circles in the patch of short, coarse hair that led to his cock. She nibbled his jawline, tasting the crisp, earthy freshness of the spring-fed lake. It had just a hint of brine. Her core was clenching and desperate to feel him inside her. She nipped his ear, and strong fingers clenched her ass, pulling her tight against his long, hard cock.

"I'm game if you are," she said.

His answer was to remove his bathing suit and affix it to the rope with the waistband tie. His movements were effortlessly efficient, even with her hanging on him. She rubbed her hands over his wonderfully chiseled chest and licked tangy lake water from his neck and shoulders while he worked. Once he'd secured his swim trunks to the line, he backed her up to the rope once again, his eyes regaining their sexy glint. Firm fingers gripped her wrists, pushing them into the scratchy rope.

"Turn around."

The seductive command made her thighs tingle.

"Put your arms over the rope and don't let go."

Normally, she didn't like being ordered around. She'd had way too much of that when she'd been sick, but his commands were like a siren's call. Impossible to ignore and sexy as hell.

She slid her arms over the bristly rope and closed her fingers tightly around it. Her breasts and stomach tingled with anticipation. She could sense him behind her, but she knew he didn't want her to turn and look. Knew he liked the idea of her waiting for him to touch her.

"Close your eyes."

His tone was one of bone-melting promise.

Calloused fingers brushed her thighs. Strings tightened then loosened, first at her back, then at her hips. Her swimsuit fell away. Cold water flowed freely over her exposed rear and the apex of her thighs. She was naked.

Completely bare.

Then emptiness was replaced with Aleksei. He was everywhere at once. Biting her back. Stroking her ass. Bending her neck backward to possess her mouth with his insatiable, exploring tongue. Fingertips alternating between gently squeezing her breasts and tugging firmly on diamond-hard nipples.

It felt like he was a part of her. A piece she had been missing her entire life.

He was seeing her as she was. Completely bare except for the bathing suit cap she needed to wear to keep her wig in place. She had a strong body but was far from model-perfect. She was twenty-seven years old and shockingly short on life experience. Yet he was consuming her like a starving man at a feast—as if she were irresistible, as if her body enflamed him to unbridled passion, as if he thought she was perfect.

"Please tell me you're ready. I'm so fucking desperate for you, Rose. I don't think I can wait one more second. But I will. I'll wait as long as you need me to."

His hot length was sliding between her legs, grazing her core with each thrust. His hand was playing her breast like a concert pianist. His teeth and tongue were exquisite torture on her neck and shoulder. His hot breath tickled her ear as he murmured the depths of his need against it.

"I can feel your slick heat against my cock. I'm dying to be inside you. I thought about fucking you the entire hike back. My dick was so hard watching your ass move in those leggings, I could barely walk."

Her clit pulsed. Flames licked at her thighs and breasts. She needed him inside her. Now.

"Please," she begged, pushing her core against his hard length.

He thrust between her legs one more time, the tip of his dick pressed so firmly against her clit that she almost came. Then he was gone. She heard sloshing water, and the coarse rope bounced. Her core was empty and yearning. Her clit was throbbing, and the darkness, the waiting, the not knowing when or where he would touch her, fueled the delicious sensual anticipation.

Then he was there, his firm chest against her back. His stone-hard dick pushed against her ass and thighs.

"Open for me," he commanded.

The words made her quiver. She separated her thighs, cool water flowing between them, quickly replaced by the heat of his dick at her entrance. He thrust. Flame-covered steel filled her, stretched her, and brushed against that precious spot deep within her.

"Yes!"

A thought of the public beach tickled the edge of her mind and was immediately erased by the next thrust. He set a fast pace, almost frantic. Firm fingers tightened around one breast. A calloused hand kneaded her ass. The rope scraped her arms and ribs. She tried to hold on tightly so the strength of his movements didn't push them over it, but her fingers had no grip. Her arms had no strength. Her mind had no thoughts. All that existed was the mounting fire within her, stoked by each stroke of his dick.

Tension coiled in her abdomen. Her clit throbbed and tingled. She was screaming, begging, but she didn't know what words were spilling out of her mouth. All she could focus on was that cyclone of need whirling within her, spinning faster and faster with each thrust.

It was too much, and it wasn't enough.

"I need....I need."

His hand gripped her hip tighter. His voice, rough with desire, filled her ear. "Tell me what you need, my soft, lovely, precious Rose," he said slowly, punctuating each endearment with a stroke of his dick.

Lust overwhelmed her natural shyness.

"I need you to touch me."

"Tell me where," he demanded as he slowed his pace.

He was torturing her, drawing out her need. He knew what she wanted. Knew she was desperate to come. But he wanted to hear her say it. Her need was so intense, she'd tell him anything.

"My clit. I need you to touch my clit. I want you to feel me come on your dick."

He growled, the sound deep and feral. Cold water teased her nipple as his hand shifted from her breast to the apex of her thighs. Between the water and her own wetness, his finger slid easily between her folds, stroking the epicenter of her need. He quickened the pace of his thrusts, matching the speed with which he was circling her clit.

Her thighs quivered. Every muscle in her body grew tighter, tighter, tighter. Molten steel filled her faster and harder. Stubble grazed her back. Deep grunts mixed with her own pleas of "Don't stop! Don't stop!"

"You're going to make me come," Aleksei growled into her ear.

Two fingers pressed firmly against her clit, then circled again.

Fireworks exploded behind her eyelids.

And they both flew apart.

Chapter Sixteen

A snake of dread slithered down Aleksei's spine as they entered the homey cabin. They'd both used the hot water showers near the beach to warm up when they got out of the lake, but Rose's full lips still had a slightly blue cast. He normally preferred tent camping, but he was grateful she'd rented a modern cabin. He hated the thought of her being cold. As she flipped on the lights, he found the thermostat and ratcheted up the heat while the dogs barked and scampered excitedly around them.

"I'm going to change into clean clothes." Rose gave him an impish grin as she walked toward her bedroom with Thor at her heels. "It seemed like such a good idea to go in the lake, but I didn't think about having to put back on my gross, sweaty hiking clothes."

"I'll change too," he said.

His legs felt heavy as he entered his tent and changed into clean underwear, a T-shirt, jeans, and a flannel. The snake in his stomach had grown into a full-blown den. When he went back into the cabin, he was going to have to sit Rose down and tell her the truth. The entire truth. Not just the bits and pieces of honesty he'd mixed in with feigned coincidence and omission.

He still wanted to nail Moresco. Needed to. He'd never be content until Phillipe's murderer was brought to justice. But his feelings for Rosemary had grown too strong too fast. Admiration had blossomed into affection, and now affection seemed far too weak a word for the intense emotion that stretched his carefully walled-off heart.

He hadn't meant for it to happen, but loyalty to Phillipe and loyalty to Rose now held equal sway. It was time to come clean. Even if she knew Moresco was a little shady, there was no way she knew the extent of his crimes. She'd never knowingly be involved with someone like that. Her spirit was too pure and bright.

He couldn't think of one good reason to put off telling her the truth. He wasn't worried that she'd tell Pannetone or Moresco about him. Even if she was furious with him for lying, she'd never intentionally put him or anyone else in danger. Her heart was simply too good. His real fear was that she would shut him out. He had to find a way to convince her to help him. The problem was, every variation of the conversation he envisioned ended with her kicking him in the nuts and telling him she never wanted to see him again.

He pressed two fingers into the bridge of his nose. If there was an afterlife and Phillipe was watching him, Phillipe would tell him he was a royal fuckup. And he'd be right. Even Jaka seemed to be giving him the side-eye from where she lounged in the corner of the tent. *The law of Karma is inexorable and impossible of evasion.* That's what Phillipe would say. The fucking Gandhi quotes always hit the nail on the head.

Karma was coming for him. Better to tell the truth now and get it over with, or the payback would just keep getting worse.

The door was heavy in his hand, and his sneakers felt like they were lined with concrete as he entered the cabin. He could see straight through the living area to the kitchen. The sight that greeted him nailed his leaden feet to the floor despite Jaka pulling at her leash.

Rose stood in front of the stovetop, her hand on a spoon submerged in a large silver pot. She looked cozy in black sweatpants and a gray sweatshirt that read THEODORE'S DANCE ACADEMY in pink lettering. Puffy pink slippers covered her feet where Thor sat, tail wagging in excitement. The heat had returned the pink hue to her lips and cheeks, but her mouth was pushed up into an uncomfortable smile. It wasn't her clothes or slippers or face that froze his limbs. It was the almost pearly white shine of her completely bare head.

Rosemary had taken off her wig.

She looked different, yet the same. Her skull was paler than her face, but the difference wasn't striking. The lack of hair highlighted her features. Her long straight nose seemed straighter. Her sultry, blue eyes looked larger and sexier. Her lush pink lips appeared fuller, her cheekbones higher, the curve of her jaw more pronounced. The absence of hair gave her an aura of strength. As if a mask of softness had been stripped away, leaving only a rock-solid core.

He knew he was staring, knew he should say something, knew too many wordless seconds were passing, and that she might misinterpret his silence. But his mouth wouldn't move. He'd never frozen in battle, never frozen on an op no matter what he'd faced, but terror had now overtaken his initial shock. Rose standing before him, bare and exposed, was more expressive than any words she could speak. This was a sign of faith, a sign of trust.

She was trusting him with her true self. Trusting him to accept her.

And it was fucking terrifying.

He didn't care that she was bald. He would be attracted to her no matter how she looked because her soul was beautiful. But he didn't want this show of trust. He couldn't handle the expectation implicit in her action. She hadn't even let her sister witness her bare head. With this one action, she'd elevated him above her family.

It was too much.

She'd rewritten the rules of the game, and he'd frozen because he had no idea how to make another move. In the water, she'd said she wanted them to enjoy the moment. That they didn't need to worry about commitments or the future. That she didn't want anyone to feel responsible for her.

But this leap of faith undercut every one of those words. This was a sign that she was opening her heart to him, that she was trusting him to accept her and do the right thing by her. It was the kind of trust one partner put in another. He couldn't live with that kind of responsibility.

Not again.

Panic squeezed his ribs. He felt like he was in a falling elevator. He internalized his emotions, but they were there, silently screaming inside him. He'd fail her just like he'd failed Phillipe. He'd already failed her with his lies and omissions. By having sex with her before telling her about his mission. Once he told her the truth, she would hate him. And even though he couldn't let himself be bound to her, couldn't trust himself to take care of her, the thought of losing her was a knife to the chest.

She broke the silence. "Shut the door. You're letting the cold air in."

Her voice was calm and even, as if he hadn't gaped at her for two minutes in utter silence.

He couldn't move. He was like the mythic soldiers who hadn't averted their eyes from Medusa. The concrete in his shoes was turning his entire body to stone. As soon as he shut that door, he would be trapped. He would have to face the trust Rosemary was thrusting on him.

The warm air in the cabin was pregnant with expectation. Her baldness was the elephant in the room. The soul she'd bared when she'd taken off her wig hung in the space between them, eager for acceptance. Her hope was like an anchor around his neck.

He couldn't think. He had no fucking clue what to say. The woodsy crispness of the cool air flowing through the open door was a tantalizing temptation.

It smelled like peace. It smelled like escape.

"I forgot a razor. I'm going to run up to the park office and see if they have one."

The excuse was weak, but it was the first thing that popped into his mind. He needed time and space. He needed the brisk, clean air to clear his head. He needed to put distance between himself and Rose before he found himself making promises he couldn't keep. He needed to be free from the nervous hope that filled her gaze. He needed to delay the inevitable expression of disgust he would see when he told her the truth.

He tugged on Jaka's leash, pulling her out the door with him. He couldn't get to his truck fast enough.

He was a fucking coward.

His heart was still hammering in his chest when his phone sprang to life, jumping and buzzing in the cupholder as he rounded the last bend in the road leading to the park office. It didn't stop until after he'd turned into the parking lot and backed into one of the parking spots. He hadn't had cell service since he pulled away from the office last night. Several rural parks still lacked consistent service, so he wasn't surprised when it conked out. What did surprise him was the dance his phone had just done in the cupholder.

He grabbed the phone, still chilly from resting in his hiking pack all day. He'd brought it with them on the hike and checked it multiple times, but service had never kicked in. Now he had thirty-six text messages, thirteen missed calls, and five voicemails. In less than twenty-four hours.

"Shit."

His back stiffened. Moisture evaporated from his already too-dry mouth. Since Phillipe died, an all-consuming fear flowed under the surface of his skin, waiting to break through at any hint that something could be wrong with someone he cared about. He wanted to double down and ignore the bad news that had been sitting, waiting to spring to life on his phone screen, but guilt from walking out on Rosemary had already become acid in his gut. He wasn't going to let fear win again.

He took a swig from his water bottle, but the liquid did little to alleviate the sand-parched feeling in his throat. He entered his passcode and braced himself. All the voice messages and calls were from his mother and sister. Most of the texts were from them as well, and they all had the same theme:

I heard about the fire.

Are you all right?

Call me.

I'm getting really worried.

Call me.

Where are you?

Please call me!

He climbed out of the truck while he scrolled, his taut muscles relaxing. No one was hurt. His mother was fine. His sister was fine. His nephews were fine. He had no clue what fire they were talking about, and Mom and Zina would give him an earful for making them worry, but he didn't mind. Relief was like that. He was so happy everyone was okay, the idea of getting harassed by his mom and sister suddenly didn't seem that annoying.

The last unread text he clicked on had been the first one to come in. It was short and to the point.

Call me. Now.

Kemper was never one to waste time on too many words.

He hadn't spoken to Gary since his mom told him about Gary's visit to her house. He'd been too pissed off. Showing up at his mom's house looking for Phillipe's notebook was a dick move. Aleksei had been waiting for his temper to cool before confronting Gary about it. His blood still ran hot at the thought of Kemper dragging his mom into all of this, but Gary would know what the hell had gotten his mom and Zina all worked up. Better to get the facts from Kemper before calling his family, in case he needed to do some spinning.

Kemper answered on the first ring. "Where the hell are you?"

"You first," Aleksei retorted. "You owe me answers. What the hell were you doing at my mother's house? I told you everything I had was in Philly, and you go to her goddamn house and try to bully her into giving you Phillipe's notebook?"

Kemper sighed into the phone.

Aleksei had known Gary long enough that he could visualize the irritated head shake that came with that sigh. Kemper was full of tells. He shook his head when he was exasperated. He flicked his thumb when he lied. He squeezed his ear when he was desperate for a cigarette. Aleksei heard footsteps through the phone, followed by the opening and closing of a door and then that all-too-familiar strike of a match—long inhale and exhale.

"No one could ever bully that woman, and you know it."

"What the hell is wrong with you? There was no reason for you to go there. No reason to drag her into this."

"But you went there, didn't you? What reason did you have?"

Aleksei's jaw clenched. "I don't need a reason to visit my own mother."

"Your accent gets heavier when you lie. Not a lot. But enough."

His teeth pressed together even more tightly. Kemper had been the one who taught him to focus on body language, so he shouldn't be surprised that Gary had discovered some of his own tells. "What are you getting at?"

Another inhale, exhale, and sigh of contentment.

"When we spoke Friday night, your accent got thicker when you were talking about the notebook, so I knew you were lying. I wasn't sure if it was about whether you had the damn thing, where you were keeping Phillipe's things, or something else—but I knew you weren't telling me the whole truth. You can't get out of your own head, Thompson. Ever since Phillipe died, you've made everything about you. You're obsessed with your own loss and blind to everything else and everybody else. I know Phillipe was your best friend. I feel bad for you. I really do. But I was the leader of that unit. Phillipe was *my* responsibility. He was murdered on *my* watch."

Another inhale and exhale, and then Kemper's voice was calmer, placating. It was the kind of voice you used when you explained something to a kid for the fourth time, trying not to lose your patience.

"I know you think I let brass sweep this under the rug, but I didn't. Unlike you, I didn't go off half-cocked and quit the FBI. I used my fucking brain and waited. That's what I've been doing this whole time...waiting until there was some kind of break. This isn't just your chance for redemption—it's mine too. And I'm not going to let you fuck it up by lying to me. If you lie to me, I'm going to go around you. You lied to me about the notebook, so I went around you. It's that simple."

Kemper's words brought a hot blister of shame. Gary had said the same thing Zina and his mom had been saying to him for the past two years. The same thing Rosemary had said last Friday night. He was letting his loss blind him to other people's pain, blind him from seeing or understanding other perspectives.

What else has this whirlpool of grief kept me from seeing?

He pushed the thought away. This was not the time for psychoanalysis. He'd have to figure his shit out later.

"Fine. We'll call a truce, but I need you to tell me what the hell is going on. My cell service has been shit since last night, and now I have a ton of frantic messages from my mom and sister. They said something about a fire."

Kemper took another drag on his cigarette. A really long drag. Aleksei's spine tensed.

"The shit hit the fan," Kemper said.

"Not helpful," Aleksei responded. "What shit? What fan?"

"Pannetone & Associates blew up. And so did your apartment."

No preface. No warning. Gary had done nothing to soften the blow.

Aleksei leaned against the park office building, giving his body physical support so his mind could fully process the information. "Do you mean actually exploded?"

Kemper's "yep" sounded like a grunt.

His apartment was gone. He hadn't lived there in years, but it still felt like his home had been ripped away.

"Could the explosions have been accidental?"

He knew the answer even as he asked the question. The coincidence was too great. The chance of accidental explosions at both the accounting office and his apartment was fingernail-thin.

"The bomb techs confirmed explosive devices were present at both locations," Kemper answered.

His home was gone. Rose's workplace had been attacked.

Kemper was right. The shit had definitely hit the fan.

"When?"

"Pannetone's office blew just before ten this morning. Your apartment went about an hour later."

The first thing you did after an attack was assess the damage.

"Casualties?"

Kemper sighed. "I played your connection to the bureau, the link between Pannetone and Moresco, and our prior op to get the FBI to take jurisdiction. With two explosions, they were probably going to step in anyway, but I didn't want to waste time and let the locals fuck it up. Since I'm based in Chicago now, I'm not assigned to the case, but I was able to get some inside info. Your apartment building was empty, but the investigators found three bodies at Pannetone's: two male, one female. All burned beyond recognition. There are six employees, and the only one the bureau located is the receptionist. She got lucky. She was in the stairwell when the bomb went off. She was injured, but it looks like she's going to be OK. She's been in surgery, so no one's talked to her yet. They don't know who the deceased female is."

Kemper's voice trailed off, his last sentence a question. Aleksei knew what Gary was asking.

"It's not Rosemary. She's with me. She's safe."

"Thank God," Kemper said. "With what the informant said about Moresco having her followed, I was worried she was the target."

"Maybe she was. She told me her vacation was a last-minute thing, so maybe whoever planted the bomb expected her to be at work. We need to find out who the other survivor is. Maybe he's behind this whole fiasco. What's the initial read?"

Silence from Kemper.

"What's the initial read?" Aleksei repeated.

"You're the prime suspect. The current working theory is that the Pannetone explosion was a revenge hit. Moresco was grabbing coffee in the gelato shop when the bomb went off. He was at Pannetone's for a meeting and left a few minutes in because the espresso machine in the office broke this morning. He got lucky."

If Moresco had left a few minutes later, he would be dead right now—incapable of hurting anyone else. Instead, Moresco had been spared, and Aleksei was a fucking suspect. Maybe karma was already kicking in.

"How did they come up with the crazy-ass idea that it was me?"

"That's partially my fault. I wanted the bureau to jump on the case, so I told them that you were working solo, tracking down a lead at Pannetone's regarding Phillipe's murder. If I'd known Moresco was anywhere near that building, I would have kept my damn mouth shut. Now, some newbie has the ass-backward theory that you planted the bomb to hit Moresco. I told him he was off the mark, but you know how things get a life of their own around here."

Yeah, he knew. Some agents were great, and others couldn't solve a goddamn Scooby Doo mystery. Him as the prime suspect made no sense. No fucking sense.

"Don't they think the timing of Moresco's coffee trip is a little too convenient?"

"I mentioned that," Kemper responded. "And you know what else seems a little too convenient? There were two localized explosions at Pannetone's. One on the second floor and one in the basement. The structure of the building is intact, and the gelato shop wasn't damaged."

"Let me guess. Moresco owns the building and the gelato shop."

"You should play the lottery," Kemper said. "You'd be a goddamn millionaire."

"But instead of blaming Moresco, some shit-for-brains rookie is blaming me? Why would I blow up my own goddamn apartment?" A passing park ranger gave him an odd look. Aleksei took a few steps away from the office and lowered his voice. "What's their reasoning for that?"

Another long suck and an exhale. He made a mental note to start sending Kemper quit-smoking reels when all this was over.

"They think it was an accident," Kemper said. "They think you had explosives in your apartment from building the bomb that took out Pannetone's, and they blew. I told them that was bullshit. I told them you wouldn't hit Moresco, and that if you did, there was no way you'd take innocent lives in the process. I also told them that you know your way around explosives and were too goddamn smart to blow up your own building."

If the idiots took a minute to look over his FBI file, they'd know all of that too.

"I take it they didn't believe you?"

"They want you to come in. They want to talk to you."

Of course, they did. Shit was hitting the fan from every direction.

"There's one more thing," Kemper said.

He hadn't thought things could get worse.

"What?"

"After the explosion, I flew to Philly and went to Rosemary's apartment. I was hoping that maybe I would find her there. When I arrived, the door was ajar. Her place was ransacked. Ripped apart. Someone was looking for something."

It had to have been Moresco. Maybe he thought there was a leak. Maybe Pannetone and Moresco had a falling out. Maybe Moresco decided to have a different firm cook his books and wanted to eliminate all loose ends. But none of those scenarios explained someone ransacking Rose's apartment. Maybe Moresco had seen that Rose wasn't at the meeting, had sent someone to take her out, and the guy had trashed the place in frustration. Or maybe Rose had something Moresco wanted.

The options were endless.

The only thing he knew for sure was that they were doubly fucked. Rose was in danger, and the FBI was after him. It was only a matter of time before the investigators tracked down Sage and learned that he and Rose were camping together at Ricketts Glen. They might already know. Kemper wasn't directly involved in the investigation, so the information he had was likely hours out of date. Agents could already be on their way, and he had to assume whatever info the agents had, Moresco had as well. Moresco's men might also be coming.

He and Rose had to get the hell out of here.

"I have to go."

"Tell me where you are. I can help," Kemper offered.

"At this point, the less you know, the better."

"Dammit, Thompson, don't shut me out." Kemper's tone danced between worry and frustration. "I thought you were in Philly. I thought you were in your apartment. I thought you might have gone up with that goddamn building. I can't handle losing another man."

He hated stressing out Gary. The guy had done his best by Phillipe. Was doing his best for him right now. But Kemper was still FBI, which meant his loyalty was to the bureau first and foremost. It was safer to keep him in the dark.

"I'll check in with you soon. I promise."

He hung up, turned off his phone, and dumped it in the trashcan.

Rose was not going to be happy when he did the same thing to hers.

Chapter Seventeen

He'd left her. He'd stared, uncomfortable and silent, then turned around and walked out the door. She'd laid herself bare before him, and he'd run for the hills. Well, the park office—but he flew out of the cabin as if his sneakers had wings.

The closed door looked like a gaping mouth. She wished it would swallow her whole. Maybe that would ease the tightness in her ribs.

She turned the burner off on the chili she'd been reheating and collapsed into one of the kitchen chairs. Her legs were like overcooked spaghetti, and her head was spinning. The chair was firm and solid. Firm and solid was what she needed. Firm and solid was what she was supposed to be. She was stronger than this. Rejection shouldn't make her feel like she'd come down with an instant case of the flu.

She glanced back at the door, then looked away. She was acting like a dog eager for their owner to return. Thor plopped his head on her knee as if to emphasize her behavior. She was pathetic. What had she been thinking, taking her wig off like that?

It was too much too soon.

Aleksei had tried to slow things down between them at the lake. He'd said he didn't want to have the responsibility of another person in his life. That he wasn't ready for a relationship. But she had pushed anyway and then taken the fact that he'd had sex with her as a symbol of some deep emotional connection.

She'd obviously misinterpreted his feelings. He'd told her straight up that he didn't want a commitment, and instead of listening to him, she'd let her heart read his compliments, kindness, and concern as a level of affection that simply didn't exist. He wanted a casual relationship, and she'd gotten swept up in him like a middle schooler with her first crush.

Her neck and cheeks burned. She'd acted like a fool. What was even more ridiculous was that she'd been so goddamn proud of herself. She thought she was being so brave greeting him *au natural*, putting her bald head on display while she serenely cooked at the stove. She'd wanted him to know her. Truly know her. She didn't want the wig to create awkwardness between them, in bed or out. She'd wanted to be her true self in front of him. Open. Real. Bare.

Well, she'd certainly accomplished that.

Sitting with Thor in the too-quiet and now too-warm cabin, she couldn't ignore the truth. Her quest for independence had been a façade. At the first hint of a chance at a relationship, she'd thrown her whole self in and completely ignored the deep, unspoken intimacy that standing bald in front of Aleksei would create. The gesture screamed of her desire for a deep connection. It screamed of expectation, and Aleksei had been clear that he didn't want any of those things. The urge to turn back time and make a different choice—the choice to keep her wig on—was so strong, she could almost feel the silky strands of hair on her fingers.

But there would be no turning back time. No amount of wishing something were different would change it. She'd learned that a long time ago.

She rubbed Thor's ears and then stood, shaking her head to clear it while imagining strength flowing into her legs. She might have been a needy fool, but at least she'd been true to her motto of living life to the fullest. She'd swung for the fences and struck out. She wasn't going to allow herself to feel any shame in that. She'd get the chili on the table so Aleksei could have some dinner before he headed back to DC. She'd vacation for the next few days solo and make the most of it. She would take care of herself. That was what this trip was supposed to have been about in the first place.

The front door flew open with a loud thud. A gust of chilly, pine-scented air rushed into the kitchen. Thor barked in surprise, but Aleksei ignored him, rushing into the kitchen with Jaka at his side. "Where's your phone?"

She glanced up from where she'd been setting the table and pointed calmly to the counter. She would not let him see that his abandonment had shaken her.

"It's right there, but I don't have service. You can normally get service up by the park office. Didn't you try when you were up there?"

He pushed the door closed and crossed the room to the counter, his long strides making quick work of the short distance. His face was like marble. Stern and rigid. Instead of playing, both dogs sat, alert, sensing the tension emanating from him. He palmed her phone, squeezing the side buttons with his thumb and forefinger.

"What are you doing?" she demanded.

"I turned it off. We'll throw it in the dumpster on our way out. You need to pack. Now. We need to be out of here in five minutes."

What the hell?

She wasn't going to pack up and leave just because Aleksei said so. She'd bared her true self to this man, and he'd walked out the door. Then stormed back in, ordering her around, expecting her to leave her vacation with no explanation.

Not happening.

"You can't be serious."

"Unfortunately, I am," he said as he took the silverware she was holding out of her hands and set it on the table with a clink.

Those long, lean fingers that seemed to instinctively know exactly how she liked to be touched closed around her shoulders. She met his gaze, taking in the grim line of his mouth before reaching two orbs of flat slate. There was no mirth or flirtatious twinkle in his eyes. Her sexy, fun hiking companion was gone, replaced by a soldier.

He *was* serious.

Her pulse raced. Her heart fluttered in her chest. Icy fingers of doubt dug into her rib cage. The shift in Aleksei's personality, the iron demands—they didn't make sense.

Had she made a terrible mistake trusting this man?

She didn't want to be wrong about him. She didn't want to believe her instincts could be so horribly off, but going with him felt like one of those decisions teenagers make in horror films that the entire audience knows is going to end in disaster.

She stepped out of his grasp, backed away, and dashed into her bedroom. She needed a minute to think. She stopped short, staring at her long blonde wig on the dresser. Removing her wig had been a leap of faith, and she'd fallen flat on her face. The decision about what to do next was going to be made with her head, not her heart. To face Aleksei on equal footing, she needed her armor.

She settled her wig cap on her head and grabbed the wig from its stand. The one she'd worn in the lake was still wet, but this one was dry, the strands soft and smooth on her fingers.

"Are you packing?"

Aleksei's voice startled her.

She whirled toward the doorway. "Why are you acting like this? Why do we need to leave? Why?"

That last word held all the other questions she didn't know enough to ask. Questions Aleksei better damn well answer if he truly expected her to leave Ricketts Glen when he was acting like a paranoid maniac and her vacation had barely started.

"You're in danger. Someone's after you. I promise I'll tell you everything once we get on the road, but we need to get out of here. Now."

This wasn't real. No one was after her. She was just a normal person. There was no reason for her to be in danger. What if Aleksei was lying? What if he wasn't the person she thought he was? She'd seen his FBI consultant ID, but credentials could be faked.

Sage had begged her to let Ryker's PI run a background check on him, but like an idiot, she'd refused. It didn't feel right. From the first moment she met Aleksei, there had been an instant connection, as if their souls recognized each other. Running a background check felt crude, almost offensive.

"Do you realize how crazy this sounds?"

"I know. I'm sorry, but you have to believe me. You *are* in danger, and we need to get away from here as soon as we can. I'd never forgive myself if something happened to you."

His voice was softer now, less demanding and more pleading. His tone pulled at her, making her want to trust him, to do as he asked. His body was rigid. His eyes were dark. He looked grim and haunted. Her fingers ached to stroke the stress from his expression.

Damn her soft heart. All it had gotten her so far was reeling rejection.

Head not heart. Head not heart. Head not heart.

"I don't know what to believe. I don't even know whether to believe you're with the FBI."

Hurt tracked across his marble features and then disappeared. "What happened? What did I do to make you think I'd lie to you?"

If he didn't recognize his rejection and understand the impact it might have on her, he really wasn't the man she thought he was.

Before she could answer, his words cracked through the silence like thunder. "Scratch that. I know what I did. I know we need to talk, but right now, we don't have time. Once you get your things together, I need you to get in your car and follow me to the park office. We can use your phone for one quick call to my former boss before we ditch it. He can verify my identity for you."

"How can I trust him? He could be some random person playing a part. You go. I'll stay and take my chances."

The words felt like dirt in her mouth, gritty and foul-tasting. She believed Aleksei thought they were in danger, but she was still stinging from his rejection, and the wounded animal within her was striking back.

His lips became a thin, flat line. "I didn't want to tell you like this, but I talked to my former supervisor when I was up at the park office. There was an explosion at Pannetone & Associates today. There were three casualties: two males and one female. There was an explosion at my apartment too. The investigators think the events are linked. Someone also ransacked your apartment. I don't have details or reasons, but we are both in danger. I'm not leaving you here alone. If I need to sit here all night and answer your questions, I will, but please at least pack and drive up to the park office with me to talk. Sage knows you're here, and other people likely do as well. The campsite is registered in your name. It's not going to be hard to find you. If we stay at this cabin, we're sitting ducks."

Thoughts clogged through her mind, quick, heavy, and frantic, like Irish dancers.

Most of her coworkers were dead. She'd escaped death. Again. It didn't seem fair.

Who else had survived? Were they feeling that same twist of survivor's guilt she was?

Had Sage heard? If so, she'd be nauseous with worry. Two males? Who had been spared? Nick? Armando? Dante?

One female. Was it Marge or Lily?

She should have tried harder with Lily. Been kinder. Been more understanding. Maybe it was neither of them. Maybe there was a visitor.

She shouldn't pray for it to be other people, but death was so much easier when it was someone you didn't know. But it shouldn't be. It shouldn't be easier.

Strong arms pulled her into a firm chest. Aleksei's sweatshirt was cool on her cheek and smelled of spiced pine and night air. It felt good to rest her head against something solid. To have his strength ground her and pull her thoughts out of their spiral.

"Shhh. It's OK. Don't cry. It's going to be OK."

She lifted a shaking hand to her exposed cheek, and her fingers touched wetness. She hadn't realized she was crying.

This was not the time to fall apart. They could be in danger. But it didn't make sense. There was no reason for anyone to want to hurt her. It had to be a mistake. However, if what Aleksei was saying was true, they should get moving. Until they figured out exactly what was happening, leaving Ricketts Glen was the best choice.

But she wasn't just going on faith anymore.

She would call Sage to reassure her that she was okay, and then she'd ask to talk to Christian. She hated asking for favors. She'd spent way too much of her life beholden to all the people who cared for her when she couldn't care for herself, but with his job in the FBI cybersecurity division, Christian should be able to confirm whether Aleksei was telling her the truth. She needed that answer, even if it meant having to ask Christian for help. If Christian needed a little time to work his magic, she'd sit in the park office parking lot until she heard back from him.

It was head over heart from now on.

She packed quickly, shoving towels and linens into a plastic trash bag. The food she'd brought was quickly tucked into reusable grocery store bags and her cooler. Makeup and toiletries were unceremoniously dumped into her shoulder bag. She hadn't unpacked her suitcase, so it was easy to shove in the few things she'd taken out. The only thing she was careful with was the wig she'd worn earlier in the day. She hated packing it still damp, but she'd pull it out to dry wherever their next stop was. She slid it into its satin-lined bag and gently laid the bag on top of her clothing, zipping the suitcase closed.

Aleksei had managed to pack, dismantle his tent, and load all his things, the cooler, and the food bags into his truck in the same amount of time it took her to get her suitcase and toiletries together. Annoyance pricked at her as she looked at the neatly covered truck bed barely illuminated by the moon. Night had fallen quickly, and the small, remote overflow parking lot they now occupied was blanketed in darkness. She was glad they were in separate cars. It was hard to think in his brooding presence.

She'd spoken quickly to Sage and more at length with Christian. During her call, she watched Aleksei walk the perimeter of the parking lot, slide a gun from his waistband, slip on a silencer, and shoot out the two streetlamps in the lot. The effortless efficiency of his movements was like being doused with a bucket of ice water.

Aleksei Thompson was a dangerous man.

She should feel unsettled. The gun, the switch in his persona from sweet, wounded potential boyfriend to dangerous protector. She should feel nervous around him, wary, at least until she got confirmation from Christian that Aleksei was who he claimed to be. Instead, his presence made her feel safe and protected.

Head over heart. Head over heart.

She needed to keep reminding herself of that.

She looked at the time illuminated on her dashboard: 9:15. It was time to turn her phone back on again. Christian said he'd call her back in thirty minutes and had directed her to turn her phone off while she waited. The time had passed like molasses, and she had to battle to keep herself from leaving her car and climbing into Aleksei's truck. She'd let herself fall so fast, believing they were forming an intimate bond. She now knew he didn't feel the same way she did, but her brain was struggling to convince her heart to adjust to the new reality.

The phone sprang to life in her hands, startling both her and Thor, who lay dozing in the back seat. She answered, and Christian's voice boomed through the speakers in her car.

"Hey, Rose. You still hanging in there?"

She generally despised nicknames. If people shortened her name, they mostly called her Roe, and she would firmly tell them she went by Rosemary. She only let Christian shorten her name because he was the sweetest future brother-in-law anyone could ask for, and Rose was much nicer than a pile of fish eggs. But when Aleksei had called her his soft, lovely, precious Rose in the lake, her bones had melted. She'd loved the sound of the nickname on his lips.

She forced her mind back to Christian. "I'm OK. What did you find out?"

It felt rude to skip the normal small talk, but time was of the essence. She and Aleksei were in danger, and Christian was still recovering from surgery. He should be resting.

"Good news. I was able to worm my way into the personnel files, and your guy's story checks out. Aleksei Thompson. Thirty-four years old. Graduated from college in three years at the age of twenty. He was in ROTC. After graduation, he served five years in active duty, receiving multiple commendations. He was Special Forces, but I couldn't get details on his missions without hacking into the highly confidential stuff and sending off alarm bells. After the Marines, he spent seven years with the bureau. Sky-high marks on his entrance exams. Excellent tactical skills. Glowing annual evaluations. Passed all the psych exams with flying colors. Shifted from active agent to a consultant trainer at Quantico two years ago."

The vise grip around her ribs eased with each sentence. Her instincts hadn't been wrong. They might be in a crazy situation, and by taking off her wig, she might have pushed the relationship too hard, too fast, but her heart had read Aleksei correctly. He was one of the good guys.

"Thank you. I really appreciate your help."

"Of course. Any time. I feel bad for the guy. From the files, it seems like he's really been through it. It looks like he retired after his partner was killed during an undercover organized crime investigation. I don't blame him for taking one last shot at putting this Moresco guy away. It seems like the entire team thought Moresco was behind the murder, but there was no proof. The murder hit the headlines, so they had to shut the op down."

If she wasn't already sitting, she'd have dropped to the ground. "Salvatore Moresco? From Philadelphia?"

"Yeah. There's an addendum to the personnel file. It looks like it was added earlier today. It says Thompson initiated contact with an accountant at Pannetone & Associates a few weeks ago to follow up on a lead pertaining to Moresco. Potential money laundering. I assume that's when he contacted you. There's no more detail other than a link to an active investigation, which I assume is the explosion at your office that you told me about. That file has a higher classification, so I can't easily access it. I'm sure I can get in if you need me to. I just ran out of time."

Her throat constricted. Her blood went hot. She might actually vomit. What was the phrase Christian used? *Initiated contact with an accountant.*

He'd initiated contact with her all right.

The words made it sound so official, but there wasn't anything official about it. He'd tricked her. He'd used her. He'd known who she was from the beginning. He'd played her, and she'd gone right along like an eager-for-attention golden retriever, thrilled with every scrap of attention he'd thrown at her.

She'd been gullible. Now she knew better. Step one was making sure Christian knew exactly what Aleksei had done.

"He didn't tell me he was investigating Moresco. He acted like we were dating." She hated how weak and shaky her voice sounded.

"Oh shit, Rose. That sucks. I'm sorry." His tone was sympathetic, but he sounded nonplussed.

"You're not surprised, are you?" she asked.

"He's an undercover man. That's how they catch criminals. It's not pretty, but it works. Thompson needed information and likely didn't know if he could trust you. He approached you in a way that made sense."

That type of deceit would never make sense in her world. But she wasn't in her world anymore. She was in a world of pretense and lies. A world where men handled guns with silencers as comfortably as a pen. A world where people dumped phones so they couldn't be tracked. A world with explosions. A world where bodies were burned beyond recognition. A world that was not safe.

A world she didn't have the skills to navigate alone.

"Can I trust him?"

"Come to DC. I'll get to the bottom of this. I'll protect you."

She wasn't going to DC. There was no way she was dragging Christian deeper into this mess than she already had. Sage and Ryker had saved her life. Literally. If she went to DC, she'd bring the danger that was stalking her to all of them. She would never do that. She loved them all too much.

"Can I trust him?" she repeated.

"Rose, this is not the time for you to be stubborn. Come here. Let me help you."

She asked a third time, pouring ice and determination into her tone. "Can. I. Trust. Him?"

Christian sighed wearily. She didn't know if he was still tired from surgery or exasperated by her refusal.

"Men like Aleksei Thompson don't change. He has excellent skills, and they're still sharp. He wouldn't be a trainer if they were rusty. Soldiers and agents don't get the commendations and reviews he received unless they're loyal and willing to serve at any cost. He might lie to you. He might do things you don't like or agree with, but a man like that would give his life to keep an innocent civilian safe. A man like that would die for you if he had to."

And that was the kicker, wasn't it? Her heart hadn't been wrong in recognizing the goodness in Aleksei—it had just been wrong in interpreting his general goodness as affection for her specifically. Being around him, knowing that he'd played her, knowing their deep conversations had been faked and that his feelings for her were an act was going to be hard. Really hard.

But whether she liked it or not, if she wanted to live through this, staying with Aleksei was her best option.

Chapter Eighteen

Rosemary jolted awake in the passenger seat of Aleksei's F150. The last thing she remembered was him eating a toxic-looking egg sandwich and studying a paper map in the parking lot of an all-night gas station while the dogs snored, snuggled together in the back seat. She hadn't seen anyone navigate using a paper map since she was a kid, but he seemed comfortable doing it. It was probably a military thing. She wasn't going to ask. She needed to work on creating distance, not on getting to know him better.

She rubbed her gritty eyes, trying to figure out where they were. When she'd asked him where they were headed, he'd said, "working on it." Maybe he hadn't figured it out yet. Maybe he was intentionally keeping her in the dark. It didn't matter. At this point, she had no choice but to follow his lead. She'd left her car in a remote parking lot at Ricketts Glen and ditched her phone. She'd followed orders like a robot, the pain of his betrayal leaving her numb.

Sleep had helped. Now, curiosity nipped at her.

The truck was stopped on a dirt road. The headlights illuminated a steep hill to the left and a sharp drop to the right. It was hard to see in the darkness, but the few trees out her window appeared to be growing sideways, giving her a sense that the road was too narrow for the truck. At any moment, it seemed they would tumble over the edge. She gripped the armrest as if her fingers had the power to hold the tires to the road. In the rearview window, there was nothing but black. The quiet of the forest around them was ominous. This place felt unwelcome.

Of course, maybe it was the giant fence topped with wicked-looking barbed wire blocking their path and the huge No Trespassing sign that was creating the vibe.

"Wait here," Aleksei said as he jumped out of the truck, leaving the driver's door ajar. Cold air nipped at her face while she watched him jog to the side of the road and fiddle with a square metal box on a post. Worried that her wig might have shifted while she slept, she flipped the visor down and ran her nails under the edges, giving her scalp a good scratch before ensuring the wig was straight and firmly in place. A soft creak brought her attention to the road, where the fence was parting in the middle, swinging inward.

Aleksei hopped back in, an expression of relief on his face. "I wasn't sure if that was going to work. If it didn't, we'd be making camp right here on the road, and Virus would be pissed. Scratch that. More pissed than usual. His everyday mood is pricklier than a puffer fish."

She rubbed her eyes again. He wasn't making any sense. She wasn't sure if it was because she was still groggy from sleep or he was talking nonsense.

"What didn't you think would work? And did you say *Virus*? Is that a person?"

He laughed as the truck engine roared to life. It was a deep, warm rumble that made her think of morning-after breakfasts and kisses over coffee. Her mind jumped away from the image like a hand that got too close to a flame. Her subconscious needed to stop filling her head with romantic images.

"Sorry. There's a fingerprint sensor near the gate. We're in Trout Run. Virus is a friend of mine. He's not particularly friendly, but he is a friend. We can trust him."

He'd said *we,* not *I*. As if they were a couple.

Head, not heart. Focus on the facts.

"Where's Trout Run? Why are we here? And if this guy is so unfriendly, do you think maybe you should avoid calling him Virus?"

More warm rumbling laughter turned her bones to marshmallow, but the sound was shorter this time. Aleksei's hands gripped the wheel firmly, and he continually scanned the sides of the road. The ground to her right slowly leveled out as they drove. Now she saw only thick trees on both sides and the dusty gray-brown road that cut through them.

"We're about seventy miles west of Ricketts Glen, but it took us several hours to get here because I took all the back roads. I wanted to avoid cameras on the highways. The route I took is rural, so we won't be easily trackable like we would on the highway. We need a safe place to rest and regroup, and I don't think anyone will think to look for us here—at least not for a few days."

"And Virus?" she prompted.

"His real name is Petros Grigoris. When I finished ITC, he was in the unit I was assigned to. He's one of the toughest guys I know. Fiercely loyal. Not much of a talker and has no patience for bullshit, but a good friend."

"He has no patience for bullshit but is fine with people calling him Virus?" she asked.

His cheeks lifted, but the smile disappeared quickly, replaced with alert concentration. "It was his nickname when I met him. The story goes that the first day he arrived for ITC—that's what they call special ops training—he was sick as a dog. Pale, fever, puking. The way the guys tell it, they make it sound like he was half dead. He didn't want to get behind, so he wouldn't go to the infirmary and wouldn't sit out. Apparently, he had some super contagious flu, and nearly everyone on base ended up getting sick. One of the SOOs started calling him Virus, and it stuck."

Warmth seeped through her chest. It was a nice story. Funny and personal. She liked hearing him talk about his past.

Then doubt chilled the heat. Was the story part of the role he was playing? An anecdote intended to relax her, to gain her trust?

"Is it true?" she asked.

"Is what true?" he asked, his tone distracted.

"The story about Virus. Is it true or is it another lie? An interesting personal story meant to lull me into a sense of comfort."

His hands tightened on the wheel. "I never lied to you. There were things I kept from you—serious, important things I should have told you a hell of a lot sooner—but I never lied to you. Everything I said about my life, my family, Phillipe, and myself. It was all real."

Her ribs felt constricted, like there was a boulder on her chest, making it difficult to breathe. She didn't know what to believe. She didn't know if it mattered what she believed. What she did know was that she didn't want to feel like a fool again.

"I made a gesture of faith by coming with you. Now you need to do the same for me. Promise me there will be no more lies. No more omissions. Big or small. Going forward, I want you to be completely honest and upfront with me. If you can't do that, I'm leaving."

She meant what she said. Staying with Aleksei until the danger passed was the safest thing to do, and she wanted to be safe, but she could not handle being lied to and used. If he couldn't promise honesty, she'd face this thing on her own.

"All right. I promise. You can ask me anything, and I'll tell you the truth."

"I want more than that. I don't want to have to ask. I don't want you holding back information and then using the fact that I didn't ask a question there was no way I could know to ask as an excuse. I want you to tell me everything. Everything. Keep me fully informed."

Her voice sounded harsh and angry. It should. She was furious. But deeper than her rage was a sorrow so strong, her stomach ached from it. The butterflies of joy and excitement that had danced inside her during the past week lay still and bleeding, cut down by betrayal. Hopefully, her anger masked her suffering. She didn't want him knowing how much he had hurt her.

"I promise."

He spoke the words like a vow. His voice shimmered with guilt and regret, seeping through her own anguish, igniting her instinctive need to comfort. She clasped her hands together in her lap, fighting the urge to reach out and lay a reassuring hand on his muscled thigh. To get through the next few days with him, she needed to keep that innate desire in check. She was with him for protection, not to build a relationship.

That thought, and the raging heat in the car, was making her nauseous. Aleksei had turned up the heat to battle the chill that filled the truck while he'd opened the gate, and now she was sweating.

Her scalp twitched.

She glanced at the dashboard. It was 4:00 a.m. Other than the short break at the cabin while she cooked, she'd been wearing a wig for more than nineteen hours straight. She'd never worn one this long. Putting the wig on was normally the last thing she did before leaving the house, and she took it off the minute she got home.

The twitch was now an itch. Itches, really. Several of them. She pressed her fingers to the sides of her head, but instead of soothing her scalp, the pressure set off a chain reaction of prickly, itchy sensations that made her want to jump out of the truck and chuck the wig into the eerie dark woods.

"Would you turn off the heat?" she asked.

"Sure," he answered as he adjusted the knob. "Are you okay?"

She was now gripping the console and the overhead handle so tightly that her fingers were tingling.

"Yes. Just a little carsick," she lied.

There was no way she was telling him what was really bothering her. From now on, she was communicating with him out of necessity, not desire. She'd already shown him too much vulnerability. She wasn't making that same mistake again.

* * *

Aleksei knew Rose was lying to him, but he didn't have the right to demand the truth. He'd fucked up. Really fucked up. He could hear her distress in every word she spoke. Pain she was trying to hide from him. Pain he'd inflicted. He'd been so focused on his goals, driving the train down the tracks, zooming right past flashing lights and warning signals.

He hadn't meant to hurt her.

He hadn't intended to start dating her. He hadn't intended to trick her with romance. His plan had simply been to meet her and then make it up as he went along. He hadn't expected to be attracted to her. He hadn't expected to feel that instant spark of connection. But he had. And when that happened, he should have changed direction. But he didn't.

He'd asked her to dinner. He went with her to the theater. He took her to McGillin's of all goddamn places. He snuggled with her on his couch in the firelight, kissing her, reveling in her moans as he caressed her soft curves. He texted and called her. He crashed her vacation, made her breakfast, hiked with her, flirted with her, and had mind-bending sex with her in that freezing cold lake. And through all that, he lied. Not actual lies, but it was just as she said. The things he hadn't told her, the truths he kept from her—they were the same as lies.

His gut turned sour as he faced his own choices. He'd chosen to cut himself off from his friends and family. He'd fought the therapists every step of the way, so he hadn't processed his emotions. He'd stayed laser focused on Phillipe's death, so the pain never lessened, and his need to avenge Phillipe only grew. By the time he met Rose, he was like a shriveled plant in the desert. Her kindness and compassion were like water. Irresistible to a parched man.

That was the reason he invited her to dinner.

He should have changed course right then. Come up with an alternate plan. Instead, he'd chosen to lean into her soothing comfort, even while using her to avenge Phillipe. He'd wanted to have his cake and eat it too, and in his selfishness, he'd hurt her. Grievously. Possibly irreparably.

Phillipe would be ashamed of him.

No matter what the newspapers or Internal Affairs said, he was certain Phillipe had been a good man. He saw it in the way Phillipe treated Samantha like she was precious. He saw it in Phillipe's endless patience with his kids. He saw it in how Phillipe always minimized his role in any accomplishment and made sure everyone else involved received praise. Phillipe never assumed someone was a criminal simply because they were a suspect. If someone had committed the crime, Phillipe would try to understand the circumstances that drove them to make the choices they had. Phillipe always looked for the good first, no matter what.

Kemper's accusation last night, that he was obsessed with his own loss and blind to everything else, was a seed in his mind, growing buds and shoots. The rebuke had the feel of an uncomfortable truth. Aleksei had quit his job. He barely visited his mother and sister. He couldn't remember the last time he reached out to one of his friends. He spent most of his free time alone, hiking, working out, going over old notes from the Moresco op, and keeping tabs on the Philly mob. When Phillipe died, Samantha and the kids had been his lifeline. When she cut him off, he'd cut himself off from the rest of the world.

Rose had said that her sister held on so tightly that, sometimes, it made it hard to breathe. Was that how he'd made Samantha feel? Had he been using her to hold on too tightly to Philippe, pinning her to that point in time so she was trapped, feeling like she was slowly suffocating?

The anger toward Samantha that he thought he'd previously let go suddenly dissipated, unraveling one of the tightest knots in his constantly constricted chest. Samantha had done what she needed to do to survive. Just like he had been doing. But Samantha was stronger. She had the strength to let go and move forward, and he'd stayed entombed in the past.

Was he truly seeking revenge for Philippe? Or did he want to bring Moresco down to assuage his own guilt?

He pushed the questions away. They were moot. The chess pieces were already in motion. He'd have to finish the game.

Step one was rest. His body had been in fight-or-flight mode since he'd spoken to Kemper. He'd driven for hours. The hike and time in the lake with Rosemary felt like a week ago instead of yesterday. Once they were settled in Virus's cabin, they'd be safe, and he could sleep. Virus wouldn't be thrilled to see him. He wasn't ever thrilled to see anybody, but this was the most secure place Aleksei could think of. His body had literally sagged with relief when he spotted how close Trout Run and Ricketts Glen were on the map.

It had been a few years since his last visit. He and Phillipe had come here to hunt. Virus had a woman in his life back then. She had encouraged Virus to invite them. She said it would be good for him to spend more time with friends. The woman had been good for him. He was happier than Aleksei had ever seen him. Virus hadn't known Phillipe, but he'd been warm and welcoming. Unfortunately, the relationship ended soon after. Virus provided no details, and Aleksei had never been invited back again.

His friend was up here alone, fighting his own demons, but Aleksei hadn't reached out once in the past two years—and now he was showing up unwanted and unannounced. What Kemper said about him was dead on. He was so obsessed with his own suffering, he hadn't spent one goddamn minute thinking about anyone else. He was a fucking asshole.

He could only hope Virus was in a forgiving mood.

As if called to the flesh by his thoughts, about fifteen feet in front of them, Virus stepped out of the shadows, an M4 pointed directly at them.

Chapter Nineteen

Rosemary dug her feet into the floorboard, pushing herself backward, but there was nowhere to go. The seat was firm against her back, preventing her retreat. Her heart stuttered, then sprinted into overdrive. Sweat pooled at the edges of her wig. Instinct demanded she wipe the perspiration away, but she was afraid to lift her hands, afraid to move at all. She didn't want to do anything to startle the man with the giant gun.

Strong fingers squeezed her thigh. "It's all right, Rose."

Aleksei put the truck in park and climbed out slowly, keeping his arms away from his body, bent up at the elbows, his fingers splayed wide. He left the door ajar. Was it because he wanted to leave open the option of a quick escape? Or because he hadn't wanted to turn his back on the gun to close it? Neither option was comforting.

"Hey, Virus," Aleksei's voice floated in through the open door.

He sounded calm and pleasant, as if he was greeting a friend in the supermarket, not facing an irritated, broad-shouldered, sober-faced, former Marine holding what looked like an automatic weapon. Not that she knew anything about guns. The first time she'd seen one other than on a screen was when Aleksei had shot out the streetlights in the parking lot at Ricketts Glen.

"What are you thinking sneaking up on me in the middle of the night, Thompson?" an unfamiliar voice asked.

Aleksei's rumbling laughter filled the air, and her shoulders dropped a fraction of an inch. She didn't find anything funny about this scenario, but if Aleksei was relaxed, things must be okay. Maybe this was some weird type of Marine humor.

"You know damn well I'm not sneaking up on you. Your motion sensors and cameras picked me up the second I turned on the road, and I used my fingerprint to open the gate, so you knew exactly who was driving up. Stop acting like a dick, put the gun down, and open the gate. You're giving my girl a panic attack."

He'd called her his girl. She should be offended. She was a woman, not a girl, and after the shit he'd pulled, she certainly wasn't his, but her wishy-washy, traitorous heart still softened. Was this endearment part of his act, him trying to lull her into believing his affection? He'd been an undercover agent, so he was, essentially, an expert con artist who just happened to work for the good guys. His con job had definitely done a number on her. She hated feeling like she couldn't trust her own mind or heart.

"I'm not running a bed and breakfast here. You know my place is rustic." Virus waved the butt of his rifle toward the passenger seat. "You sure she's up for it?"

"Rose is as strong as either of us. And she's a hell of a lot nicer." Aleksei's tone shifted from light to weary. "Now, please open the goddamn gate. We're in trouble, and I'm so goddamn tired I can't think straight. We need to rest."

And just like that, no questions asked and no explanations demanded, Virus slung the gun over his shoulder and opened the gate. Rosemary released the breath she'd been holding in a long, slow exhale. She wasn't sure how to feel about this grumpy, gun-toting, former Marine, but like Aleksei, she was too damn tired right now to think about it.

An hour later, as she was sitting on a metal four-poster double bed, brushing out her wig, her opinion of Virus had already shifted toward the positive. She'd visited the outhouse and used the basin of warm water Virus had placed on an antique-looking dresser to wash her head and face and brush her teeth. The smile he'd given her when he'd told her she should call him Virus instead of Petros was brief but kind. He didn't know her, but he'd helped her anyway, and he hadn't lied to her. So, at this point, in her book, he already had more points than Aleksei.

She shifted on the surprisingly comfortable bed. Despite the spare furniture, the lack of an indoor shower and toilet, and the fact that the cabin looked like it might have been built in the 1800s, the linens Virus gave her to make up the bed smelled freshly laundered, and the mattress was a modern pillow-top style. She glanced at Thor, who covered half the bed, snoring. She should change his name to Benedict Arnold. When Aleksei had come to collect him for dinner and a quick walk with Jaka, Thor had trotted along happily without hesitation. They were in full role reversal. Now, Thor was the one who adored Aleksei, and she was the one with reservations.

She blew out a breath, rustling the hair on the wig in her hand. It felt like betrayal, but at least it assured her that Aleksei was trustworthy at a basic level. If he weren't, Thor wouldn't want Aleksei anywhere near her, and that would make things challenging, since it seemed they'd be cooped up in the small cabin for at least a day or two.

The house was a single story with only three rooms. The combined kitchen and living area was similar to the cabin at Ricketts Glen, but Virus's sink had an old-fashioned hand pump instead of a regular faucet. Hopefully, she'd hidden her shock when she saw it. She didn't want Virus to think she didn't appreciate what he was doing for them.

The other two rooms in the cabin were bedrooms. Virus's eyebrows had winged up when Aleksei announced he would sleep on the couch, but he hadn't commented. He hadn't said much at all since they'd arrived. Aleksei had shown her the outhouse and explained that there was a cistern outside that fed a cold-water outdoor shower.

Despite it being spring, the temperature was in the forties, so she skipped the shower and used the basin. At least the cabin had electricity.

She gave the wig one last brush. She didn't like the idea of sleeping bald when she was separated from both men by only thin sheets of plywood. Her soul was battered, and the wig was her protective armor, but she could not put it back on right now. By the time she'd gotten settled in the room, her head had been so itchy and irritated that it had taken multiple washes with the blessedly cool water to settle it down. Her scalp needed some time to recover.

She rose and pulled her two wig stands from her suitcase on the floor and set them on the dresser. She placed both the wig in her hands and the damp wig she'd bagged up earlier on the stands. She was exhausted. The last thing Aleksei had said to her before she shut the bedroom door was, "Don't worry. You're safe here." Maybe it was wishful thinking or fatigue slowing her brain, but she trusted those words. She climbed under the covers with Thor snuggled next to her and taking up more of the bed than she did. When she closed her eyes, sleep came hard, fast, and dreamless.

Woof, woof, woof.

The barks jolted her awake. She reached for her phone to check the time, but it wasn't on the nightstand next to the bed. Right. It was in a dumpster at Ricketts Glen.

There was no clock in the room, but the sun shimmered brightly around the curtains. She climbed out of the cozy bed and pushed one of the tree-patterned panels aside. The sun was high in the sky. Did that mean it was after noon? A grin spread across her lips. She was acting like a pioneer woman, trying to tell the time by the position of the sun.

Thor barked at her again, standing tall in front of the bedroom door.

"All right. All right," Rosemary muttered.

She preferred to ease into the morning, but Thor always woke up ready for action. That was one of the very few downsides of pet ownership. She found a sweatshirt in her suitcase and threw it on over the tank top she'd slept in, settled her cap and wig into place, and slipped on her Uggs.

Thor barked again.

"I know. I know. You need to go out. I hear you. I need the outhouse too."

Floorboards creaked under her feet as she made her way to the front door. The house was empty and quiet. A coffee machine with a half-full coffeepot sat on the counter, tempting her.

Bathroom first. Then coffee.

She opened the cabin door, and the beauty of the land nearly stopped her forward motion. She was in the mountains surrounded by trees. A large area behind the house had been cleared and turned into fields, gardens, and a small orchard. Behind the clearing, the landscape shifted back to thick forest. She could hear a creek rushing in the distance. Last night, Aleksei had mentioned the property was more than five hundred acres.

Her mother would have loved it here.

Thor dashed up the dirt and gravel road that ran in front of the house. Aleksei had let the dogs run off leash last night, so Rosemary assumed it was okay. She didn't want to do anything to irritate Virus. Not just because he was a mean-looking, gun-toting, former Marine who thought grunts were an appropriate form of speech, but also because he had allowed them into his home when everything about his body language said he preferred to be alone. She was grateful for that and wanted to be a respectful houseguest.

After both she and Thor had taken care of their personal needs, the house was still empty, so she helped herself to coffee and made toast with butter and homemade blackberry jelly she found in the fridge. It was a simple breakfast, but the jelly was the best she'd ever had, just the right mix of sweet and tart, and the coffee was pure heaven. Relaxation flowed through her with the first sip. It was always that way with coffee. And wine.

Deep voices and the crunch of footsteps on gravel interrupted her peaceful moment. Thor leapt up from lazing in a sunny spot on the kitchen floor. He barked as Aleksei and Virus entered the cabin with Jaka. Aleksei kicked off his sneakers and headed directly for the coffeepot, poured a cup, and sipped it black. Thor and Jaka wrestled on the floor of the sitting area in front of Virus, who sat on the couch, unlacing thick brown work boots.

Virus nodded toward Thor. "Quite an animal you got there. Looks more like a cow than a dog. He probably weighs as much as you do."

Aleksei coughed, spewing coffee onto the kitchen floor. "Living out here alone seems to have rusted your charm," he said as he cleaned up the mess with a wet paper towel.

She knew her build wasn't slim and petite like her sister's, but she liked her figure. It was the perfect mix of athletic and curvy. She was fit and strong but still felt soft and sexy.

"It's okay," she said, smiling and shifting in her chair to face Virus. "He's a Great Dane Dalmatian. Last time he was at the vet, he weighed 175 pounds, so yeah, he's a big dog."

"You're lucky Rose is as sweet as her name. Any other woman would punch you if you compared her to her dog," Aleksei said, a teasing note in his voice.

"Shut the hell up, Thompson. I should just shoot you and keep Rosemary for myself."

Warm laughter tickled Rosemary's throat, but she didn't set it free. In the homey cabin, with the sun shining, gorgeous views through large windows, and the comfortable banter, it was easy to forget what had brought her here. She couldn't let herself be distracted. Someone had set off a bomb in her office. Most of her coworkers were dead. If someone was after her, they might also go after Sage, Ryker, or Davis. Now that she'd rested, she needed to focus on figuring out what the hell was going on.

"Any chance you have internet access?" she asked.

Aleksei straightened and set his coffee cup on the counter with a *thunk*. "Tell me you don't have a computer with you."

She didn't like his tone. "I have a work laptop with me."

"Do you normally bring your work computer with you on vacation?" he asked, his tone still terse.

"No. But when Dante suggested it, I felt like I couldn't say no. Especially since I was leaving him and Armando with such a mess."

Virus sprang up from the couch and headed toward the kitchen. His movements were swift and agile, but his gait was slightly uneven.

Aleksei squeezed the bridge of his nose. "Please get the computer."

Invisible hands squeezed her ribcage. "You didn't ask me about a computer. You only asked about my phone."

"If they can track a phone, they can track a computer."

"Even if it's turned off?" she asked.

"Yes."

She hadn't thought about the computer. She'd just put the backpack that held it with the rest of her things for Aleksei to load into the truck. She wasn't used to worrying about her location being tracked. She didn't even know someone could track the location of a computer that wasn't connected to the internet. Aleksei had worked so hard to cover their tracks and get them to safety, and she'd left a trail of breadcrumbs.

Virus laid a bulky, thick-knuckled hand on her shoulder. "It's okay. It'll only take me a few minutes to pull it apart to make sure there's no tracker inside and get the location services turned off. Computers aren't the same as phones. There's a good chance there's nothing to worry about. Plus, there are motion sensors and cameras around the perimeter of the entire property. If anyone sets foot on my land, I'll know." He glanced toward Aleksei. "Grab the laptop, and we'll all head to the basement."

She grabbed the computer from her room, and they descended into the basement through a door in the living area that she'd assumed was a closet, leaving the 1800s vibe of the cabin far behind. Multiple surveillance screens hung on a wall over a long counter that housed a few laptops, several desktop computers, and multiple computer screens. A wheeled office chair sat in front of the counter.

The room also held a round dinette set, a mini-fridge, a TV, and a comfortable-looking couch and loveseat. Books were scattered around, a plate and coffee cup sat on a side table, and a gray-toned flannel shirt was slung over the back of one of the dinette chairs. It looked like Virus spent more time down here than he did upstairs.

Virus ushered them toward the table, walking briskly but still with that slightly uneven gait, his jeans swishing with each step.

"Is your leg all right?" she asked.

Both men whirled to face her. Aleksei grabbed Virus's shoulder, but Virus pulled out of the grasp, his eyes sharp and lip curled in a sneer.

"No. My leg is not all right," he snarled as he bent at the waist, lifting the left leg of his jeans. There was no skin above his white sock. Instead, there was just a shiny, silver rod.

They all stood frozen.

She didn't know what she should say or whether there was anything to say. Sympathy spiked through her. Sympathy for Virus, for his injury, and all the unspoken anguish in his surly response. Sympathy for all the people she'd judged for staring at her wordlessly when she'd told them about her cancer. Maybe she'd been too harsh. Maybe they, like her, were silent because they couldn't find words to express the empathy cracking their hearts.

"Seen enough?" Virus growled, releasing the leg of his jeans.

Words eluded her. She understood his anger. Had felt it herself as her hair came out in handfuls. Felt it as she donned baseball caps and wrapped scarves around her head. Felt it every day when she stared at her gleaming white scalp before putting that goddamn wig on her head. Felt it as the few people who knew that her hair had never grown back glanced speculatively at her wig. She knew raw, boiling rage.

Without her hair, she felt like a piece of herself was missing.

"Go upstairs, Aleksei," she ordered, breaking the silence that was as thick as stew.

Aleksei crossed his arms over his chest and didn't budge.

"Go. Upstairs," she repeated, emphasizing each word. "I know what I'm doing."

He glanced between her and Virus, then stomped toward the stairs. A few thuds followed, then silence. She could tell he'd only gone partway up, but it was enough to block his view. That was good enough.

She closed her eyes, blew out a slow breath, reached up, and pulled off her wig. "I've had cancer three times. I'm lucky to be alive, and I'm grateful for that. Truly. But my hair will never grow back. I'll be bald the rest of my life. I don't know what happened to your leg. I can't imagine what you went through, and I would never presume to say I know how you feel. I don't. Hair is such a small thing compared to a limb."

She laid a hand on his forearm. His sleeves were pushed up, and his skin was hot and thick with muscle.

"Life has a way of turning out so differently than what we imagine. The medicine that saved my life killed a part of me. I feel vain and stupid and ungrateful, but I loved my hair. I feel like less of a female without it. Less human." She shook her head to clear it. She was babbling. "Anyway, I just wanted to tell you that I'm sorry for what you've been through. Whatever happened. Whatever you suffered. From my soul, I'm sorry. I know you don't need my sympathy, but you have my empathy if you'll accept it."

She pulled her hand away and walked on wobbly legs over to the dinette table. Sitting down, she resettled her wig on her head with shaking fingers. Adrenaline was a bitch sometimes.

Virus plopped down in the chair next to her with a loud grunt. He laid one large, tan-skinned, big-knuckled hand over hers. "I'm sorry. Sometimes I forget that some scars are easier to hide than others."

Rosemary relaxed into the warmth of their connection. Sometimes, she did too.

Chapter Twenty

Virus was being charming. Fucking charming. Aleksei wouldn't have believed it if he wasn't seeing it. Virus was joking with Rose as his fingers disassembled and reassembled the laptop with a dexterity that shouldn't seem possible from such bulky hands.

"No tracker," Virus said, beaming as he pushed the computer toward Rosemary. "Nothing to worry about."

The statement lifted the jungle of anxiety that had rooted in Aleksei's neck and shoulders the second Rose had mentioned the computer. At least now he knew they hadn't been advertising their location the entire time they were traveling. If they got online, that would be a different story, but Virus had enough equipment and skills to block their location for at least a short while if need be. They'd cross that bridge when they came to it.

"I'd never forgive myself if something happened to either of you because I didn't mention this computer," Rose said, looking down at the closed laptop in front of her.

She looked so unhappy. He'd trade ten years of his life for a do-over of the last half hour.

"It's not your fault. This shithead," Virus said, pointing his thumb toward him, "should have asked you whether you had any other electronics with you. There's no way you could have known. If it's anybody's fault, it's his."

Yep. Rose had made a friend for life, and now he was the one in the doghouse.

"Well, this shithead thinks that we should fire this thing up and see what's in here," he said.

Rose's head snapped up, her blue eyes flashing. "You want to start the computer? After you yelled at me for bringing it with me? I thought you said they could find our location if I logged in."

"They can only track the IP address if we get online. Pannetone's office was targeted, and you said that you'd found something concerning in one of the client files before you left. Was it about Moresco?"

Rose bit her lip and pressed her hands into her temples.

Virus shifted in his seat, a glare on his face, but he didn't speak. Aleksei knew he wouldn't. Virus might not like seeing Rose upset, but he understood the need for answers. Aleksei had brought Virus up to speed during their morning walk. Virus knew how dangerous Salvatore Moresco was. Knew the choices Aleksei had made and why. He disapproved, but he understood.

The timing of Rose's discovery and the explosion were too close to be coincidental. Moresco wanted Pannetone, his people, and his entire business gone, so the first step in figuring out what was going on was getting the details around whatever Rose had discovered.

"I feel like I'm breaching Armando's trust," she said.

"Think about it as trying to pin down Armando's killer," he offered.

He didn't add that they couldn't even be sure Armando was dead. One man had survived the explosion.

Virus grasped Rose's right forearm, gently pulling it away from her head and toward the table. "Aleksei's correct. Right now, your computer is the only potential lead we have. I know you're angry with Aleksei, and you have every right to be, but it doesn't make him wrong about this. We need to get to the bottom of this shitshow before someone else gets hurt. You need to tell him what was going on at work."

She opened her eyes and smiled at Virus, a sweet, grateful smile. "Thank you. This entire experience has been very unsettling. I appreciate how kind you're being to me."

He wished Virus hadn't reminded Rose that she had good reason to be pissed at him. He wished that warm smile was for him.

She might never smile like that at me again.

The thought was like stitches without anesthesia, but there was no time for self-pity or regrets. They had work to do.

"What did you find?" he prompted.

"I found a couple of invoices on Moresco projects for work that was never done," she said. "They were for elevators in single-story warehouses. I told Armando about them right before I left for vacation. We started reviewing files on other Moresco projects to see if we could find more suspicious invoices, but there are hundreds of files, so we didn't make a lot of progress. Armando wanted to get his arms around the issue before discussing it with Sal."

Of course he did. Stealing from the mob was a life-ending choice. If Armando was the one generating the fake invoices, he would have wanted to divert suspicion away from himself. On the other hand, if Armando was cooking the books for Moresco and missed someone else stealing, he'd be shitting bricks as well.

"Log on," he encouraged, waving his hand toward the computer.

Rose's fingers trembled slightly as she opened the laptop and entered her login and password. "I don't think this will be of any use without connecting to the server. All the Moresco files were on a local server in the basement. I assume it was destroyed in the explosion."

"It wasn't cloud-based?" Virus asked.

She shook her head, fluorescent light glinting off long blonde strands. "No. Dante, the IT guy, is actually Sal's nephew. He said that his grandfather is a stickler about cybersecurity. Apparently, for a long time, he refused to allow electronic records, but that wasn't practical. Dante said all the Moresco files were on the server in the basement and locked down so they couldn't be copied or emailed outside the firm. If the server was destroyed in the explosion, there's nothing left."

Shit.

"That explains the localized explosions," Aleksei said.

Both Virus and Rose looked at him expectantly.

"Kemper told me that there were two explosions. One on the second floor and one in the basement, but there was no damage to the structure of the building or to the gelato store on the first floor. Kemper said Moresco owns the building. If someone wanted to make sure that everyone who worked on Moresco projects and all their records were destroyed, but still protect the building, localized explosions would do it."

Sal would definitely want to protect his investment. He was notorious for squeezing every last dollar he could from every enterprise, regardless of who got hurt.

Aleksei didn't like mafioso, but he understood them and, on a certain level, even respected them. In some ways, the mafia was like the military. It was a community with an established hierarchy that worked together for a common goal and adhered to a specific code of ethics. Just like a military unit, mafioso stuck together. They protected each other. Loyalty was rewarded.

But Salvatore Moresco was different. Aleksei had studied Sal when he was undercover. Moresco wielded power without respect. He put himself before the family.

Rose stood from the table and crossed the room, stopping near the couch, with her head down and her arms crossed over her chest. She was a strong, athletic woman, but her oversized sweatshirt and baggy pajama bottoms combined with her hunched posture made her look delicate and fragile, like the old cards and letters his mother kept in a box in her closet. Every time he touched them, he felt like they would crumble in his hands.

He would not let Rose crumble.

She was angry with him. He knew she might never forgive him, but he had to try. He'd hurt her.

And it wasn't just Rose he'd hurt. In trying to protect himself, he'd screwed over lots of people he cared about. He envisioned Samuel's face at the bar, a mix of pleasure and disappointment. They could have grieved together. He could hear the disappointment in Zina's tone when he'd told her time and again that he couldn't come for dinner or to the boys' games—and compared that to the rush of hugs he'd received when he walked in the door this past weekend. There were all the unreturned calls and texts from the guys in his unit. His mother begging him to let her come visit. Virus, out here alone in the woods.

Rose, standing in the cabin kitchen, brave and nervous, her scalp shining white, baring herself to him.

He'd been too afraid to accept the gift she'd offered.

It was as if Phillipe was here, whispering in his ear, quoting Gandhi.

The enemy is fear.

Aleksei's body moved toward her of its own volition, like the instinct of a cat finding its way back home. Her shoulders were shaking. She'd angled her body away from the table, as if she were trying to hide her anguish. He stepped in front of her and wrapped her soft, quivering body in his arms. Her back stiffened, but she didn't push him away. He squeezed tighter, trying to still the sobs racking her body. Tears wet his neck.

He'd do anything to fix this. Anything. But for now, all he could do was hold her and whisper assurances that everything would be OK. And it would. She'd put her faith in him, and he was damn well going to make sure nothing bad happened to her. Not on his watch.

He wasn't going to fail again.

* * *

She shouldn't let Aleksei comfort her. His arms shouldn't be the grounding force holding her together. She didn't want him to see her this vulnerable, but if he let go, she might shatter.

"How can you do it? How can you talk about death and destruction as if it were normal? My coworkers are dead. My apartment was ransacked. Yours exploded. You smashed our phones and shot out streetlights. We're holed up in a compound, worried that people are tracking our location. You discussed Moresco destroying the office and killing the people I worked with every day, as if it were logical. This is not normal, but I'm the only one freaking out."

His arms squeezed even tighter. Her ribs barely had room to expand as she breathed, but it felt too good to ask him to loosen his grip.

"I was trained for this. I've had a long time to get used to guns, violence, and always having to look over my shoulder. You're doing great. It's natural to need time to adjust. The first time I saw someone shot, I lost my goddamn mind. It took Virus a week to talk me off the ledge."

"True that," Virus called out from the dinette.

She felt a smile tug at the edges of her lips. The light moment made her feel better. She pushed her forearms against Aleksei's chest. The hug had gone on too long. She didn't want him to think she'd forgiven him.

"Not yet," he whispered, his breath tickling her ear. "I need to apologize for the way I acted yesterday. I am so sorry."

She wanted to push harder. She wanted to tell him to take his apology and shove it, but she also wanted to hear what he had to say. Her heart was still bleeding. She wanted to know if any part of their relationship had been genuine or whether it was all just an act.

"You were beautiful yesterday, standing there at the stove. That was my first thought. That you were so fucking beautiful. Every part of you. Inside and out. With or without hair. You were so incredibly brave and open that it scared me. I panicked. I'll regret walking out of that cabin, the way I did, for the rest of my life."

More beautiful words. His lilting cadence was hypnotic. An image of herself as a bird being drawn into the mouth of a Phrygian dragon with eyes the exact storm-gray as Aleksei's flitted through her mind—but she would not be afraid of words. She would decide what she believed. She would decide how to react. They were going to be stuck together for a while. It would be good to clear the air between them.

"What were you scared of?" she asked.

"My feelings for you. I was afraid of disappointing you. I was afraid of losing you. I'm still afraid. For the past two years, I've been ruled by fear. I thought I was controlling it, but it was controlling me. I pushed everyone away because I was afraid of losing them, afraid of failing them, like I failed Phillipe. You stood there gloriously bare, trusting me to accept you, silently asking me to join you in living life like there's no tomorrow—and instead of grabbing the amazing gift you were offering, I ran. I ran because I was afraid of what losing you would do to me. If I never had you, I would never feel the pain of that loss." His voice cracked. "I was so stupid. I wish I could turn back time, walk into that cabin, and make love to you on the kitchen floor. I don't want to live in fear anymore. I want you. Can you forgive me? Will you give me another chance?"

Fear. She knew all about fear. She'd been afraid most of her life. He was right. When fear sank its claws in, it did control you. It had controlled her for years, and like him, she hadn't recognized it. Death, or the specter of death, had a way of doing that. It wasn't until her last bout with cancer that she'd realized how small her world had become, how much fear had stolen from her. That was when she decided to fight back.

Her skin felt tight. She'd been angry at Aleksei for lying to her, but he had been doing his job. Could she be so sure she wouldn't have done the same thing if it were her best friend who'd been murdered? And how could she judge him for his fear when hers had been just as potent? Him walking out of that cabin had shredded her soul, but knowing his actions sprang from fear softened the ragged edges of the wound.

Since she'd met Aleksei, she'd felt more alive than she ever had.

When she'd finally beaten cancer, she'd rejected fear, promising herself to live life to the fullest. There was something about this man that sang to her soul. Giving him another chance meant risking having her heart crushed again, but giving up on him would be climbing back into the safe, protected cocoon where she'd spent most of her life.

And she'd vowed she was never going back there again.

She curled her arms around him, pulling him closer. "No more lies. No more omissions. No more hesitation. If you're not willing to give me one hundred percent, then let's not do this again."

His gentle hand trailed up her arm and over her shoulder, cradling her face. His calloused thumb stroked her cheek, wiping away some of her tears. She relaxed into him, letting herself savor the heat of his body. Being back in his arms felt like coming home.

His breath warmed her temple as he spoke. "I want to do this. I need to do this. No more lies. No more omissions. No more hesitation. If you want one hundred percent, I'll give you one hundred fifty. I am so sorry. I don't want to lose you. I know we can build something amazing together."

She believed him. This thing between them was honest and true. He'd lied, but that was in the past. Things had been hard and were probably going to get harder, but the best things weren't gained easily.

Aleksei was worth the time and effort.

"I think we can build something amazing together, too," she whispered into his flannel shirt, its fuzz soft against her mouth.

His lips touched her forehead first, warm, firm, and comforting, and then brushed against her eyes with a gentleness that felt like reverence. He kissed her nose in a playful peck and then grazed the edge of her lips in teasing promise. The gentle hand that had caressed her face dropped to the side of her neck. When he finally kissed her mouth, the energy between them crackled.

His tongue thrust her lips apart, and met her own tongue, darting and swirling. His exploration bordered on the edge of plunder, igniting her senses. She leaned closer, relishing the sensation of his muscled chest against her breasts. He shifted his hips, and his hard length pressed against her stomach. The hand that had remained on her back dropped to her ass, squeezing while his hips rolled against her. Fire shot to her core.

This was what living life to the fullest should feel like.

"Still here," a rumbling voice invaded the haze that had overtaken her senses.

Shit! Virus was still at the table waiting for them, and she and Aleksei were acting like teenagers after prom.

Aleksei ended the kiss with one last soft touch of his lips to hers. He raised his right hand in the air, middle finger extended toward Virus. "You never give an inch, do you?"

"I gave you lovebirds ten full minutes. It was getting so hot in here, I was starting to sweat. Plus, we have work to do. I need Rosemary to look at this."

Aleksei stepped away with an exaggerated sigh.

She didn't want to leave the sweet escape of his arms, but avoiding their situation wasn't going to make it better. She walked to the table and sat back down in her chair, uncomfortable with the sight of Virus at her work computer. It probably violated every rule in the employee handbook, but Pannetone & Associates didn't exist anymore, and she was way out of her depth. If Virus accessing her computer would help figure out who had murdered her colleagues, it was the right thing to do.

"What do you need me to look at?" she asked.

Virus angled the laptop toward her as Aleksei hovered behind them.

"Is this what normally happens when you log in?" Virus asked. "This spreadsheet just automatically loaded."

She studied the document. There were only twenty-two lines of data, but her scalp instantly began sweating. Columns listed various Moresco projects, invoice numbers, dates, amounts, payees, and methods of payment. She immediately recognized the elevator invoices for the Girard and Penrose projects, as well as the suspicious duplicate sprinkler and lighting invoices she and Armando had identified. She wasn't familiar with the project names or information for the other listed invoices, but they totaled close to fifteen million dollars and had all been paid within the past five years.

"What is this?" Aleksei asked as she scrolled.

She shook her head quickly, brushing him off, as she absorbed the data. She clicked around, pulling up the document details. Pannetone & Associates' system automatically labeled documents with a number and the initials of the document creator. Each had a section for notes, which they often used to list information a team member didn't want to include in the body of the document, but that would be helpful if another person needed to work on the file.

The notes section read: "If anything happens to me, get this laptop to my grandfather."

The document author's initials were DMB.

Dante Moresco Bianchi.

An image of Dante sitting on the couch in Armando's office, working away at his computer, flashed through her mind. He'd told them he hadn't found any other anomalies.

"He must have lied."

"Who?" Aleksei and Virus asked in unison.

She ignored them and clicked on the yellow file folder icon at the bottom of her screen, pulling up the local drive. She found a folder labeled Moresco and opened it. There were hundreds of nested folders with project names. Her heart stuttered. She scratched around the edges of her wig with her left hand while her right hand clicked on folders and documents. Every document she clicked on grayed out immediately after she opened it, and a password box popped up. She couldn't see any specific data, but based on the file organization and names, she was fairly certain what was on the laptop.

"I think this computer has every file, document, and invoice for every Moresco project. If I'm right, there are years of data here. I think the initial spreadsheet that popped up is a list of the fraudulent invoices Dante was able to identify before I left for vacation. Unfortunately, that seems to be the only document I can access. All the others require a password."

"So, all these files aren't normally on your computer?" Aleksei asked.

She shook her head, her mind still reeling over the cache of information on the laptop. "Pannetone treated the Moresco files like Fort Knox. I had very limited access, but this isn't my normal laptop. It's a loaner. Dante said he needed to update my computer and gave me this one to use while I was away. I don't normally bring a computer on vacation, but he pressed it on me as I was leaving." She lifted her head. "It's almost like he knew something bad might happen to the server and wanted a backup. Do you think he suspected Armando was involved?"

"Since Dante is part of the Moresco family, maybe he was the one who planted the bomb. Maybe the Morescos were done with Pannetone & Associates, and this was their way of severing all evidence and still retaining the business records they needed. We won't know until we have more info," Aleksei said. "What I can tell you is, the FBI would have a field day with those files. The Morescos are involved in just about every illegal activity you could think of. Gambling, extortion, drugs, prostitution, money laundering. You name it, they do it. Set the geek squad on that laptop, let them follow the money, and they could probably find enough dirt to put Salvatore Moresco away for the rest of his life."

Her stomach felt like she'd just ridden a roller coaster with too many loops. There was no way Dante had hurt innocent people. "Do you think Sal's behind it all? Do you think he could have done this?"

Virus made a sound of disgust. "If the Morescos would kill a cop, they certainly wouldn't hesitate to take out a bunch of accountants. Let's just hope they don't find you here. You survived. You have what they need. They're going to be coming for you."

Chapter Twenty-One

Virus had always been a man of few words, and when he did speak, he usually cut right to the heart of the matter. Aleksei took Rosemary's wide eyes, ghost-pale face, and rushed breath as hard proof that Virus's approach wasn't always best. If she didn't slow her breathing, she was going to pass out, and he might just have to kick Virus's ass.

He rested a hand on her shoulder, her weathered sweatshirt soft and fuzzy under his fingers. He pressed firmly, hoping the weight of his palm would ground her. He took a few slow, audible breaths. Thank God she latched onto their connection and matched her breathing to his. Her shoulders slackened, and he imagined he could feel her heartbeat slow to beat in time with his.

She laid a pale hand over his. "I'm okay. Really. I'm just not used to people wanting me dead."

He shot Virus a death glare, which resulted in a sheepish shrug and a mumbled apology. His sweet Rose brushed it off as unnecessary. In his view, it was most definitely necessary.

Satisfied with the pace of her breathing and the pink that had returned to her cheeks, he removed his hand from her shoulder and began walking the length of the room. The feel of the hard floor under his pacing feet organized his erratic thoughts.

"Tell me more about Dante," he said.

"He is, or maybe was, the IT guy for Pannetone & Associates. Like I said, he's Sal's nephew. He's young, sweet, and a little quirky. I can't imagine him hurting anyone." She waved toward the screen. "There's a comment in the spreadsheet notes. It says he wants me to give the laptop to his grandfather. It's so bizarre. He told me his grandfather lives in Italy. I wouldn't have a clue how to find him."

"He'll probably find you," Virus commented. "Especially if his grandson died in that explosion."

Aleksei shot him a second death glare, and Virus lifted both his hands in surrender. "Got it. No more keeping it real."

"If the Morescos wanted to cut ties with Pannetone and destroy all the records at the office, I don't understand why Dante wouldn't transfer the records to his own laptop or back them up somewhere," Rosemary said.

Virus inverted his lips.

"Spit it out." Aleksei said. "Just no more murder and doom and gloom."

"Grandpa's paranoid about cybersecurity, so there's no way Dante can email or do anything that might put the Moresco files in a hackable domain. The Morescos are mafia, which means they have to assume they're always being watched. Maybe they thought it was safter to use you to get the records out of the office. No one is watching you."

Except the CI who told Kemper he'd been hired by Moresco to follow Rosemary.

Aleksei kept pacing, unease inching up his spine with every step. "It doesn't make sense."

"What doesn't make sense?" Rosemary asked.

"Legal or illegal, businesses need records, and the mafia is just like any other business. They need a firm grasp of income and expenses so they can track profit and make sure no one's stealing from them. That's why they use accountants. They always have and always will. They need those records."

"So, it seems a little far-fetched that Moresco would destroy the server and leave the only copy of the records with me," Rose said.

"Maybe Moresco was the one stealing," Virus offered. "Doesn't he have to report up to his dad? Maybe he wanted more than the percentage the old man was letting him keep?"

"Maybe," he said, but it didn't sit right. "What's the total amount of the invoices on that spreadsheet?"

Rosemary looked down at the computer screen. He liked watching her work. Even in pajama bottoms and a sweatshirt, she looked intelligent and efficient.

"Almost fifteen million."

"And what's the date of the earliest invoice?"

"About five years ago."

"That's right around the time the bureau started focusing on the Morescos. I wasn't involved then. The surveillance and background team gathered intel for about eighteen months before Phillipe and I went under." Aleksei paused for a moment. It was still so fucking hard to say Phillipe's name out loud. "Sal's grandfather, Lorenzo, moved to Italy about six months before that. He stepped back so his son could take the reins. Sal is the functioning head of the family. I hate the guy, but I just don't see him faking invoices. Yeah, the honor payments to Lorenzo are a percentage of the profits, but the percentage is so small that faking invoices to inflate expenses so the profit looks lower and they pay less in honor payments seems like a lot of work for what's probably a few hundred thousand dollars."

"It's not worth it to risk betraying his father for that," Virus said.

Aleksei agreed.

"Maybe Armando was embezzling money and the Morescos found out. And then they thought they had to get rid of the server and eliminate all the people who knew the details of their business, so Dante sent the laptop with me on vacation to preserve the records,"

Rose suggested, and then scrunched her pretty pink lips and shook her head, rejecting her own theory.

"If the Morescos really do need their records, it's too big of a risk to throw them on a laptop and assume they'd be safe with me. I could've spilled coffee on the laptop or accidentally dropped it into the lake, or found the spreadsheet, gotten suspicious, and called the cops. It would make more sense to leave the server alone and just address the Armando issue."

She'd just voiced the same theory he'd been tossing around in his own mind, and she rejected it for the same reasons he had.

"Like I said, it doesn't make sense. Giving you that laptop doesn't feel planned to me. I think it was a spontaneous decision."

Weeeoooo. Weeeoooo. Weeeoooo.

A three-toned siren emanated from speakers in the ceiling. Virus stiffened and spun his head toward the wall of screens.

A black Ford Bronco was climbing the hill toward the same chain link fence Aleksei had used his fingerprint to open last night. Virus shifted from the table to the chair in front of the counter. His fingers flew over buttons on a keyboard, and one of the screens zoomed in on the driver's face.

"Any idea who that is?" Virus asked.

Gary fucking Kemper.

He'd known Kemper would find him eventually. But this was quicker than he expected. If Gary had found them so easily, Moresco might not be far behind, and if Gary had made the trip all the way out here, the pile of shit they were in had likely gotten a hell of a lot deeper. He needed to know how Kemper had found them and what other fucknado had struck to bring him here.

"Let him in."

* * *

Special Agent in Charge Gary Kemper seemed uncomfortable in the old armchair next to the wood-burning stove. Rosemary had a hunch that Virus had intentionally placed him there and then turned up the heat. Literally. She found Virus's living area on the main floor cozy and inviting with its woven rugs, mismatched furniture, and curtains that featured moose and trees, but Agent Kemper was sweating.

Of course, the fact that Virus was sitting on the edge of a rocking chair, glowering while cleaning a wicked-looking rifle he'd set on a tray table in front of him, could also be the source of Agent Kemper's perspiration. The man looked stiff, hot, and itchy. She'd been there too many times to count. Sympathy gnawed at her stomach, but neither Aleksei nor Virus appeared concerned. Instead, they both seemed irritated by his presence. She was the only one happy to see Agent Kemper.

Gary. He kept telling her to call him Gary. She needed to remember that...and happy wasn't really the right word for her current emotional state. She was more relieved. Gary had brought news that Sal knew she had the laptop and wanted it back. He hadn't gotten into the details yet, but she considered it progress. She hated the idea of sitting around waiting for something bad to happen.

"How did you find me?" Aleksei asked.

Snuggled next to each other on the couch, she and Aleksei fit together like a lock and key. Being tucked in tightly next to him with his arm heavy around her shoulders filled her with a soothing, slow warming, hot-tea-on-a-brisk-fall-morning feeling. She could stay here forever.

"It wasn't hard," Gary answered. "The field team finally got in touch with Rosemary's sister. She told them Rosemary was camping at Ricketts Glen State Park. I figured that's where you'd called me from, so I pulled up Google Maps, skimmed around, and saw Trout Run. I remembered you and Phillipe talking about a hunting trip here to visit one of your buddies from the Marines. I put some tech guys on finding the names of your unit members and cross-checking them with the real estate records in Trout Run. I had the address in an hour."

Aleksei's body tensed against her side, but his tone remained cool. "I'm surprised you didn't come with a SWAT team. I thought I was the prime suspect."

"That changed when Sage told the investigators Salvatore Moresco called her, demanding to know where Rosemary was and threatening bodily harm if Rosemary didn't return the laptop to him at one of his warehouses by midnight tonight. Sage said he was emphatic on the deadline and that Rosemary come alone."

Every bit of warmth leached from Rosemary's body. The quick summary Gary provided when he arrived was that Moresco wanted the laptop returned. He hadn't said anything about Sal calling her sister. He hadn't said anything about Sage being in danger. She had to keep her sister safe. She wouldn't survive if anything happened to Sage. Especially if it was her fault. Sage had given everything to take care of her. Everything. Sage had saved her life. Rosemary was not going to let anyone hurt her sister.

"You have to protect her." Her voice was a croak, as if her vocal cords had fallen victim to the glacier slowly overtaking her body.

"She and her fiancé are already in protective custody," Agent Kemper responded.

"And Christian?"

"He's safe."

"Can I talk to my sister?" The need to hear her sister's voice, to have audible proof of her safety, was as primal as the need to breathe.

"I'm sorry," Gary answered. "That would compromise their safety."

Of course. That made sense.

"What about Davis?"

"There's a team at your stepfather's house. We won't let anything happen to your family," Gary assured her.

But something had already happened. Sage had been threatened, and her family had been forced into hiding. They wouldn't be safe unless Rosemary returned the laptop. She would do it. In person.

Alone. By the deadline. Just like Moresco wanted. She didn't care about the risks. She would die protecting her family if she had to.

"What aren't you telling us?" Aleksei asked.

How did Aleksei know there was more?

"He said they would know if the files had been accessed, transmitted, or copied."

"Shit. Shit. Shit."

Kemper nodded. "That about sums it up. The bureau sent me to get Rosemary and the laptop. The plan is to copy all the data and, hopefully, find something to base an arrest warrant on so they can send a SWAT team in to pick up Moresco before the deadline."

Aleksei leapt up from the couch. "If they do that, Rose will never be safe."

Goose bumps rose on every piece of skin where Aleksei's body had touched hers. If she wouldn't be safe, her family wouldn't be safe either.

"I'm not giving my computer to the FBI. I'm not putting my family at risk," she said.

Gary sighed and shifted his chair a few inches away from the stove. His features were handsome, but he looked weathered and beaten down, as if he'd carried too heavy a burden for far too long.

"I'm not asking you to. I've had a bad feeling about this from the get-go. I had the same feeling with the first Moresco op, and one of my best men ended up dead. The tech guys are good, but there's no guarantee they'll get into those files or that Moresco won't know they accessed them. I want to nail Moresco, but I'm not going to risk you or your family. I already have too much blood on my hands." Gary mopped sweat from his brow with a tissue. "I'm not asking you to give the computer to the FBI. I want you to give it to me. I'll take it to Moresco for you."

She rose from the couch, her limbs stiff and shaky. Her family had sacrificed their entire lives for her. Her mother had made her health the focus of her life—attending every appointment, holding her head while she'd vomited from chemo, scrubbing the house and wearing a mask, and staying in an unhappy marriage for financial support. Sage had foregone dating. Sage skipped parties, dances, and weekend trips to stay home with her to watch movies and play board games. Her sister had stripped to pay their bills after Davis abandoned them. Sage had gotten her the experimental drug that had saved her life.

Now it was Rosemary's chance to rescue her family. Her turn to be the strong one. Her turn to do what had to be done to protect her sister, no matter the cost. She wasn't going to let anyone else suffer or take risks for her. Not Sage. Not Virus. Not Aleksei. Not Kemper.

This was something she had to do herself.

"I appreciate your offer, but I won't risk you or anyone else getting hurt. I'm going to take the laptop to Moresco myself, and I'm going to do it alone."

Chapter Twenty-Two

Aleksei could not believe what he was hearing. Rosemary had just said she was taking the laptop to Moresco herself, and Kemper was offering to give her a ride, all nice and easy, as if she needed a lift to the goddamn grocery store. As if she wouldn't be walking into a room full of criminals who likely wanted her dead. That laptop was the only leverage they had, and Rose's brilliant plan was to walk into the warehouse and hand it over like a deer trotting into a hunter's cabin.

"You are not fucking serious."

The words flew out of his mouth unedited. He might have chided Virus earlier for being too direct, but this was not the time to temper his words. This was a shit idea, and he was going to let Rose know it.

Her lovely pink lips pressed into a straight line. "I am absolutely serious."

"You really expect me to let you go in there alone?"

Her eyes flashed. "I expect you to respect my decisions. I'm a grown, capable woman, and this is *my* family at risk."

"Being grown and capable is irrelevant. You're way out of your league here. These are dangerous men. You don't have a weapon, and you don't know how to fight. You're walking into a deathtrap. You don't have the expertise or training to deal with a situation like this. Kemper should know that. If he doesn't have the sense to keep you out of there, then I will." He squeezed the bridge of his nose, trying to make his tone reasonable. "If you go in there alone, there's no way I can keep you safe. I won't be able to forgive myself if something happens to you."

"You can't always keep everyone you care about safe," she responded.

"I wouldn't have to worry about keeping you safe if you weren't being irrational."

Thor and Jaka's barks emanated from the bedroom where he had shut them in when Kemper arrived. They didn't like the raised voices. He called out to settle them.

Kemper stood, lifting a hand in a calming gesture. "This isn't my first rodeo. I've got a team on call. I'll wait until we're close and then let them know Rosemary insisted on taking the laptop in herself. We'll cover her entrance and exit. If we hear anything, we'll rush the place."

Aleksei snorted. He'd already assumed Kemper would have a team on the ground to swoop in if the shit hit the fan, but that could be too late.

"She could be dead by then," he said, intentionally trying to shock Rose into seeing reason.

"It's her family. Her life. Her choice," Kemper responded.

He studied Rose. Her skin was blanched white, her eyes were glossy, and whether she knew it or not, she was shaking. He reached out and ran a finger down her soft cheek.

"Let's compromise. I'll go in with you. That way you won't be by yourself. If shit goes sideways, I'll be there to help."

She leaned away from his touch. "I have to do this alone."

The rubber band that had been holding his temper in check snapped. He leapt to his feet.

"You're acting like a fool! You spent half your life relying on other people to care for you, so now you think you have something to prove.

You're so hell-bent on standing on your own that you're being foolish. You think an offer of help is an insult, and that accepting help is weakness, but it's the exact opposite. Your stubborn insistence on doing this alone is going to get you killed, and I'm not going to stand outside that warehouse and do nothing while it happens! I'm not losing another person I care about on my watch. Phillipe went in alone and look where it got him."

He was yelling, the dogs were howling, and he didn't fucking care.

"Guess what, Aleksei? Not everything is about Phillipe! You've spent the last two years wallowing in guilt because you can't accept that you're not responsible for another man's choices. You want to come with me because you want to avenge Phillipe. I'm not risking my family so you can assuage your guilt. Preventing me from saving my family isn't going to bring him back. It's only going to rip us apart. So, which one of us is the fool?"

She was right. Phillipe had made his own choices. He'd chosen to go out alone that night. He'd chosen not to wake Aleksei. Phillipe hadn't wanted his help and, apparently, Rose didn't want it either. Her rejection felt like a hot knife pressed to his skin.

He'd opened his shuttered heart for her. He'd said he wanted a relationship with her. By offering a future together, he'd taken a step he'd sworn to himself he would never take again. He'd taken responsibility for her. She knew about Phillipe. How could she not see that, if anything happened to her on his watch, it would destroy him?

He couldn't survive having his failure result in the death of another person he loved.

His jaw ticked, and his fists clenched. Her choice was betrayal. Just like Phillipe's had been. If Aleksei stayed in this room one more second, he was going to say something he would regret. Something that might irreparably damage their budding relationship. He snatched one of the burner phones he'd pulled out from Virus's cache that morning from the coffee table and strode out the cabin door.

He kept walking until a bead of sweat trickled down his back. A chilly breeze nipped at his cheeks, but the late afternoon sun and his brisk pace were keeping him warm even though he hadn't grabbed a jacket. He'd thought the walk would calm him down, but his temper was still blazing. Rose was being selfish and unreasonable. He had no fucking clue how to convince her that walking into that warehouse alone was a huge mistake. He pulled the phone out of his back pocket and did what he had done every time he'd been at a complete and utter loss.

He called his mom.

He veered off the dirt road onto one of the narrow walking trails, taking his time telling her the complicated story while robins whistled, blue jays cawed, and stones and twigs crunched under his feet. Her murmured *hmms* and *go on* assured him she was following. When he got to the end, he'd convinced himself that not only should Rose not be going into the warehouse alone, but that she shouldn't be going at all. If she truly cared for him, she'd stay at Virus's cabin and let him go for her. He had the skill set and training. He was probably the only one who had a chance to get in and out alive.

"She thinks you want to go to the warehouse with her because you want to be the one to arrest Moresco?" his mom asked.

"I didn't ask for that," Aleksei said. "I'm willing to give Moresco his goddamn records back and walk away. If I never avenge Phillipe, so be it. I'd give up pursuing Moresco to protect her, but she isn't willing to stay back here where it's safe. If she cared about me, she wouldn't risk her life when she knows I can't protect her. She wouldn't ask me to watch her walk into that warehouse to meet the man who killed Phillipe."

"Ahhh. So, we finally get to the root of it."

Her tone rankled him. He'd called for sympathy and affirmation. She should be telling him to do everything in his power to protect Rosemary, even if that meant locking her in a room until he worked their way out of the fucknado they'd been sucked into. And then she should be reassuring him that Rose would still want him after he did it. That Rose would realize he'd been right all along.

Instead, he was getting the patronizing condescension she'd used on him when he was a headstrong teenager.

"The root of what? She won't listen to me. If she goes to meet Moresco, she'll be walking, innocent and unarmed, into a roomful of criminals. If something happens to her, I'll never forgive myself."

"Just like you'll never forgive yourself for what happened to Phillipe. You're just like your father." His mother's last few words were laced with the same wistfulness she always had when she talked about his dad.

That was exactly why he didn't want Rosemary putting herself in danger. They'd only known each other a short time, but she already felt like a part of him. He couldn't imagine a future without her. He was in love with her.

He was in love with her.

The seeds had been planted that first night when she'd danced down the concrete steps, eyes twinkling, bell-like laughter filling the air. Deep conversation, laughter, and an effortless, bone-deep intimacy were the fertile soil and rain that fed them. Love had bloomed. She had opened parts of him he thought he'd shut down forever.

And now he was bare. If he lost her, there would be no barrier to protect him from the pain.

"I want to be like Dad. I want to save Rose just like Dad saved you."

His mother sighed softly. "Saving me was the easy part. The hard part for him was forgiving himself. His guilt almost ruined us."

His father was the knight in shining armor who fought dragons and rescued the princess. He had nothing to feel guilty about.

"What are you talking about? Dad was a hero."

His mother's silence was too long, and Aleksei stopped walking. He was about to learn something he didn't want to hear.

"You know the story. The police were investigating a gambling ring. Instead, they found human trafficking. Your dad wanted to get me out the first day he met me, but I insisted on staying. I wanted those bastards to pay for what they did to us. I wanted to make sure the DA had an airtight case. I wanted to make sure the police knew every location where women were being held. It took almost two weeks. Those two weeks were...difficult."

Acid burned the back of his throat. His mother didn't need to spell it out. He'd never been assigned to the sex crimes unit, but he knew what human trafficking entailed. He'd just never thought it through when it came to his mom. Or maybe he hadn't wanted to know the dark side of the fairy tale.

"You were sexually assaulted."

His mom's voice was brisk. "I was. Multiple times. I didn't tell your father about it until after we'd been dating for a while. He was angry, so very angry, and he felt like he'd failed me. He grew overprotective. He didn't want me taking my law school classes because he was worried about me walking to my car at night. He felt so helpless that he almost quit the force, and to be honest, I almost quit him. He couldn't get past my tragedy, and I wasn't willing to let it sit on my shoulders my entire life."

His parents had always seemed blissfully happy. He couldn't imagine them splitting up.

"What happened?"

"I reminded him that I was the victim, and that bringing the people who had preyed upon so many innocent women to justice was something I needed to do and would do all over again, regardless of the consequences. I convinced him that respecting me meant respecting my choices, even if he didn't agree with them. You're right. Your father was a hero, but not because he always kept me safe. He was a hero because he realized that, in his fear, he was trying to take away my volition. He was a hero because he went to therapy, worked through his guilt, accepted my choices, and chose to continue in law enforcement, knowing that things weren't always going to work out exactly as he wanted every time."

He heard her message loud and clear.

Loving someone didn't mean always protecting them or keeping them safe. It meant supporting them even when it was difficult. It meant respecting Rose's decision. It meant accepting Phillipe's decision to go out alone that night. It meant letting go of the guilt he'd been carrying every day for the past two years so it didn't destroy his chance at happiness with the woman he loved.

Shit. Why did his mother always have to be right?

He retraced his steps back to the cabin at a run. He was going to go to Philadelphia with Rose. He was going to give her the one hundred fifty percent commitment and support he'd promised. He'd wrangle a sniper rifle from Virus and plant his ass at the best vantage point he could find. Watching her walk into that warehouse by herself was going to be the hardest thing he'd ever done, but he'd do it for her.

But when he got back to the cabin, Rose and Kemper were gone.

* * *

It was nearly 9:30 p.m. by the time they reached the deserted industrial area where the warehouse was located. They were close to the airport. The car shook every few minutes as planes buzzed by. A spring wind blew a few wrappers, chip bags, and other trash to join the water bottles, beer cans, broken glass, and car parts that lay on the sides of the road.

"How much farther?" she asked.

The long car ride had been spent mostly in silence. Rosemary didn't feel like talking. Her mind warred with itself, rehashing that horrible argument with Aleksei and second-guessing her decision. The choice had seemed so clear at Virus's cabin, but a sense of unease tapped at her ribs as soon as she entered the car. The tapping had slowly increased to a steady thrum.

Gary slowed and made a quick right, pulling behind a large dark building. Most of the lights in the parking area were broken, creating an eerie darkness full of black holes and shadows.

He faced her. "I'm sorry. You seem like a nice woman."

Sorry?

"Sorry for what?"

"Give me the laptop."

She clutched her backpack like a security blanket, the disquiet in her chest a frantic drumbeat. "We decided this already. I need to be the one to return it to Sal. I need to convince him that I haven't done anything wrong. I need to make sure my family will be safe."

He sighed and pulled a gun from the holster on his chest, aiming it toward her. "Don't make this harder than it has to be."

Fear slithered through her veins. Gary had agreed to her demand to take the laptop to Moresco herself so easily, almost too easily, and he'd hustled her into the car right after Aleksei had stormed out of the cabin. She'd assumed he was helping her avoid further argument, that he was rushing so they would have time to meet with his on-site team before she met with Moresco. Have time to plan her entry. Time for the FBI to do everything they could to keep her safe.

Had Gary just wanted to get her away from Aleksei? They'd been in the car together for hours, and he hadn't made one phone call. Wouldn't he need to be coordinating with his team?

Her stomach dropped the way it had when she'd ridden the Double Shot at the beach for the very first time last summer. She and Sage had held hands as long as they could and screamed like teenagers. That stomach drop was terrifying joy. This one was simply terror.

"You're working for Moresco."

"You're a smart woman. Too smart, and too curious for your own good."

Her scalp started to itch. "What do you mean?"

"Lily's been slipping extra invoices into the Moresco files for the past five years, and nobody noticed until you came along."

It didn't make sense. Why would Sal ask Gary to give Lily fake invoices to put in the file? And how the hell did Kemper even know Lily?

Five years.

Images of Lily's tear-stained face in the stairwell filled her mind. Lily had been waiting for her married boyfriend to leave his wife for five years.

"You're Lily's boyfriend."

A genuine smile wiped away Kemper's haggard expression. He looked handsome. Trustworthy.

"I really do love that woman. She tipped me off as soon as she realized you were messing around in the Moresco files. Our plan was perfect. The office explosion would destroy all the evidence, and the bomb at Aleksei's apartment would make him look like the perp. Everyone knows he hates Moresco. Moresco would be dead, Aleksei would take the fall, and I, broken by it all, would retire to Borneo, where Lily would join me a few months later."

Gary wasn't helping Sal. He was stealing from him.

"You were the one embezzling the money. You're the one who planted the bombs."

Kemper nodded, relaxing his arm a bit so the gun pointed toward her abdomen instead of her chest. She needed to keep him talking while she figured out how to get out of this.

"Don't you have a family?" she asked.

Her family was everything to her. She couldn't imagine heading to Asia and never coming back.

"My wife and I divorced a few months ago. The house is sold, and she got a one-time payout. Of course, she doesn't know about the money I have squirreled away in a foreign bank account."

There wouldn't be any record of it. Pannetone paid most of the invoices via wire. The funds would go from a Moresco account to some foreign account that may or may not even be in Kemper's real name. It was brilliant.

"What about your kids?"

"I barely know them. This job is long hours, tons of travel, and shit pay. I started selling tips to Moresco to help pay for college. I betrayed the FBI, my wife handed me divorce papers, and the kids all took her side. It's the bureau's fault. I gave them everything and got shit in return. I deserved more, so I created a situation where I got more. It's the American way."

Murder was not the American way.

"What happened to your perfect plan?" she asked.

"Dante never showed up. Moresco went out for espresso, and you went on an unannounced vacation."

Ice seeped into her bones. They'd wanted her to die in the explosion. Her, Dante, and Sal.

"Lily saw the Moresco kid give you the laptop, but she didn't think anything of it. After the explosion, when we realized you weren't in the office, she panicked. She knew you, Pannetone, and the Moresco kid were concerned about some type of fraud. She'd seen Dante leave for the night empty-handed"—he waved the gun toward the backpack on Rosemary's lap—"so she thought there might be something incriminating on that laptop."

Gary had orchestrated the whole thing.

"Does Sal even know about the laptop?" she asked.

"I have no fucking clue."

"So why bring me here? Why not kill me up in Trout Run or somewhere along the way?"

He rolled his eyes. "Too many loose ends. I arranged to meet Moresco tonight at his warehouse"—Gary flicked his gun toward the back of his car—"over there. I've got another bomb in the trunk. I shoot you, put your body near the warehouse, and then blow that. When they investigate, they'll assume Moresco killed you and Aleksei planted the bomb. He was always so goddamn sure that Moresco was responsible for Phillipe's murder. Everyone will assume it was revenge."

Her bones turned so cold she felt like they would crack.

"What do you mean 'assumed'? Didn't Moresco's men murder Phillipe?"

Gary didn't answer, and her blood dropped to the same frigid temperature as her bones.

"Did you kill him? Did you kill Phillipe?"

Gary hesitated and then shrugged. "He found out. I have no fucking clue how he figured it out, but he did. Not all the details, but enough. He knew I was in with Moresco. He knew I was seeing Lily." He snorted. "He was so fucking naïve. He actually thought I would turn myself in."

Fire mixed with the ice that had taken over her body. "You killed one of your own men, and you're setting up another to go to prison. Everything was a lie. Sal never threatened my sister. My family was never in danger."

"I needed to get you away from Aleksei."

She'd made it easy for him. She'd let her need to prove that she could stand on her own go too far. After she was declared cancer-free, she'd thrown herself into the job Davis found for her so she could show him she didn't need his financial support. Insisted her sister move out of their shared apartment so she could prove she could live alone. Declined invitations from friends because she didn't want to be around people who remembered what she was like when she was sick. Looked wistfully at signs for hiking clubs but refused to join because she wanted to prove she could do it on her own.

Her living life to the fullest motto was a façade. She'd been so proud of herself for being self-sufficient and free, but she'd actually trapped herself in an invisible prison of her own making. She'd been so worried about not being a burden on anyone that she'd missed opportunities for new relationships and adventure. Her need to prove her independence had led her to refuse Aleksei's help tonight.

Aleksei was right. She was way out of her league. She didn't have the expertise or training to deal with a situation like this. Her stubborn insistence on doing this alone was going to get her killed.

Realization hit her like a frying pan to the head. She'd made a terrible mistake. She had nothing to prove. She hadn't been a burden on her family. She had simply been loved.

In loving Aleksei, she'd wanted to do everything in her power to keep him safe but hadn't respected his need to do the same for her. In maintaining her autonomy, she'd taken away his. Just like her desire to keep Aleksei away from this shitshow stemmed from love, his anger at her walking into it may have been love, too.

Maybe he loved her. Maybe he didn't, but she was certain that she loved him. Hopefully, she didn't die before she got the chance to tell him.

Either way, she wasn't going down without a fight.

She faked a coughing fit, slipping her arms through the straps of the backpack and pushing the unlock button on the door. Then she used the only weapon she had.

She pulled off her long blonde wig, threw it over Kemper's face, opened the door, and ran.

Chapter Twenty-Three

Aleksei's hands shook as he flipped through Phillipe's old notebook. He'd gone back to it because he had no place else to turn. He didn't know where Kemper was taking Rosemary, and he had no one to ask. Kemper wasn't answering his phone, and he'd let the other friendships he had within the FBI fade after Phillipe's passing.

Now he had no one close enough to be willing to put their job on the line and share the details of a covert op. Especially not when he might still be on the suspect list.

And Virus was no fucking help. He was hanging out in his goddamn rocking chair, cleaning his fucking gun like all was right with the world.

Aleksei's frustration popped like a pressure cooker bomb. "Why the hell did you let her go?"

Virus arched an eyebrow. "Are you really asking me that question?"

Aleksei's fingers pressed so hard into the notebook that the page started to rip. "Yes! Don't you see Rose is putting herself right in the line of fire? Why didn't you stop her? I thought you liked her."

Virus put the gun down on the tray table with a hard *thunk*, then began slowly massaging his left knee. After a few minutes of silence, he spoke.

"Let me see. She has evidence some mafia dickhead wants. If said dickhead doesn't get it, he's going to hurt Rose or her family. Kemper has a stick up his ass, but at least he offered her a solution other than keeping her head in the sand and hoping it all works the fuck out. He kept it real with her, gave her a choice, and respected her decision. He's putting his job on the line for her, and he's going to have an entire unit ready to bust in if things go south. If you were so goddamned worried, you should have kept your temper—and your ego—in check and gone with her. At least then you could've busted in with them."

Shit. There wasn't one fucking thing he could say to that. Everything Virus said was something he already knew.

"I'm frustrated."

"If you want someone to blame, look in the fucking mirror."

Classic Virus. He was never one to mince words.

Aleksei rubbed a hand over his head. His close-cropped hair prickled his palm. "Yeah. I know. I'm sorry."

He was sorry. So fucking sorry he'd let his anger get the better of him. So fucking sorry he'd walked out. Of course, Rose went with Kemper. If it were his sister, he would have done the same goddamn thing.

He straightened his shoulders and turned his attention back to the notebook in his hand. He couldn't change the past. All he could do now was focus on the only shred of hope he had—the notebook. If he were somehow able to figure out where Rose was going and get to her, there might be something in the notebook that could be a bargaining chip—information Rose could take in with her to use as leverage.

Or maybe he was bullshitting himself. Maybe he'd gone back to the notebook because he'd fucked things up beyond recognition. He was lost and alone and needed his best friend. Holding the notebook was comfort, but like every other time he'd looked at it, it yielded no clues.

The thing was exasperating. It was part diary, part planner, part sketchbook—a mishmash of doodles, sports scores, reminders, addresses, inspirational quotes, books to read, a few recipes, and even Christmas gift ideas for Samantha. He'd pored over it before, reading and rereading it in the months following Phillipe's death, but he hadn't found the answers he was looking for. He hadn't found anything that explained why Phillipe would go out for an unplanned meet, alone, in the middle of the night.

There was a reason Phillipe had left the notebook on the table that night. There was something Phillipe wanted him to see. Something Phillipe wanted him to know. He was sure of it. But whatever it was continued to elude him.

He threw the notebook across the room. "Damn you, Phillipe. Damn you. Damn you. Damn you. Why the hell aren't you here when I need you?"

The notebook bounced off the wall and flopped to the floor, the well-worn spine lying flat, the hot air from the woodstove flipping the pages.

"You all right there, friend?" Virus asked.

"Yeah, I'm all right," Aleksei said, distracted. His eyes fixated on the slowly turning pages. The scent of myrrh filled the air. A chill raced down his back. It smelled just like that fancy English cologne Phillipe used to wear.

An odd sensation tickled his spine, and the aroma grew stronger. Magic tingled in his veins.

Phillipe was here with him.

He crossed the room, the floorboards creaking under his feet, and carefully plucked the notebook from where it had fallen. The cardboard cover was smooth in his hand and warm from the heat of the stove. A large printed Gandhi quote spanned both pages:

THE LAW OF KARMA IS INEXORABLE AND IMPOSSIBLE OF EVASION. THERE IS THUS HARDLY ANY NEED FOR GOD TO INTERFERE. HE LAID DOWN THE LAW AND, AS IT WERE, RETIRED.

He'd concentrated on that quote so many times before, trying to divine its meaning—even considered whether it was a coded message—but this time, with the waning sunlight flowing through the window, the words blurred, and his attention was drawn to the tiny sketches at the corners of the pages.

Phillipe's sketches were always precise and lifelike. Although small, these were no different. The drawing on the bottom left was of a beautiful arched window. The one on the right showed two men in business suits.

One man was tall, with slicked-back hair and an outstretched hand that offered a stack of cash. His posture exuded authority and condescension. The other, shorter man lazed against a wall with an air of bored indifference. He had one arm extended, as if reaching for the money. A cigarette hung between two fingers of his other hand, a thin line of smoke floating up into the lined white pages.

Recognition hit like a sucker punch.

It was Kemper and Moresco.

Phillipe had no reason to draw them together. Kemper had never met Moresco in person. He'd only seen him on surveillance tapes. Or so he'd said.

It could be an imagined scene, but any time Aleksei had seen him sketch, Phillipe had drawn something right in front of him—their server, a dog, a building they were staking out. That meant there was a good chance Phillipe had actually seen them together.

Kemper and Moresco. Together.

Son of a bitch.

He ran a finger over the image of the arched window, trying not to vomit. At the point of the arch, there was a hammer crossed by a saw and encircled by leaves. He knew that window. There were three of them over the front door of the building where Phillipe was murdered.

The sketch of the window and the sketch of the men were on opposite pages, but his instincts told him they were connected. Did the payoff happen in front of that building? He knew Phillipe. Phillipe always looked for the best in everybody. If Phillipe saw Kemper take money from Moresco, he would have confronted Kemper about it face-to-face. He would have given him a chance to explain.

And what would Kemper have done in response?

The smoky, earthy scent of myrrh tickled his nostrils again. He lifted his head. Virus sat in the rocking chair, head down, focused on cleaning his rifle. No candles were lit. No incense was burning. Aleksei ran his finger over the drawing of the arched window, letting his mind wander back to that terrible morning, allowing the images of Phillipe's dead body to settle in his mind instead of pushing them away as he had in the past.

Phillipe was face down, parts of his skull shattered by the close-range gunshot. Dried blood spattered and pooled on the walkway near his head and the stubs of his hands. Then the medical examiner had flipped him over. Aleksei saw Phillipe's wide, glossy eyes and the grayish-black smudges that dirtied his face and speckled the front of his white shirt. That night, his only thought was that he wanted to wipe those marks away, that Phillipe shouldn't have dirt on his face.

He mentally zoomed out to take in the entire scene. Cigarette ashes littered the ground. Now, he saw those smudges for what they really were. Ashes. Ashes on the ground weren't surprising, especially in a warehouse in a blue-collar part of town, but something about the scene didn't sit right with him.

Puddles.

There had been puddles on parts of the walkway, too. The fluorescent crime scene lights glinted off the wet grass. Ashes littered the walk, as if someone had smoked while pacing.

It clicked.

If the ashes were old, the rain would have washed them away. The ashes were fresh, and there were a lot of them. But no butts. Someone had smoked multiple cigarettes while waiting for Phillipe but hadn't left one single cigarette butt—someone smart and cool-headed enough to think about DNA evidence in the face of murder.

He flipped the pages of the notebook, studying the drawings on each page, looking at them as if they were one complete picture instead of random, disjointed doodles. He found a few other sketches of Kemper—one with Moresco and others with a woman who looked vaguely familiar, but he couldn't place her. It didn't matter. Her identity wasn't the priority. If Kemper was on Moresco's payroll, Rose was in even more danger than he'd thought, and he couldn't think of one friend he had in the bureau who would believe him.

It doesn't have to be my friend!

He may not have a friend in the FBI who was close enough to call, but *Rose* did. She had Christian. When she'd called him, Christian had put his job on the line, skulking around FBI files to get her the information she wanted, no questions asked. If Christian thought Rose was in danger, he'd likely do anything to help her.

As he flipped more pages, Aleksei thanked the gods of preparation and paranoia. Before they'd trashed her phone, he'd told Rose to copy down all the phone numbers she might need. Neither of them had paper, so they'd written them down in the back of Phillipe's godsend of a notebook.

Rose said Christian was a cyber whiz. Hopefully, he could access Kemper's files and figure out where the hell Kemper was taking Rosemary.

* * *

Gunshots exploded behind her. The sounds were almost deafening. A streak of white-hot pain seared her arm. Rosemary stumbled but kept running. A car door slammed, and an engine revved. In front of her was a sea of blacktop. To the left, a concrete curb and a field of grass filled with a line of craggy trees separated the parking lot she was in from the one for the group of buildings next door.

She cut left, aiming for the trees, her arm burning and her knees shaking. The moon had not risen, so it was hard to see. She tripped over the curb, onto the strip of greenery, and then ran face-first into a chain link fence.

The force of the hit rattled the fence and her lungs, but she ignored the sensation. She was used to ignoring pain. She was used to pushing through. Her fingers gripped cold metal, and her hiking boots found purchase on the chain links. She climbed, tuning out the sound of the approaching engine.

If Gary got there before she made it over the fence, she was a dead woman.

Her strong arms pulled her up despite the fiery throbbing that ran from her wrist to her shoulder. She threw one leg over the top and jumped just as the Ford Bronco crashed through the fence and into a tree. She landed hard, twisting her ankle. She risked a glance over her shoulder. Smoke billowed from the hood of the SUV, creating an eerie fog in the headlights.

Shutting out her sore ankle, she scrambled to her feet and ran.

She stuck to the shadows, heading in the direction Kemper had indicated Moresco's warehouse was located, being as quiet as she could despite the agony in her ankle and arm. She jogged around the edges of two parking lots and climbed another fence, her lungs aching from stress, constant motion, and the weight of the backpack. Finally, she came to a warehouse where light emanated from the narrow windows above the loading bays. At the end of the building, two large men stood on either side of a door illuminated by an overhead light. They both held weapons similar to the one she'd seen Virus holding.

It looked like she'd found Moresco's warehouse.

She glanced behind her. Darkness. She heard no footsteps, but Kemper could close in on her at any minute.

It was now or never.

She raised her hands, her injured arm screaming at the motion, and walked into the light. "My name is Rosemary Cashman. I'm an accountant. I worked for Armando Pannetone. I need to see Mr. Moresco. It's an emergency."

She'd never been frisked before, but she didn't flinch as rough hands groped her, ostensibly searching for weapons. She'd seen so many doctors that she was used to strangers touching her body. She tried to object when one of the men—Nico, if she could trust what the other called him—took her backpack from her, but he ignored her protests. He opened the door and waved her forward. His partner remained outside.

The sound of the heavy door slamming behind her sent her already erratic heartbeat skittering. This was a terrible idea. Maybe she should have kept running and tried to make her way out of the industrial park. Maybe she could have found a Good Samaritan to take her to a police station.

Or maybe Kemper would have found her and shot her.

At least with Moresco, she had a chance of getting out of this alive.

But she started second-guessing that assumption as soon as Nico pushed open the door that separated the small foyer they'd entered from the main warehouse. Floor-to-ceiling shelves filled with pallet after pallet of boxed TVs, computers, video games, high-end mixers, and loads of other stuff took up most of the building. She'd feel like she was in Costco if it weren't for the six empty poker tables, bar, and improvised lounge that occupied a small portion of the warehouse.

Costco didn't have an opulent sitting area with jewel-toned couches, chairs with plush pillows, and exquisite tables decorated with candles and fresh flowers. It also didn't have numerous oversized men holding automatic weapons.

Salvatore Moresco's icy, accusatory gaze also ratcheted down the happy shopping vibe.

Nico dropped her backpack on the ground. A man with a leashed German shepherd approached. The dog sniffed the backpack for a minute, then pulled away. A second man approached and waved a metal wand over the bag. The wand's slow beeping didn't change. Moresco nodded, and Nico picked up the backpack, set it on the closest poker table, and pulled out the laptop.

Shit like this did not happen in real life.

Moresco lifted both hands, palms up, and raised one bushy eyebrow. "So, Ms. Cashman, what are you doing here?"

The sound of his voice was like a thousand tiny spiders crawling under her skin. She could see the evil in his near-black eyes. She'd sensed a darkness in him during their first meeting, but it had been muted. Now, the force of it staggered her. She'd miscalculated.

She would have been better off running.

Get your shit together. You're imagining things.

She pointed to the bag, trying to keep her hand from shaking. "I think that laptop has your business records on it. The files are password-protected, so I can't be sure, but I could see the names of the files, so I think they're there. Dante gave me the laptop when I left for vacation. I know the servers were destroyed in the explosion. I thought you'd want it back."

Moresco stepped toward her, and she had to look up to meet his gaze. He was trying to intimidate her, trying to make her feel small and inconsequential. It was working, but she wasn't going to give him the satisfaction of showing she was afraid. She stood her ground, allowing him to encroach on her personal space.

"How did you know where to find me?"

This was the meat of it. She was here to bargain, and by running his mouth, Kemper had given her a better bargaining chip than the business records. He'd made her a pawn in his game, so now she had no choice but to play.

"Agent Kemper brought me here." She lifted her bleeding arm. "He shot me, but I managed to get away. He's been embezzling from you for years. The records on the laptop will prove it. Kemper found out that I told Armando and Dante about some accounting anomalies and was afraid you'd discover what he'd been doing. He's the one who planted the bomb at Pannetone & Associates. He tried to cover up the embezzlement by destroying the servers and"—she swallowed—"murdering all those innocent people. But he didn't count on you stepping out for espresso and Dante giving me the laptop."

Moresco's sallow cheeks flushed, and his lips pressed into a thin line. "Where is Kemper?"

Her palms were sweating. Her armpits were soaked. She fought to keep the nervous quiver out of her voice as she pointed in the direction of the smashed fence and smoking car.

"He wrecked his car chasing me. The last time I saw him, he was in a parking lot over that way. I ran and didn't look back."

Moresco jerked his head toward two burly men with dead eyes. "Find Kemper. Dispose of him."

Despite the chill in the warehouse, perspiration continued to trickle down her lower back. Habit made her squeeze her hands into fists so she wouldn't scratch her head, but she realized that, for the first time in months, her scalp was cool and comfortable. Not that it was any consolation. Moresco had just given his men a not-so-veiled order to kill an FBI agent. She hadn't considered that Moresco would kill Kemper. If Kemper hadn't gotten his ass out of here, his blood would be on her hands...and since Sal had issued the order in front of her, she likely wasn't long for this world either.

Hot tears pricked her eyes. The Fates really were fickle. When her doctors told her that her cancer had returned for a third time, she'd examined her life, said her apologies, asked for forgiveness where it was needed, and prepared her soul. But then, a miracle happened: Remiza healed her. She let go of death and embraced life.

Now, she was going to die in a desolate industrial park without saying goodbye to her sister, without setting things right with Aleksei, and with the responsibility of putting Kemper's life in danger clouding her karma.

Moresco stepped away from her, the air around her sweeter in his absence. He picked up a martini from the bar and took a sip, sighing with pleasure. He waved an elegant, tan hand toward Nico.

"Thank you for the laptop, Rosemary. Now, be a good girl and go with Nico. He's going to take you for a walk. You're a bit pale. You look like you need some fresh air."

She opened her mouth to protest, but her tongue was too dry to form words. All she could do was wrap her arms around herself to try to quell the tremors coursing through her body as Nico's hot, beefy hand settled on her back and shoved her toward the door.

This was going to be the last walk of her life.

She was going to die with her last words to Aleksei having been angry and harsh. She was going to die without telling him she loved him.

Chapter Twenty-Four

Cold air rushed over Rosemary's hot face as Nico pushed the warehouse door open.

"Where the hell is Frankie?" he muttered, the fishy smell of his breath assaulting her nostrils.

Whoosh.

Something whizzed past her ear.

Nico grunted, gripped his neck where a dart protruded, and toppled with a mushy whomp, like a felled tree in the forest. Adrenaline flooded her already overstimulated body, making her lightheaded. She glanced right and then left but couldn't see anything beyond the small sporadic lights affixed to the warehouse.

Run. Run.

But her body was frozen, the proverbial deer in headlights. A dark figure appeared in the shadows. She managed a few steps backward, her fingertips grazing the knob of the door she'd just come through. Which was safer? Staying out here alone with Kemper or facing the sinister mob inside?

"Rose!"

Her name floated on the breeze as the figure moved closer with swift, agile grace. Her knees weakened.

Aleksei!

She rushed forward, flinging herself into the safe heat of his embrace, relishing the strong arms crushing her against his muscular chest.

"I'm so sorry. I'm so sorry." Warm breath caressed her neck as he repeated the words.

"I'm sorry too. I shouldn't have cut you out. I shouldn't have left without you. I should have let you help me."

Firm lips grazed her forehead and cheeks. "I shouldn't have gotten angry. I was so intent on keeping you safe that I didn't respect your choices. I was wrong. Love isn't control, even when it's well-intentioned. Love is letting people make their own decisions, even when it's hard."

"You were right," she admitted. "I didn't want to be weak. I wanted to be strong enough to do this alone, but what you said is the truth. Accepting help when you need it is strength, not weakness."

Warmth seeped into her bones. They'd both been wrong, but everything was going to be all right. A wry laugh shot up her throat. "I just wish I figured that out before Kemper tried to kill me."

He laid calloused palms on either side of her face. "And I should have figured out that I loved you before I almost lost you."

She felt weightless, as if his hands on her face were the only things keeping her from floating away.

"Did you say that you love me?"

He lowered his head, and her eyes shuttered in anticipation of his kiss. Firm lips brushed against hers as he said, "I love you, my lovely, bright, precious Rose. I love you."

Her chest was so full, it might burst. This fierce man who'd been shattered by his best friend's death was willing to trust her with his heart.

She followed his lead, letting her own lips move against his. "I love you too."

His tongue invaded her mouth. His hands roamed her back and ass, rubbing and kneading. Her breasts were crushed against his hard chest. Her head spun.

And then he stepped back, chilly air filling the gap between them. The sound of their heaving breaths danced on the breeze. He grasped her hands in his strong, rough fingers.

"We've got to get out of here. It's not safe."

His words cut through the blissful haze. He was right. They needed to go. There would be plenty of time for kisses later.

Before they could take a step, the sound of revving engines assaulted her ears. Headlights blinded her as cars screeched into the lot, halting directly in front of them. She lifted her free hand over her eyes to block some of the glare. Bulky men in dark suits spilled out of two large black SUVs. Goose bumps pricked her skin. They looked way too much like Moresco's henchmen for her comfort. Aleksei tugged at her hand, trying to pull her behind him, but she stood her ground. She had already been seen. There was no point cowering behind him.

One of the men pulled open the back door of the second car, and a tall, thin, silver-haired man emerged, carrying a cane. The man's sharp, accented voice cut through the heavy silence that had settled over the parking lot.

"*Voi pirla*! Turn off those lights. You are blinding *la ragazza*!"

One of the men reached into the car and clicked off the headlights, but her eyes still retained bright, shimmery halos of light. Another car door slammed, and a stocky man in joggers, high-tops, and an Eagles jacket bounced around the car to join the older man.

For the second time in minutes, joy flooded her body. If they lived through this, it would take weeks for her adrenal system to recover from the pendulum swings.

"Dante!" she called, dashing forward to embrace him. His body was thick with muscle, and he smelled like sandalwood. "I'm so glad you're all right."

A throat cleared behind her. She turned to find more guns than she could count pointed toward her, and an amused smile on the older man's face.

He waved an arm toward his guards. "*Voi pirla!* Put down the guns. You will scare the life from *la ragazza*!"

He waved again. This time toward Aleksei, who was being held back by two of the overfed giants. "Let the boy come, but take his weapons first."

Dante's bulky hand gave her shoulder a reassuring squeeze. "Rosemary, this is Don Lorenzo Moresco, my grandfather," he offered, his voice warm with affection.

She shifted her gaze away from the guards who were disarming Aleksei and focused on Dante's grandfather. Don Lorenzo Moresco was an aged version of Sal, a mirror image of his son, just older, thinner, more wrinkled, and silver-haired—except for his eyes. Where Sal's eyes were hard pebbles of arrogant disdain, Don Moresco's were gentler, suggesting wisdom tempered by compassion.

Her mother always said you could read a soul through a person's eyes. She hoped her mother was right, and that the kindness in Don Moresco's eyes would extend to Aleksei and her.

Having been released by the guards, Aleksei sidled next to her, circling a steady arm around her waist and pulling her close. Dante positioned himself on her other side. She was sandwiched between one man who loved her and another who respected her enough to trust her with his family's secrets. Despite the dark parking lot and the guns, she felt safe. Just like she'd always felt with her mother and sister.

It felt good to have people to lean on. This caring was what she'd given up by trying too hard to prove her independence. If she and Aleksei got through tonight safe and sound, she was letting go of her guilt. She was going to accept the support of her friends and family. She was going to accept Aleksei's love and work on building something special together.

"Let's go inside and sit while you tell me what's happening," Don Moresco said. "I am old. I do not like to stand in the cold." A large gold ring glinted in the light as he raised a graceful hand toward her. "My grandson says you are a smart woman, but you do not have the good sense to wear a hat. You must be cold as well."

A hat? No one else was wearing a hat, but now that he'd put the idea in her mind, her head actually did feel chilly.

Aleksei's arm tightened around her. "She doesn't need a hat. She's a warrior. Her scalp is a badge of honor. She has every right to show it if she wants to."

Her scalp is a badge of honor. She has every right to show it. She slowly lifted a hand to her head and felt nothing but cool, smooth skin.

Her wig was gone.

She was standing completely bare in front of all these people.

Of course her wig was gone. She'd thrown it at Kemper. She'd been bald since the moment she ran from that car. Every person she'd come in contact with since then had seen her bald head. Frankie and Niko. Sal and his posse of muscle. Now Dante, Don Moresco, and their guards. The world hadn't ended. She was still standing. Standing with a friend on one side and the arm of the man she loved around her.

Aleksei.

She'd been bald and bare in front of Aleksei this whole time, and he hadn't said a thing. He'd held her. He'd told her he loved her. He'd kissed her so fiercely, her mind had blanked on the danger they were in. He hadn't seen weakness or sickness. He's seen only her.

She dropped her hand from her head, straightened her spine, and pushed her shoulders back. There was nothing to be embarrassed about. Like Aleksei said, she was a warrior. It was time to start acting like it.

"I don't think your son wants to see me," she said to Don Moresco. "I think he wants me dead."

The old man's eyes turned to polished granite, and she saw a glimpse of what had made Lorenzo Moresco the don.

"You will be safe. My son will do as I say."

Don Moresco's voice was strong and sharp as a blade.

She believed him.

* * *

Sitting on a luxurious couch in the middle of a warehouse surrounded by armed mafioso and stolen goods was not the way Aleksei thought he would spend the night, but Don Moresco had been true to his word so far. Rose was safe, at least for the moment, and tucked at his side. It was the most he could ask for, considering the FUBAR the day and night had been.

If he and Rose got through this, he would have to tell his mother she was right. The Romani luck she always said he was blessed with had come through in spades.

Christian had answered on the first ring and readily agreed to help, throwing stealth—and likely his job—to the wind by hacking into Kemper's personnel file, pulling Kemper's phone info, and then feeding him Kemper's location. He and Virus had found Kemper's abandoned, crashed car and then located the only warehouse with lights on. He'd incapacitated the guard at the door and left Virus in the bushes, covering the warehouse while Aleksei circled the building. He'd come around just in time to see that asshole push Rose out the door. Virus had made a perfect shot with that tranquilizer dart.

He glanced over to where Salvatore Moresco and Don Moresco were in deep discussion at a poker table. Dante sat on the other side of the table behind Rose's laptop and a shitload of other computer equipment he'd hauled in. The tension in the warehouse was thick as morning fog.

Don Moresco's arrival appeared to be unexpected. Sal looked like he was going to have an aneurysm, and his men were restless. Aleksei could hear snippets of whispered conversations about what it meant. He eyed the door, hoping Virus had the sense to keep his ass outside for the time being. At this point, a puff of wind might start a gunfight.

"Rosemary, please come here," Don Moresco called.

Aleksei rose with her, gripping her smaller, pale hand in his own. She gave him an encouraging smile that didn't quite reach her eyes. He slid his palm around her neck and pressed his lips to the cool skin of her forehead.

"I'm here."

That was all he could say. That was all he could be. He would be there for her. Like he had been there for Phillipe. He would offer love and support, but it was up to Rose to choose which paths she walked alone and which paths she asked him to join her on. Just like it had been Phillipe's choice. Love was letting people make their own choices and respecting them.

"Come with me," she said, and his heart soared. They would face Lorenzo and Salvatore Moresco together.

"Tell me. Was my son really going to kill you?" Don Moresco asked after they were seated at the poker table

Sal's olive skin looked more green than tan.

Rosemary flinched. Aleksei squeezed her fingers reassuringly. If only he could get her out of this place and away from the evil in the room. She was too good to be here.

"I...I don't know. He didn't use those words. He told Nico to take me for a walk."

He hated the quiver in her voice. Hated that the only comfort he could provide was the connection of their joined hands.

"And what about this FBI agent? This Phillipe Forcheaux. Was my son involved in his death?"

Phillipe. Aleksei was sitting at a table with the man who'd been responsible for his best friend's death, yet he didn't feel the overwhelming rage that had consumed the past two years of his life. The pain was less now, more subtle. It was the ache of a healing wound rather than an open one.

Yes, he hated Salvatore Moresco. Yes, he wanted him to pay for what he'd done, but loving Rose had shifted something inside him. Living had become more important than revenge. The future had become more important than the past. Love had become more important than hate.

"I don't think so," Rose said. "Kemper told me he did it. Kemper killed Phillipe because Phillipe found out he was taking bribes from your son. Phillipe confronted him, and Kemper killed him."

Rose's answer felt like a too-low jump when you know your chute will be late, no matter how fast you pull it. The words hit with the force of gravity and hard ground.

Kemper had murdered Phillipe. Kemper had betrayed the badge and his own man. The idea had skimmed across Aleksei's mind when he saw those sketches in the notebook, but it hadn't seemed possible. Kemper had joined them for beers dozens of times. He'd spoken at Phillipe's funeral. He'd held Samantha while she sobbed in his arms.

It was so much worse than Moresco. So, so, so much worse.

Smooth hands squeezed his fingers and rubbed his arm. A warm, soft body pushed into his side, offering strength and comfort. The need to lean into the solace Rose was offering was basic and primal. His wounds needed her soothing balm, needed her to fill the holes in his heart and soul, needed her to make him whole again.

But what would happen to those holes if he lost her?

His years with Phillipe flashed through his mind. Playing hangman and telling stupid jokes on long stakeouts. Arguing over who had the best cheesesteaks in Philly. Celebrating their softball league victories at McGillin's. Drowning their sorrows over their softball league losses, also at McGillin's. Holding Phillipe's newborn sons. Playing wiffleball with them at picnics. Hunting. Fishing. Eagles and Phillies games.

If he hadn't chosen Phillipe's friendship, he'd have missed out on every one of those perfect moments. If he didn't choose Rose's love, he'd miss out on perfect moments with her. He wanted to experience all the wonderful things he knew they could do together. He wanted to live. He wanted to love. He wanted Rose.

He rested his head on her shoulder and let her citrus ginger scent slide through him, softening the edges of his pain, replacing sorrow with hope.

Creak. Creak. Crackle.

He lifted his head. The noise was coming from the shelves of stolen goods.

Creak.

His ears zeroed in on the sound, and his eyes followed. A gun barrel slid between boxes, followed by a shadowed silhouette. Someone was hiding among the pallets. He followed the direction of the circular metal. The gun was pointed toward Don Moresco and his son.

"Get down!" he yelled, jumping out of his chair and pushing Rose toward the floor.

He leapt just as a series of soft pops and flashes came from the stacks of boxes. He stretched out his arms, and his body crashed into the chairs occupied by father and son. Hard concrete knocked the wind from his chest. Wood splinters poked his thigh. Soft flesh spared his head from slamming against the floor. He rolled, sucking air into his lungs, and found what he was looking for—the table legs. He yanked hard, flipping the heavy poker table.

Chaos erupted. Guns blasted. Men yelled. Furniture splintered. Bullets chipped wood. Cold metal pressed against his hand. He whirled his head. Don Moresco crouched behind him, shoving a gun into his hand. He checked the weapon automatically and then peered around the edge of the poker table, his gaze locking on the narrow space among the pallets where the tiny lights flashed.

He aimed and fired, emptied the weapon, and watched Gary Kemper fall to the ground.

Phillipe's murderer was dead.

His best friend could finally rest in peace.

Aleksei fell back against the carpet, letting adrenaline and relief claim him. Lying flat with his head angled, he had a perfect view of Kemper's motionless body. Blood leaked from his head and hands. The location of Kemper's injuries mirrored Phillipe's.

Gandhi was right. The law of karma was inexorable and impossible of evasion.

Gentle hands probed his body. He turned his head. Rose knelt next to him. Warm tears fell from her eyes and dripped onto his face. A table lamp glowed behind her, making her appear as if she had a halo. She looked like an angel. Her lips moved, but he couldn't hear what she was saying over the constant ringing in his ears.

"What?" His throat was dry, but he forced the word from his mouth.

She leaned closer. "Are you hurt? Please tell me you're okay."

He laid a palm over one of her scraped, injured hands, pulling it to his heart. "How could I be anything other than okay? I have you."

Don Moresco barked at the guards in Italian as they helped the don, Sal, and Dante to their feet. Footsteps thudded, and strong hands pulled Aleksei up. His lungs were still aching, but he stepped in front of the burly guard before he could touch Rose, giving her the opportunity to rise on her own. Father and son stood side by side, the don leaning on his cane, and Sal directing his gaze at the floor.

The don reached forward and rested a light hand on Aleksei's shoulder. "You saved our lives. I thank you. I ask that you leave the computer here with me and speak nothing of this night. If you do these things, you and Rosemary will have my protection, and there will be no more trouble from my family. You are free to go."

Aleksei nodded his assent and then glanced toward Kemper's dead body. If questions were raised, he would tell the truth. He wasn't sure if it was his gun or the guards' that had finally taken Kemper down, but all the bullets had been fired in self-defense. The only one to blame for Kemper's death was Kemper himself.

He pulled his gaze away. He was done dwelling on death and pain.

Instead, he let his eyes feast on Rose. Her white scalp gleamed in the harsh warehouse light. Her pants were ripped. Her face was dirty. Her eyes were red and puffy. Blood seeped through the arm of her sweatshirt. And he'd never seen anyone more beautiful. His woman was a fighter. He knew she would pour all that fierce dedication and resolve into loving him. Her gentle strength would carry them through good times and bad.

He took her skinned and bleeding hand in his own and led her out of the warehouse into the brisk, chilly night. The moon had risen, shining down upon them. They were both leaving their pasts behind to build a future of light and love together.

Epilogue

6 months later

The September sand was warm and grainy under Rosemary's bare feet. Hot tears stung her eyes as the lilting strains of a string quartet playing "Lost in Your Eyes" floated through the air. Only her sister would choose to walk down the aisle to Debbie Gibson.

Sage looked stunning. Her tanned skin glowed against the bright white sheath of her dress. Her maple-syrup brown hair hung nearly to her waist, with only a few strands pulled away from her face. Ryker stood tall and darkly handsome in a sea-glass blue suit, watching her sister approach as if she were the most amazing person to have ever walked the earth.

Rosemary sniffed and pressed a finger under her eye in an attempt to protect her makeup. Strong, calloused fingers slid a tissue into her hand, and she met Aleksei's gaze. He wasn't watching Sage or Ryker. He wasn't admiring the splendor of sunset on a Cape May beach or watching the dolphins frolicking off the coast in the white-capped waves.

He was looking at her. Looking at her with the same bright intensity she had just seen in Ryker's gaze. Looking at her with the same depth of emotion she'd seen in those storm-gray eyes the night they'd walked out of the Moresco warehouse, hand in hand. They'd been grateful to be alive, grateful to have the past behind them and their future ahead of them, and grateful for each other.

Aleksei shifted closer to her side, pressing a warm palm against the small of her back. Minty spice filled her nostrils. Her bones melted. They'd been together for months, but the smell of him still intoxicated her. His touch still took her breath away.

His breath tickled her ear. "You look absolutely radiant."

She didn't always feel beautiful, but she did feel beautiful today. She loved the Grecian-style bodice and flowing length of the maid of honor gown she and Sage had chosen together. It made her feel like a goddess. She ran a hand down the long, silky, rose-pink scarf that covered her head. She'd knotted the scarf at the side of her neck, creating the illusion of a long ponytail.

She'd debated wearing her wig, but late September had brought an 80-degree day, and she'd stopped choosing vanity over comfort the night she'd walked out of the Moresco warehouse completely bald in front of more than twenty men.

Her hair didn't define her. Her cancer didn't define her. The choices of her friends and family didn't define her. Even her relationship with Aleksei didn't define her. It had been a long road, but she'd finally come to understand that she defined herself.

She squeezed Aleksei's hand and leaned her head into his suit jacket, breathing him in. He slid his palm from her back to her waist, pulling her even closer. Aleksei may not define her, but being with him brought her incredible joy. She felt like she was living a dream.

She loved sharing her Philadelphia rowhouse with him—the four of them, Aleksei, Thor, Jaka, and her, all cozily settled together. They were building a life together. They traveled, hiked, camped, walked the dogs, went to museums, cafés, and bookstores, and explored Fairmount Park. They played board games with Sage and Ryker and visited Aleksei's mother and sister as often as they could. He'd started working for a friend's private security company, and she'd gotten another accounting job—one at a reputable firm with no secrets and no mafia connections.

They'd even set up a small remembrance table in a corner of the living room with pictures of her mom and dad, Aleksei's father, Phillipe, and her coworkers who'd lost their lives. It felt good to see those faces every day and reflect on the joy they'd brought to the world instead of focusing on the loss. Life was meant to be lived fully and celebrated.

Firm lips brushed against her temple. "Your love saved me."

She shook her head. "It was accepting love that saved us both."

His eyes twinkled. "Maybe we can sneak back to the hotel and accept each other's love between the ceremony and the reception."

She gave him a sexy smile.

That sounded perfect.

* * *

Thank you for reading! Did you enjoy? Please add your review because nothing helps an author more and encourages readers to take a chance on a book than a review.

Want to see what coming next from Elisabeth Caldwell? Then, read STRIP, available now. Turn the page for a sneak peek!

You can also sign up for the City Owl Press newsletter to receive notice of all book releases!

Sneak Peek of Strip

Sage Cashman wasn't afraid to perform. She'd been dancing for nineteen years. Granted, most of that time she hadn't been wearing a G-string and five-inch heels, but those things weren't responsible for the nausea swirling in her gut. She'd accepted them months ago. It was what was riding on this one shot, do-or-die audition at the Black Cat that was testing her nerves.

How was this the most important audition of her life?

Sage shoved the thought away. She was being melodramatic, and she despised drama. Her sister, Rosemary, might not even be sick. Her test results hadn't come back yet, so the job at the Black Cat would be insurance. An emergency backup plan. Just in case. Sage needed to work anyway, and the Black Cat was a step up from the Horny Toad. She would make better money here. Plus, bad luck or not, she'd rather have a black cat than a horny toad.

The booming sound system rattled her molars. The club was packed. She'd been lucky to find a seat at the shiny, lacquered walnut bar. She shifted, crossing and uncrossing her legs to relieve the numbing press of the wooden barstool. It was almost her time to dance, and she didn't want her legs falling asleep.

Sage signaled the bartender for a refill of her seltzer water. What she really wanted was a glass of Torrontés or a splash of Tito's in her club soda. Her limbs were stiff, like she'd been playing too long in the snow. Rigid and jerky wasn't sexy. She needed to loosen up. Pronto.

Unfortunately, alcohol wasn't an option. She couldn't afford to be off-balance, mentally or physically. Princes didn't come riding up on white horses to save the day. If you wanted something done right, it was always best to do it yourself.

The busty, strawberry-blonde, heavily freckled bartender topped off her seltzer water. "Are you here for auditions?"

"Yep. I think I'm up next."

The bartender braced her hands on the bar, pushing herself up and forward, peeking over the edge. "No purse, no alcohol, and good solid shoes. It's not your first time, is it?"

Sage slid a hand into the top of her black, strapless, skin-hugging, snakeskin-patterned dress and flashed her cash and fake ID at the bartender. "Nope. Not my first rodeo. I've been dancing at the Horny Toad the past few months. Working there, I learned quickly to keep anything valuable either on my body or locked in my locker."

"The Horny Toad?" The bartender chuckled. "Where do they come up with these names? I heard that place can be a little rough. It's actually pretty good here. Especially with the new owner." She angled her head toward the stage. "I hope they call you soon. That poor girl is struggling up there."

Sage glanced at the twentysomething teetering around the stage. Her lilac thong was the wrong shade for her pale skin, and that was all she was wearing. She'd taken off too much too fast and didn't know how to use her hands to cover herself, allowing only teasing sneak peeks of her breasts. Her shoes were an accident waiting to happen. Literally.

"Those heels are way too narrow for dancing," Sage said.

There was a reason character shoes had thick heels. Even the best performer could stumble dancing on toothpicks. Noreen, her first and only friend at the Horny Toad, had clued her in on the tricks of the trade, and "solid, stable shoes are worth their weight in gold" had been the first bit of advice she'd offered.

The girl attempted to swing around the pole but ended up tripping over her own feet. Sage winced. Pole dancing looked easy when someone else did it, but there were physics and a heck of a lot of strength involved—and not every pole was the same. Some were stationary. Some spun. Some fast. Some slow.

Noreen said stripper poles were like people. Each had its own peculiarities. The Horny Toad had three poles. One was slim, smooth, and fast; another was thick, strong, and steady; and the third was sticky, stubborn, and creaky. That's why she'd snuck into the Black Cat a few hours before opening and tipped the janitor fifty bucks to let her check out the club's poles. She hated variables.

The girl onstage turned her ankle on her spiked heel, sending her into a graceless spin. Luckily, she didn't fall.

Sage's gaze traveled down to her own open-toed, black, patent leather stilettos. The two-inch-diameter heels and platform soles provided the stability she needed to twist, turn, and slither across the stage, and men loved the royal-blue double straps at the ankle. Still, quality shoes couldn't prevent every mishap. Even seasoned dancers took a tumble from time to time.

Her teeth dug into her bottom lip. Falling flat on her face was not an option. Not tonight.

Sage took as deep a breath as she could muster. The Lycra dress shouldn't feel confining, but the urge to gulp air overwhelmed her. Her fingers itched to lower the front zipper that ran the length of the dress for some extra breathing room, but she didn't touch it. It might be amateur night onstage, but club employees were still working the floor. She'd come dressed to impress, and every stripper's eyes were already boring holes in her back. Exposing extra skin when she wasn't onstage or working the floor could make the other dancers think she was trying to steal their regulars. No need to make enemies the first night.

A few patrons close to the stage yelled "Next!" and "Time's up!" The shouts increased in number and volume as purple-thong girl continued to flounder. It sucked to figure out when you were onstage and nearly naked that you weren't as coordinated or sexy as you thought. The poor girl was probably desperate to get back to her table.

Mercifully, the song slowed and faded. Sage laid a twenty on the bar—Rule Number One: Never piss off the bartender—and scrunched her hands into her thick, almost-waist-length waves.

Showtime.

The spotlight circled a few times before settling on her back. The DJ's rich, baritone voice cut through the laughter and conversation. "Who wants sugar when you can have spice? Our next dancer is sure to be a savory treat! Please welcome Savory Sage!"

Slipping the DJ a C-note was definitely money well spent, even it if meant she'd be eating pasta for two weeks. This was the attention-grabbing intro she'd been hoping for.

Sage spun on the barstool, uncrossing and straightening her legs simultaneously, making a quick V in the air. She pushed up from the seat, thrusting her breasts forward and hanging her head back in a catlike arch, then straightened, shimmied her shoulders, and flashed a saucy smile.

The DJ started playing her song, and Sage strutted toward the stage, working the room. She tugged on ties, tickled necks with her hair, and leaned her cleavage toward lust-filled eyes, teasing patrons as she sashayed across the club floor.

She'd scoped out the expensive watches, designer jeans, and custom-made suits while she'd waited. She focused her attention on those wealthy customers, sending a message to management that she knew how the business worked and how money was made. The stage was just a prop in the game. The real cash came from lap dances, private booths, and private rooms. A successful dancer identified who had cash to spend and convinced those men to open their wallets.

The hallway she needed to pass through to access the stage was a few feet away. A tall man stood in the shadows. The reflection of the stage lights against his polished shoes caught her attention, and his sheer size and magnetism kept it. The cut of his suit was expensive, and his posture had the quiet alertness of a lion waiting for prey. She spun toward him.

The man lazed against the wall, arms crossed. His fitted suit was not nearly as slim as the ones her friend Justin wore. Justin was thin, elegant, and dapper, and his clothing accentuated those natural traits. This man's suit was more like a disguise. The material strained slightly at his shoulders and across the thickest part of his thighs. His stance screamed confidence and power. He was a broad-shouldered, thick-legged Viking warrior, hiding his true nature in business attire.

The stage could wait a few more seconds.

Sage shimmied closer to get a better look. His strong-boned face was partially obscured by the dim light, but she could make out black, wavy hair, a straight forehead, high cheekbones, and a square chin. A three-day shadow broke through his warm, bronze skin, like he'd just returned from a beach vacation. That stubble would probably feel incredible against her skin.

Heat rushed to her thighs.

She froze.

Physical attraction to customers was not part of the game. Physical attraction to men was not a part of her life. She was here for a purpose, not to be distracted by some dark, dangerous stranger, but the spotlight still shone on her back, and at this point, retreat would look awkward.

Play the part.

Sage leaned forward and ran long fingernails down the lapel of the Viking's suit jacket. She lifted her gaze and met two expressionless circles of glacial ice.

The Viking slid strong fingers around the back of her neck, calluses electrifying her skin. Warm breath touched her ear.

"Don't waste your time on me, sweetheart. You're not my type, and I'm not a pushover like the rest of the chumps in this place."

Her cheeks blazed. Humiliation she thought she'd put behind her in her first few weeks at the Horny Toad rushed back, mixing with rage.

Who was he to judge her?

Men were all the same. They spent wads of cash to leer at naked women, then condemned them for stripping. It was a ridiculous double standard. Her knee itched to slam up. Hard. That would knock that condescending look off his face—and get her kicked out of the club faster than she could say "You're an arrogant ass."

She needed this job. For Rosemary's sake. So she flicked her long, thick, bouncy hair, spun, then strutted toward the stage, taking deep breaths to calm her pounding heart.

Sage mounted the stage just as the music changed from the slow, sexy blues tune she'd used for her approach to AC/DC's "You Shook Me All Night Long." It was a fantastic song for stripping, fast-paced hard rock, dripping with innuendo. She took a few quick, graceful steps, then launched herself at the pole, spinning sinuously around it. She slid down, landing firmly on her wide heels, spread her legs and arched her back, gripping the pole with one hand and sliding along it suggestively.

She threw herself into the familiar, crowd-pleasing routine, letting it soothe her. Dancing always calmed her, so she let the music take over. She slid her hands over her body as she shimmied toward the front of the stage. She teased the crowd by rubbing the cool zipper of her dress in her warm fingers, tugging it down just an inch. The audience cheered. A few boisterous voices yelled "Take it off!"

This was the worst part. Baring her skin was too much like baring her soul, but she'd do what had to be done, just as she had for the past several months. Rosemary needed her. That was all that mattered.

Sage eased the zipper down until her dress loosened and slid past her hips, pooling around her feet. A step and kick sent the dress flying toward the back of the stage. The overhead vent poured cool air over her body. Dancing was hot, sweaty work, so the stage area was always air-conditioned no matter the time of year. Goosebumps formed, and her nipples instantly hardened from the cold, rubbing against the red silk bows that barely covered them.

More cheers exploded, and patrons pressed close to the stage, hanging over the raised edges. This particular collection of red strings and bows was always a crowd-pleaser. There must be something about red. It was probably good she couldn't afford red shoes. They might cause a riot.

She tugged teasingly at the edges of the bows as she shook her full breasts. Years of dieting hadn't put a dent in them. Thank God her mother had talked her out of having them reduced. Sage would probably only be pulling in a third of the cash if she'd had that surgery.

Despite her teasing tugs, the bows didn't budge. Nor would they.

She'd sewn them shut with her own two hands. She never removed her thong or fully exposed her nipples. Those tiny pieces of string protected a piece of herself, a small measure of independence and pride, that she refused to give up.

Initially, management at the Horny Toad had balked at her refusal to dance fully nude, but after a week, she was the most sought-after stripper in the club. There was no challenge in the blatant nudity of her coworkers, and men loved a challenge. Every guy thought he'd be the one to whom she'd show her secret flesh. That was the game. Making each man think he was special, even though none of them would ever win the prize.

The DJ turned the volume louder, and the booming base flowed into her body, demanding motion. She threw her head back, jogged three long, graceful steps, and leaped back onto the pole, gripping the unyielding metal with her thighs.

Madame Gursky was right. Ballet gave a body the strength to do almost anything, although she likely hadn't imagined Sage hanging upside down, mostly naked, as the end goal of her years of training. And Madame had been dead wrong about Sage's body. Her full breasts and curvy hips may have been "très horrible" for ballet, but at a strip club they left the audience with glassy eyes, open mouths, and most importantly, open wallets. Her body had kept a roof over their heads and food on the table and would get her this job and the introduction she needed to the club owner. There was nothing "très horrible" about that!

A professorial-looking, gray-haired gentleman held out a twenty-dollar bill, and Sage abandoned the pole for the green, leaning backward, sliding her hands to the ground, and executing a sharp back walkover. Another cheer erupted. Acrobatics in heels was another big crowd-pleaser. She glided to the edge of the stage and shimmied down to her hands and knees, pointing to the top edge of her garter belt. The professor tucked the bill in with a polite smile. When a floppy-haired, shy-faced boy who barely looked legal waved another twenty, Sage crawled toward him and gave the same nonverbal cues.

Clear instructions avoided hands going where they shouldn't.

A group of rowdy frat boys tossed some bills onto the stage to get her attention. Sage flipped, using her left arm to arch her body into a standing position. Two quick spins brought her face to face with the group. They were young, drunk, and cocky, just like some of the guys she'd been at school with last year.

Forcing herself to retain her saucy smile, Sage pushed the bills back toward the young men with the toe of her shoe while shaking her finger in a "no, no, no, you naughty boy" fashion. Throwing cash on the stage violated club rules.

She pointed a long, painted fingernail toward the rolled cash in her red-bowed garter belt. The men got the message, picked up their bills, and slid them into her garter while she shook her shoulders and breasts to the beat of the song. The bouncer who'd been battling his way through the patrons shot her a quick, grateful smile. The bouncers always appreciated a woman who could manage the crowd.

When the song ended, Sage scooped up her dress, gave a quick wave, and pranced off the stage. Her heart hammered, and it wasn't just from the exertion of the dance. Despite the deafening applause, her nerves wouldn't settle until she was sure she had the job.

Bryce, the club manager, was waiting for her at the bottom of the stairs. He was a tank of a man, tall and wide and all hard muscle. He was so large she could barely squeeze past him. He probably started as a bouncer, and a damn good one at that. Earlier that evening, she'd seen an obnoxious customer turn tail and retreat with only a cross-armed glare from Bryce. If she hadn't experienced his warm, friendly demeanor when she'd signed up to audition, he would've seemed imposing as hell.

She traded her fake smile for a real one and pointed a playful finger toward him. "I told you they'd love me!"

Bryce rubbed a massive hand over his bald head and chuckled, his bright white teeth flashing. "You were right. Can you start right away?"

"Sure. I can start tonight."

Bryce shook his head. "Not tonight. The owner has to approve your paperwork. I'll give you a schedule for the rest of the week tonight, then call you tomorrow after he signs off so you know you're good to go. Do you have any questions?"

She was accepting the job regardless of the terms, but each club had its own financial quirks, and she needed to understand the Black Cat's.

"Do you have a price list I can see?"

Bryce pulled a folded sheet of paper from the front pocket of his black dress pants and handed it to her.

Where did he shop? His clothes fit too well for a run-of-the-mill big and tall shop, but a strip club manager likely didn't make enough to pay for custom-made. She studied the price sheet, noting the charge for lap dances by song and by time, private booths, and private rooms.

"What's the stage fee?" she asked.

"No stage fee. At least, not now. The new owner got rid of it. House gets forty-five percent of the dances. You get the rest."

"The house only takes forty-five percent? That's a pretty good deal. What about tip-out?"

"Bouncers and DJ get a dollar a dance. The new guy wanted to get rid of that too, but I told him not to shake it up too much. Folks don't like too much change at once. Do you have ID? We do everything by the book now, so you'll have to fill out a W-4."

The rumor mill was right on this one. No working under the table at the Black Cat.

Sage felt around for the little pocket sewn into the top of the dress she now held in her hand, pulled out her friend Olivia Dupree's ID, and handed it over. "Sounds like this new owner runs a tight ship. When do I get to meet him?"

"I can't say. He keeps to himself." Bryce squinted at the driver's license. "Olivia Dupree? Why did the DJ call you Sage?"

Because I'm a moron and blurted out my real name when the DJ asked me.

"That's my stage name. Sage sounds a lot sexier than Olivia."

Bryce shined a flashlight on the hard, white card, and the hologram sparkled.

Sage held her breath. She and Olivia both had brown hair, blue eyes, and a petite nose, but the similarities ended there. Olivia's face was square while hers was oval, and Olivia's straight, shoulder-length hair was light brown, nothing like the long, thick, dark, unruly waves currently sticking to her perspiration-soaked back. Plus, Olivia had a good three inches on her.

Bryce handed her back the card and thrust out his right hand. "Welcome to the Black Cat."

Relief jellied her legs and shoulders. It was a good thing everybody looks like crap in their driver's license picture.

Sage accepted the handshake. Bryce's skin was warm and dry against her sweaty palm.

"Thanks for giving me a chance."

He flashed his teeth again. "You're a natural, kid."

Being a natural at stripping wasn't the compliment Bryce thought it was, but Sage chose not to comment. She had long since resigned herself to do whatever was necessary to help Rosemary.

Once the paperwork was complete and Sage was rattling down Columbus Boulevard in her ten-year-old, dinged-up Mazda 6, she fumbled open the glove compartment and traded Olivia's license for her own. Her taillight was out. Getting pulled over with a fake ID would be a crappy end to a pretty good night.

She stopped her car on the narrow South Philly street in front of the cozy rowhouse she and Rosemary rented. It was a steal at $1,200 a month. The kitchen was dated, but the paint was fresh and the carpets were clean. A year ago, she'd never have put up with the owner's refusal to provide a written lease and demand for cash-only payments. What would have once made her suspicious was now a blessing. Anything that helped them fly under the radar was a plus.

Sage hopped out of her car, threw the two neon-orange safety cones that had been reserving her parking spot into her trunk, then parallel parked. She rubbed her goose-bumped arms as she dashed up the cement stairs to her front door. The icy door handle numbed her already frozen fingers as she jiggled her key in the finicky lock. You never knew what you'd get in January in Philly. It could be fifty degrees one day and ten degrees the next. Tonight, the temperature was hovering in the twenties.

The heavy door creaked with her hard shove, and Sage rushed inside, grateful for the dry radiator heat that rushed over her. Rosemary sat on the couch, huddled in a blanket, watching TV.

"It's nearly midnight. Why aren't you in bed?" Sage asked.

"Why aren't you wearing a coat?" Rosemary snapped back.

Because I didn't want it to get stolen.

At the Horny Toad, she locked her coat in her locker. A locker wasn't an option during amateur night at the Black Cat.

"I forgot it. I was late for work."

Sage grabbed sweatpants, a sweatshirt, and white cotton panties from the basket of folded laundry on the floor and changed her clothes in the middle of the living room. The warm, soft cotton was heaven.

Rosemary lifted an eyebrow. "It's a good thing the blinds are closed. And you're a bad liar."

"Am not." Sage flopped onto the oversized, slip-covered couch next to her sister and tugged half the knit afghan over her legs.

Rosemary clicked off the TV. "Stop before you really make me mad. I know you're lying. You didn't go to work tonight. Justin told me you were auditioning at the Black Cat club. Why didn't you tell me? Why are you leaving the Horny Toad? You said you liked it there."

"Justin needs to learn to keep his mouth shut."

"No, Sage. You need to learn to open yours. I shouldn't have to rely on whisper down the lane from Justin to get information about my own sister. You should've told me about the audition yourself. You don't have to keep protecting me. If changing jobs is about money, I can go back to work." Rosemary's face turned wistful. "I liked working."

Sage's stomach twisted. She'd rather run a marathon through a briar patch than do any kind of math, but her sister had loved her job at the accounting firm.

"I know you miss your job. I hate that we have to live like this. I know it makes you unhappy. I'm not happy. I feel horrible about it. It's all my fault."

Rosemary huffed. "Explain to me how this is your fault."

"I should've said something to Mom about Davis. She was too sweet to see him for what he really is, but I knew he was a liar and a cheat. If I'd told her he was having an affair, maybe things would be different. Maybe she would have left him." Sage hesitated. "Maybe she'd still be alive."

"That's crazy talk! The earth calls us home when it's our time. It was Mom's time. There was nothing any of us could have done to stop it. And it's not your fault we're living like this. Davis is the one who kicked us out. He's the one who threatened and attacked you. He's the one who cut us off from what's rightfully ours. That is definitely not your fault!"

"Of course it is." Sage twisted the blanket with white-knuckled hands. "I should never have confronted him. I should have pretended everything was fine. I could have said it was too traumatizing to stay in the house. We could have moved out quietly, and he never would have known I went to the police."

"That's bull crap. The police would've questioned me at some point anyway. I'm the one who can't remember seeing him at the club. I'm the one who couldn't give him an alibi. Davis is just as angry with me as he is with you, probably more."

"I'm not so sure about that. It was my accusations that set him off."

Rosemary shivered and hugged herself. "Let's not talk about him. I don't even want to think about him. It's not worth our energy, and it's bad karma. We need to concentrate on what lies ahead. Now, tell me why you're leaving the Horny Toad."

Sage didn't buy the whole fate and karma thing, but Rosemary, despite her affinity for numbers, lived by it. In Sage's mind, thinking and talking about Davis wasn't going to make things any worse. They couldn't get much worse. Well, unless he found thembut that wouldn't happen. She'd made sure of it. They'd cut all ties, except Justin. Sage only had a few close friends, and since she'd lost her mom last year and her dad and brother, Thyme, when she was eight, there hadn't been that many ties to cut.

Snap. Snap.

Rosemary's snapping fingers filled her vision.

"Yoo-hoo! Earth to Sage."

"What?"

"I asked you to tell me why you're leaving the Horny Toad. Like I said, if we need more money, I can get a job."

Sage fought for patience. "We discussed this. You're not going back to work right now. We need to lay low until Davis gets arrested or we have enough money to move and start over."

"We could save money faster if I was working," Rosemary said. "I could find something local and under the table. I could waitress. There are tons of restaurants nearby."

"That's not an option. I'm not letting you work, not with your fevers coming back." Sage pressed her palm to her sister's face and forehead. "You have a fever now."

"It's just a virus."

"When you have *Doctor* in front of your name, you can self-diagnose. Until then, you'll stay home and rest until your test results come back."

"I'm sure they'll be negative. I feel fine. You worry too much."

Sage prayed her sister was right, because if Rosemary was sick again, in order to get her well, she might have to do more than strip.

* * *

Don't stop now. Keep reading with your copy of STRIP available now.

Don't miss more from Elisabeth Caldwell at elisabethcaldwell.com and discover STRIP available now!

* * *

A dark, intense romance filled with secrets and desire.

Sage Cashman will do anything to save her sister, even if it means dancing at a gritty gentleman's club every night. She plays the part of the irresistible seductress, but everything changes when Ryker Madsen, the dark, brooding billionaire owner, starts watching her from the shadows.

Ryker is arrogant, powerful, and determined to make Sage his. But when she learns he's involved with the company producing the experimental drug that could save her sister, Sage proposes a dangerous deal: *companionship for connections*. Ryker isn't interested in emotions, but he can't resist the fiery chemistry between them. As their relationship deepens, the secrets Sage is hiding start to unravel—threatening everything she's worked for.

With time running out and danger closing in, Sage must decide: can she trust Ryker with her heart—and the truth she's been keeping from him?

A sizzling enemies-to-lovers romance full of passion, betrayal, and unexpected twists.

* * *

Please sign up for the City Owl Press newsletter for chances to win special subscriber-only contests and giveaways as well as receiving information on upcoming releases and special excerpts.

All reviews are **welcome** and **appreciated**. Please consider leaving one on your favorite social media and book buying sites.

For books in the world of romance and speculative fiction that embody Innovation, Creativity, and Affordability, check out City Owl Press at www.cityowlpress.com.

Acknowledgments

To all the women who spoke so courageously to me about their experiences with cancer and hair loss—Thank you for your honesty and candor. Without your insight, I would not have been able to write this story. You are warriors! I hope you all are living your own happy ever after.

To my husband—Your support has allowed me to live my dream. Thank you for your constant encouragement. I love you!

To my children—Thanks for enduring the embarrassment of having a mother who writes romance novels and joking about it!

To Heather C.—Thank you for talking (and texting) all things bookish with me, for bringing light to the quiet days of a writer, and for always making me laugh. You proofread, listen to my plot issues, and agonize with me over cover art and chapter images (when you should be sleeping or doing your own work). Your friendship is a welcome constant in my life, and I am so grateful for it!

To the City Owl Editorial and Design Teams—Thank you for helping me bring another one of my stories to the world. You've polished my prose and given me a gorgeous cover. I truly appreciate each of you and all your hard work!

To NJRW—New Jersey Romance Writers is an incredible organization. Every one of you is a talented writer, but more importantly, a warm, welcoming, supportive colleague. My experience with NJRW gave me the skills and confidence to embark on my writing journey, and I will always be thankful for that. Special thanks to Shari for being my accountability buddy!

About the Author

Elisabeth Caldwell is an award-winning author of romantic suspense and contemporary romance novels. She grew up a Philly (and suburban Philly) girl with thick glasses and her nose buried in a book. When she was twelve-years old, she fell into the yellowed pages of one of her grandmother's Mary Stewart novels and has been obsessed with romance ever since. She sees fairies in the trees, mermaids in the ocean, ghosts peeking through shuttered windows, and a story behind every couple that walks by holding hands.

Elisabeth lives in Bucks County, PA, with her three vibrant children, a husband who is her soulmate, and one sweet, albino corn snake. She is a jogger, tea-lover, and avid recycler. After years of practicing law and daydreaming every chance she could get, she is now living her dream and working as a romance novelist.

elisabethcaldwell.com

About the Publisher

City Owl Press is a cutting edge indie publishing company, bringing the world of romance and speculative fiction to discerning readers.

Escape Your World. Get Lost in Ours!

www.cityowlpress.com

facebook.com/YourCityOwlPress
x.com/cityowlpress
instagram.com/cityowlbooks
pinterest.com/cityowlpress

www.ingramcontent.com/pod-product-compliance
Lightning Source LLC
LaVergne TN
LVHW091120080826
845145LV00008B/1994

* 9 7 8 1 6 4 8 9 8 5 6 7 6 *